Praise for the CAT CRIMES series!

Cat Crimes

"A lively collection . . . Good entertainment for readers of both cat and crime fiction."
—*Booklist*

"Scary, funny, clever and traditional, each story has its own special flavor . . . This is a grand collection indeed."
—*Mostly Murder*

Cat Crimes 2

"Offers an even livelier selection of cat tales for reading and rereading pleasure."
—*Mystery News*

"Delightful."
—*Richmond Times-Dispatch*

Also by Martin H. Greenberg and Ed Gorman
Published by Ivy Books:

CAT CRIMES
CAT CRIMES 2

CAT CRIMES 3

Martin H. Greenberg
and Ed Gorman

IVY BOOKS • NEW YORK

Ivy Books
Published by Ballantine Books
Copyright © 1992 by Martin H. Greenberg and Ed Gorman

Library of Congress Catalog Card Number:

ISBN 0-8041-1225-8

This edition published by arrangement with Donald I. Fine, Inc.

Manufactured in the United States of America

First Ballantine Books Edition: August 1994

10 9 8 7 6 5 4 3 2

Contents

Introduction

I'm not sure why cats have found such favor in contemporary society. When I was growing up in the Midwest, cats were still seen by most people as decidedly inferior to dogs. They weren't especially cuddly, they only rarely did tricks and they certainly never offered themselves to you with the same slurpy eagerness as the canines.

When I was twelve, I lived on the edge of town and passed, once a week, a mobile library van. In memory, it's always Ray Bradbury autumn, the hills fiery with turning leaves, the air rich with the melancholy aroma of Indian summer.

It was my pleasure to lug home as many books as the somewhat aloof librarian would let me take. One day I noticed a pattern to the covers that had caught my attention.

In those days I read Ellery Queen, Erle Stanley Gardner and John Dickson Carr. I had exhausted, first, all the Hardy Boys and then, in turn, read through all the Nancy Drews. I actually preferred the latter because a) Nancy's books seemed scarier and b) I had this incredible crush on her.

But no matter who the author, I seemed drawn to books with cats on the cover. I remember a particularly stylish Ellery Queen, Jr., cover that depicted a black cat with an ominous gaze—staring, of course, right at me.

From Poe until today, cats seem inextricably bound up with the mystery tale. They're great as symbols of terror but they work equally well as serio-comic companions, as in the books of Charlotte MacLeod and M.J. Adamson.

The writers in this volume have used cats in a variety of ways, demonstrating that our feline friends are just as various in mood and spirit as their human slaves.

—Ed Gorman

Author Notes

Collaboration, in case you haven't tried it, is a tough job. Especially when the two people are married to each other. Francis and Richard Lockridge defied this truism, as did Mildred and Gordon Gordon. Now we have **BARBARA** and **AL COLLINS** turning in a fine piece of fiction and—as far as I know—still happily married. And, yes, to each other.

Herbert Resnicow has built himself a loyal audience for his particular type of mystery which is a sort of updated Golden Age fair clue puzzler presented in a variety of contemporary settings. Here he shows that he's equally at home with the short form.

Mark Zubro is rapidly making a name for himself as a writer of wry mysteries that are frequently much darker than they might seem at first. He is an active member of the Mystery Writers of America.

Matthew J. Costello is a suspense writer of increasing importance. His latest novel, *Homecoming*, won praise from virtually every corner and demonstrates that Matt's early promise is now being amply fulfilled. You'll hear a lot more about him in the coming years.

Larry Segriff is a young writer who has written two science fiction novels and is only now starting to explore the mystery form. He writes with a degree of polish that is remarkable in somebody his age. Here is his first appearance in print.

Bill Crider's novels of Texas seem to please just about everybody. Crider has several takes on his state, from the Mayberry RFD-like ambience of the Sheriff Rhodes books to the more chilling atmosphere of his fine suspense novel *Blood Marks*. In addition to this, he's one of the nicest people in mystery fiction.

Nancy Pickard will someday get her due as one of the two or three best short story writers in mystery fiction. Her novels are every bit as stunning and rich as the critics claim—but so are her rather underappreciated shorter pieces.

John Lutz has worked in virtually every sub-genre of the suspense novel except for, perhaps, gothic romance. While most people know him for *Single White Female*, one of this year's biggest movie hits, Lutz is a master of many styles. His short story "Ride the Lightning" is one of the most perfectly told stories in the history of the field.

Lisa Angowski Rogak is a non-fiction writer who is just now starting to write crime stories. This is her first sale and it's a nice one, very much her own voice and slant.

Peter Crowther is an Englishman who is infatuated with American literature of all kinds. In the past year he's started writing fiction of his own and has made perhaps a dozen sales. He's a natural storyteller with his own sly moods. He's already an accomplished tale-spinner.

DeLoris Stanton Forbes was one of the key players of the sixties and seventies. But after a flurry of books, she fell silent and is just now returning to the field. In the aforementioned flurry was at least one small, true masterpiece, *Grieve for the Past*, which somebody should soon reprint.

Wendi Lee has written six western novels, all of which have been lauded by critics and sought out by readers. Now she's going to bring her formidable talents as storyteller to the suspense field. She is presently finishing her first mystery novel.

Author Notes

Joe L. Hensley's Roback mystery novels are among the best of the "regional" series ever done in suspense fiction. Not only are they cleverly plotted whodunits, they are also tone-perfect slices-of-life of a small Indiana town colliding with the cultural changes of the sixties and seventies.

William L. DeAndrea has been entertaining mystery readers since his first novel *Killed in the Ratings* won an Edgar award. DeAndrea works in a variety of voices and forms and is remarkably adept at structure, an aspect of the craft sadly overlooked today.

D. C. Brod is a young mystery writer who is just now starting to find her audience. She crosses the private eye tale with some elements of the traditional mystery and does well by both. She will become a major player in the nineties.

Melissa Mia Hall is one of three Texans in this anthology, a slick, amusing storyteller who is always fun to read. Hall plays some stories light, others dark, but no matter what she's up to, her aim is true.

Jan Grape is another Texan, a very talented mystery writer whose name is starting to appear in many of today's best anthologies. Jan's decency as a person informs all her fiction and gives it a ring of humanity and compassion.

Arthur Winfield Knight has written several books, at least a few of which tell the true story of the beatniks (Kerouac, Ginsberg, Corso, etc.) without the burden (and deceit) of myth. He is a careful stylist and a fine writer.

Cat Got Your Tongue

Barbara Collins and Max Allan Collins

The warm California breeze played with Kelli's long blonde hair, which shimmered in the brilliant sun like threads of finely spun gold. Stretched out in a lounge chair by the pool—its water sparkling like diamonds, blinding her in spite of the Ray-Ban sunglasses—she looked like a goddess: long sleek curvy legs led to an even more curvaceous body that spilled over and out her bathing suit, as if resenting having to be clothed. Next to her, on a wrought-iron table, lay fruit, caviar and champagne. Her pouty-pink lips were fixed in a smug, satisfied smile. She was in heaven!

"Oh, poolboy!" she called out to the muscular, shirtless, sandy-haired man dragging a net across the back end of the swimming pool. "More champagne!" She waved an empty crystal goblet at him.

He ignored her.

So she stretched out even more in the lounge chair, moving seductively, suggestively. "I'll make it worth your while," she said, her tongue lingering on her lips.

Now he came to her, and looked down with mild disgust. Sweat beaded his berry-brown body. "Put the stuff back, Kel. It's time to go."

"Just a little longer, Rick," she pleaded.

"It's *time*, Kel."

She sat up in the chair, swung both legs around, and stomped her feet to the ground. "How am *I* supposed to get a tan?" she whined.

He didn't answer but stood silently until she finally got

1

up and picked up the fruit, caviar and champagne, and shuffled off to the house.

"Hurry it up!" he called after her. "They'll be home soon!"

Rick collected his gear, and after a few minutes Kelli returned, standing before him like a dutiful child.

"Everything put back?" he asked.

"Yes."

"And straightened up?"

"Yes."

"Do I have to check?"

"No."

As he turned away, she made a face and stuck out her tongue.

They left, out the patio's wooden gate, and down a winding cobblestone path that led through the gently sloping garden bursting with flowers.

"Why can't *we* live like this?" she complained.

He grunted, moving along. "Because I work for a pool cleaning company and you're on unemployment."

She sighed. "Life just isn't fair."

"Who said it was?"

They were at the street now, by his truck, a beat-up brown Chevy. He threw his gear into the back, then went around to the passenger side and opened the door for her.

"But this is *America*!" Kelli said, tossing her duffel bag inside. "Don't we have a right to *make* things fair?"

He looked at her funny.

"What?" she asked.

"Are those your sunglasses?"

"Yes, *those* are my sunglasses!" she replied indignantly. Anyway, they were now.

She got in the truck, and, while waiting for him to get in the other side, checked herself out in the visor mirror.

Now her hair looked like a cheap blonde wig, her bathing suit the bargain-basement Blue Light Special it was. She glanced down at her legs; they needed a shave. Cinderella, no longer at the palace, had turned back into a peasant!

"Where to?" she asked sullenly, pushing the mirror away.

Rick started the truck. "Samuel Winston's."

"Who the hell is he?" she exclaimed, scrunching up her face unattractively.

Rick didn't bother answering.

"Oh, why can't you clean Tom Cruise's pool or Johnny Depp's or something?"

"I can take you home."

"No." She pouted.

They rumbled off and rode in silence. Then Rick said, somewhat defensively, as he turned off La Brea onto Santa Monica Boulevard, "He's a retired actor."

She perked up a little. "Really?"

"Lives in Beverly Hills."

She perked up a lot. "Oh!" she said.

They rode some more in silence.

"With his wife?" she asked.

Rick looked at her sideways, suspiciously. "No, with his cat," he said.

Kelli smiled and settled back further in the seat.

"Isn't that nice," she purred. "I just love cats!"

With her looks, with her brains, Kelli knew she deserved better in life.

The only child of a commercial airline pilot and an elementary school teacher, she had it pretty easy as a kid, at least until the divorce. At Hollywood High, her good looks enabled her to run with a fast crowd; but it was hard to keep up, what with all their cars and money. Most of her friends had gone on to college; Kelli's terrible grades ruled that out.

She almost wished she had studied harder in school and paid more attention . . .

But what the hell: girls just want to have fun.

"Slow down, Rick!" Kelli said as the truck turned onto Roxbury Drive. She leaned forward intently, peering through the windshield, studying each mansion, every manicured lawn, as they drove by. She would live in a neighborhood like this someday, she just knew it!

The truck pulled into a circular drive.

"Here?" she asked.

Rick nodded and turned off the engine. They got out.

The mansion before them was a sprawling, pink stucco

3

affair, its front mostly obscured by a jungle of foliage and trees that apparently had been left unattended for years. The main entrance didn't look like anybody used it. Kelli frowned, disappointed.

And yet, she thought, this *was* a house in Beverly Hills.

"This way," Rick said, arms loaded with his pool-cleaning gear. Duffel bag slung over her shoulder, she followed him around the side to an iron-scrolled gate.

"Good," Rick said, swinging the gate open.

"What?"

"He remembered to leave it unlocked. I'd hate to have to holler for him till he came and let us in."

Kelli smiled at what lay stretched before her: an Olympic-size swimming pool with an elaborate stone waterfall, a huge Jacuzzi nearby, and expensive-looking patio furniture poolside. And all around nestled exotic plants and flowers and trees, transforming the area into a tropical paradise. But her smile faded when she noticed the old man slumped in one of the chairs, head bowed, snoring. He had on a white terry-cloth robe. By his sandal-covered feet lay a shaggy black cat.

"That's Mr. Winston?" Kelli whispered to Rick.

He nodded, with just a hint of a smile.

Kelli put her hands on her hips. "Why, he's older than the Hollywood Hills!"

"You just be quiet." Rick approached the old man. "Good afternoon, Mr. Winston," he said loudly.

With a snore the old man jolted awake. He focused on them, momentarily confused.

He was a very old man, Kelli thought—somewhere between sixty and a hundred. His head was bald and pink but for some wisps of white, his eyes narrow-set and an almost pretty blue; his nose was hawklike, his lips thin and delicate.

"I'm here to clean the pool," Rick said and set some of his gear down.

The old man cleared his throat and sat up straighter in his chair. "Needs it," he said.

Rick gestured to Kelli. "Mr. Winston, this is my friend, Kelli. Is it all right if she stays while I work?"

The old man looked at her. "Of course." He pointed with

a thin, bony finger to a nearby chair. "Have a seat, my dear."

Kelli sat down, crossing her legs.

"Kel, Mr. Winston worked in show business with a lot of famous people," he explained, "like Jack Benny and Houdini and Abbott and Costello ..."

"Don't forget Berger and McCarthy!" the old man said, suddenly irritable. He leaned forward and spat. "Bergen, that fraud—who *couldn't* be a ventriloquist on the radio?"

There was an awkward silence, and Kelli gave Rick a puzzled look.

Then Rick said, "Yes, well ... I'd better get to work ..." He gathered his things and left them.

Kelli smiled at the old man. "I didn't know Candice Bergen was on the radio," she said.

The old man laughed. And the laugh turned into a cough and he hacked and wheezed.

"Forgive me, my dear," he said when he had caught his breath. "I was referring to Edgar Bergen—her *father*. We were billed together at the Palace."

"The *Palace*!" Kelli said, wide-eyed.

"Ah, you've heard of it?"

"Yes, indeed," she said. She leaned eagerly toward him. "What was the queen like?"

"Not *Buckingham* Palace," he laughed, and wheezed again. "The Palace Theater in New York. Vaudeville. You're so charming, my dear ... are you an *actress*, by any chance?"

She leaned back in her chair. "I wish!" she said breathlessly.

"Well, don't," he replied gruffly. "They're a sad, sorry lot." He studied her a moment. "I'm afraid, my dear, you belong on the arm of some wealthy man, or stretched out by a luxurious pool."

"That's what I think!" she said brightly, then clouded. "But I don't have one."

"One what, child? A rich man or pool?"

"Either!"

He smiled, just slightly. He bent down and picked up the cat and settled the creature on his lap. "You're welcome to use my pool anytime, my dear," he said.

5

"You mean it?"

"Most certainly." He drew the cat's face up to his. "We'd love the company, wouldn't we?" he asked it.

"Meow." Its tail swish, swished.

"How old is your cat?" Kelli asked.

Mr. Winston scratched the animal's ear. "Older than you, my dear," he said.

"You must love it."

"Like a child," he whispered, and kissed its head. "But of course, it's no substitute for the real thing."

"You never had any kids?"

"Never married, my dear. Show business is a harsh mistress."

"What was that word you used? Sounded like a town . . ."

"I don't follow you, child."

"Something-ville."

He smiled; his teeth were white and large and fake.

"Vaudeville! That was a form of theater, my dear. Something like the 'Ed Sullivan Show.' "

"What show?"

He smiled, shook his head. "You *are* a child. The Palace, which you inquired about, was only one of countless theaters in those days . . . the Colonial, the Hippodrome . . . but the Palace was the greatest vaudeville theater in America, if not the whole world!"

Kelli couldn't have cared less about any of this, but she wanted to seem interested. "What was vaudeville like, Mr. Winston?"

"One long, exciting roller-coaster ride . . . while it lasted. You see, vaudeville died in the late 1930s. A show would open with a minor act like acrobats or jugglers, because the audience was still finding their seats, you see. That's where I began, as an opening act . . . but not for long . . ."

He was lost in a smile of self-satisfaction.

"You were a big hit, huh, Mr. Winston?"

"Brought the house down, if you'll pardon my immodesty. Before long I was a top-billed act."

Gag me with a spoon, she thought. "That's so cool. What did you do in your act, Mr. Winston?"

He laughed and shook his head. "What *didn't* I do!" he said.

The old goat sure was full of himself.

"And that's how you got rich and famous, huh?"

His expression changed; it seemed sad, and something else. Bitter?

"I'm afraid I've not been as well remembered as some of my ... lesser contemporaries have." His eyes hardened. "Sometimes when a person does *everything* well, he isn't remembered for anything."

"Oh, you shouldn't say that, Mr. Winston. Everybody remembers you!"

That melted the old boy. He leaned forward and patted her hand; his wrinkled flabby flesh gave her the creeps, but she just smiled at him.

"If only I could have had a child like you." He stroked the cat and it purred. "How much richer my life would've been."

"I'm lonely, too. My dad died before I was born."

"Oh ... my dear. I'm so sorry. . . ."

He seemed genuinely touched by that b.s.

"Can I ask you a favor, Mr. Winston?"

"Anything, child."

"Could I come talk to you again, sometime? You know ... when Rick comes to clean the pool."

His delicate lips were pressed into a smile; he stroked his cat. "I insist, my dear. I insist."

The sound of Rick clearing his throat announced that he had joined the little group; his body was glistening with sweat. He smiled at Mr. Winston, but his brow was furrowed.

"Almost done," he said.

Mr. Winston nodded and stood up, the animal in his arms; he scratched the cat's neck and it seemed to undulate, liking the attention. "Will you children excuse me? I'm going to put my little girl in the house where's it's cooler."

"Certainly," Kelli smiled, watching him go into the house through the glass door off the patio.

"I know what you're up to," Rick snapped in her ear.

She didn't reply.

7

"He's old enough to be your *great*-grandfather. And if he's interested in anyone, it'd be *me*!"

"What do you mean?"

"What do you *think*?" he smirked. "He's been a bachelor since like forever. Besides, he's no fool—he'd see through you before long."

"And if he didn't, you'd tell him, I suppose?"

"I might. Be satisfied with what you've got."

"You, you mean? A poolboy?"

"I put up with your lying ass, don't I?"

She felt her face flush and tried to think of something to say to that, but before she could, the patio door slid open and the old man stepped out.

Rick and Kelli smiled.

As Mr. Winston approached, Kelli asked, "May I use your bathroom?"

"Certainly, my dear. It's just to the left off the kitchen."

Kelli grabbed her duffel bag and headed for the patio door.

"Don't be long, Kel," said Rick behind her. She could feel his eyes boring into her back.

Inside she hesitated only a moment. She was in a knotty-pine TV room; the knickknacks looked pretty worthless, and the only stuff of value was too big to fit in her bag. She moved on, like a shopper searching bargains out in a department store, moving down a narrow hallway to the kitchen. She stopped and turned back. She plucked a small oil painting of a tiger off the wall and started to drop it into her bag. But she changed her mind and put it back; she wasn't nuts about the frame.

In the kitchen she turned to the right which opened into a large, formal hallway. A wide staircase yawned upward, as she stood in the shadow of an elaborate crystal chandelier. To one side was a closed, heavy, dark wood door. She didn't have time to go upstairs and track down the old man's pants and go through the pockets, so she tried the door. It wasn't locked.

The room had stupid zebra-striped wallpaper like the rec room at her drunken uncle Bob's; but there were also a lot of plants, potted and hanging, only when she brushed against one, she discovered all of them were plastic, and dusty. *Yuucch,* she thought. A rich old guy like Winston ought to spring for a damn housekeeper.

There was a fireplace with a lion's head over it—unlike the plants, the lion seemed real, its fangs looking fierce. Big life-size dolls or statues or something of other animals were standing on little platforms against the walls, here and there: a monkey, a hyena, a coiled snake. *Ick!* The couch had a cover that looked like a leopard's skin, and the zebra walls were cluttered with photos of people who must have been famous, because they had signed their names on themselves—she recognized one as that old unfunny comedian Bob Hope. Others she didn't know: a spangly cowboy named Roy Rogers, a guy with buggy eyes named Eddie Cantor. In some of the pictures Mr. Winston wore a weird hat that looked like something out of a jungle movie.

"Koo-koo!"

The sound make her jump; she turned and saw, among the wall clutter, a cuckoo clock. The little bird sticking its head out said its name a few more times and went back inside.

She sighed with relief; but the relief was quickly replaced with panic. She'd been gone too long! She must find something of value, and soon.

She advanced to a desk almost as cluttered as the walls and switched on the green-shaded lamp and rifled through papers, letters mostly, and a stack of photos of Mr. Winston, younger and in the safari hat. Finding nothing that seemed worth anything, she looked around the room and then she saw it.

The cat!

Sleeping in a dark corner of the room, in a little wicker bed; dead to the world . . .

Quickly she went for it, duffel bag at the ready, hands outstretched.

"Nice kitty-kitty," she smiled. "You're coming with Kelli . . ."

"What the hell are you doing?"

A dark shape filled the doorway.

"Nothing!" she said, and the figure stepped into the light. Rick.

"Don't scare me like that," Kelli said crossly.

"You have no business being in here . . . this is Mr. Winston's private collection . . . things from his career."

"Sorry," she said, almost defiantly. "Can I help it if I took a wrong turn?"

"And what were you going to do with that cat?"

"What cat?"

"Come with me—*now*!" Rick growled. "Mr. Winston's an important account, and you're not screwing this up for me!"

"Okay," she said. She glanced back at the cat, who hadn't stirred. How *easy* it would have been. . . .

On the way out she waved at Mr. Winston like a little girl and he smiled at her impishly and waved back the same way.

"Get in the truck," Rick ordered.

"Oh! I forgot something—my new sunglasses!"

"Hurry up, then."

She hadn't forgotten them, of course; she wanted to go back to make sure the gate was left unlatched.

Larry Hackett had been in California only two days, but already he wanted to go home. The vacation—his first in L.A.—was a major disappointment, from the scuzzy streets of Hollywood to the expensive dress shops of Century City, where his wife, Millie, had insisted on going, though she certainly couldn't afford (let alone fit into) the youthful, glamorous clothes.

And their stay in Beverly Hills with his wife's aunt—a live-in housekeeper for some director off on location for the summer—was also a disappointment; not that Beverly Hills wasn't nice, but he felt like a hick putzing along in his Toyota, while Porsches and Jaguars honked and zoomed around him on the palm-lined streets.

He supposed he should just make the best of the trip; sit back and look at all the beautiful women—few of whom looked back, and when they did it was as if to say, "Are you kidding? Lose some weight!"

If truth be told, the thirty-five-year-old Larry was just plain homesick. He longed to be back in his office at the computer.

"Tell us, Aunt Katherine," said Millie, pouring some

sugar into her coffee, "what famous people live nearby?"
The three were seated in the spacious, sunny kitchen, at a
round oak table, having a late-morning cup.

"Well, let's see," Millie's aunt said. She was a big
woman with a stern face offset by gentle eyes. "Rosemary
Clooney has a house just down the street. And Jimmy
Stewart."

Millie clasped her hands together. "How thrilling!" she
said. "I'd love to meet them."

"We don't intrude on our famous neighbors out here,
dear," Aunt Katherine said patiently. "Besides, I'm just
hired help, remember."

Millie frowned like a child denied a cookie.

Larry sipped his coffee.

"Well, who's next door in the Deco place?" Millie persisted.

"An Arab sheik."

"No kidding!" Millie exclaimed. "I'll bet some wild parties go on over there, don't you, Larry?" She elbowed her
husband, trying to draw him into the conversation.

He smiled politely.

"Actually," Aunt Katherine replied, "the sheik is very re-
served."

"And who lives on the other side of you, in the pink
stucco house?" Millie persisted in her questioning.

Larry rolled his eyes.

"Oh, you probably wouldn't know him," her aunt said.
"His name is Samuel Winston."

Now Millie smiled politely, but Larry sat up straight in
his chair. "Who did you say?" he asked.

"Samuel Winston," Aunt Katherine repeated.

Larry, eyes wide, turned to his wife. "Do you know who
that *is*?" he asked excitedly.

Millie shook her head.

"You know! From when we were kids!"

She looked at him blankly.

"Safari Sam!"

Millie continued her vacant stare.

Larry sighed in irritation. "Didn't you ever watch the
'Safari Sam and Pooky Show'?"

"Ohhh . . ." Millie said slowly, nodding her head,

". . . now I remember. I didn't like that show. I could never tell which animals were real and which weren't. And that Pooky scared me."

"Why would a puppet scare you?"

"It wasn't a puppet, it was a *real* cat!"

Larry leaned toward her. "How can a *real* cat play the violin?" he asked, then added dramatically, "Remember its eyes? You can always tell by the eyes."

Millie glared at him—she didn't like to be corrected—then asked innocently, "Didn't Safari Sam get his show cancelled because of cruelty to animals?"

Larry's face flushed. "That was just a vicious rumor!" he said. "Safari Sam loved those animals!"

"I know," Millie laughed, "maybe he *tortured* that cat until it played the violin!"

"Very funny . . ."

"After all," she said, continuing her verbal assault, "I heard he cut out that cat's voice box so he could pretend to talk for it!"

"He did not!" Larry shouted.

"Did too!" Millie shouted.

Aunt Katherine stood up from the table. "Larry! Millie!" she said. "Children, *please!*"

They stopped their bickering.

"Aunt Katherine," Larry said, "could you please introduce me to Mr. Winston? I'm his biggest fan."

"Well . . ."

"I know all about him . . . his career as a comedian, a magician, a ventriloquist . . ." Larry paused and stared out the window at the pink stucco house. ". . . Samuel Winston was a genius, a great man! He just never got his due. . . ."

Aunt Katherine smiled, but raised a lecturing finger. "Samuel Winston *is* a great man. He deserves respect—*and* to be allowed his privacy."

Reluctantly, Larry nodded. Millie looked sheepish.

Then Larry said, "You're right, Aunt Katherine. I'm sorry I asked."

But Larry knew he'd be asking again; they were staying all week, and he had time to work on her.

* * *

The gate creaked as Kelli swung it open; behind her Rick was shaking. The big chicken.

"I can't believe I let you talk me into this," he whispered.

It *had* taken some doing, particularly after he'd bawled her out about it in the truck when they left Winston's earlier that day.

"Jeez, Kel," he had said, the breeze riffling his hair, "if you want a goddamn cat, I'll buy you a goddamn cat!"

"But I want *that* cat!"

"Why?" he said, exasperated. "It's old, it's mangy ..."

"It's worth a lot of money," she cut in.

She had explained on the waterbed in their tiny apartment off Melrose. He'd stared at her, shook his head. "You want to *kidnap* that cat and hold it for ransom?"

"I wouldn't do that!" she exclaimed, offended, covering her breasts modestly with the sheet.

"Then what? I can't wait to hear."

"I want to kidnap the cat and collect a *reward*."

"Oh, swell," Rick jeered, "well, that's different. A reward as in somehow the cat got out and we found it and took it home, then saw the ad in the paper?"

"Exactly."

He had looked at her dazed, as if struck by a stick; but then his eyes had tightened.

"The old man *is* worth a lot of money ... and it's just a cat."

"Just a cat," she said, stroking him, "just a silly old cat."

The full moon reflected on the shimmering surface of the pool; it was the only light on the patio. The lights in the big pink house were off.

"You got that screwdriver?" she whispered.

Rick, dressed all in black as she was, swallowed and nodded.

But they didn't have to pry the patio door open; it, too, was unlocked. They moved through the house slowly, quietly, and the sound of their footsteps was something even they couldn't detect, let alone some deaf old man.

Soon they stood in the safari room; Kelli turned on the green-shaded desk lamp. The mounted lion's head and the animal shapes and the plastic plants threw distorted shadows.

"It's in the corner," Kelli said.

"You get it. You wanted it."

"It might *scratch* me!"

"It might scratch *me*!"

"Children, don't fight," said Samuel Winston, his voice kindly; but an elephant gun in his hands was pointed right at them. He had plucked it from the gun rack just inside the door.

Kelli jumped behind Rick, who put both hands out in a "stop" motion. "Whoa, Mr. Winston," he said, "don't do anything rash . . ."

The old man moved closer. "Aren't you children the ones behaving rashly? Trying to steal my little girl away from me? If you needed money, all you had to do was ask!"

"Please, Mr. Winston," Rick pleaded. "Don't call the cops. We were wrong to break in . . ."

"Very wrong, Rick. I'm disappointed. I thought you were a nice young man . . . and you, Kelli. How very sad."

Kelli didn't know what to say; she'd only been caught stealing twice in her life, and both times she'd wormed her way out—once by crying, and once with sex. Neither seemed applicable here.

"Rick can give you free pool service for a year!" she blurted. "Please don't call the police, Mr. Winston!"

"I have no intention of calling the police," the old man said.

Rick backed up with Kelli clinging to him. Seconds seemed like minutes.

Then the old man lowered the gun. "Don't worry," he said, almost wearily. "I'm not going to shoot you, either."

Rick sighed; Kelli relaxed her grip on him.

The old man turned away from them and put the gun back in its rack. "I know what it's like to live in a town where everyone else seems to have everything."

He faced them.

"The only thing worse is to finally *have* everything, and no one to share it with."

Something in the old man's voice told Kelli she was out

of danger; smiling a little, she stepped out from behind Rick.

"That is sad, Mr. Winston. I wish we could make this up to you somehow . . ."

His pretty blue eyes brightened. "Perhaps you could! How would you like to live here and share in my wealth? To be my son and daughter?"

Rick was stunned. Kelli's smile froze.

"What's the matter?" the old man chuckled. "Cat got your tongue?"

Rick stuttered, "Well, I . . . we . . ."

But Kelli rushed forward, arms outstretched.

"Daddy!" she cried.

"Koo-koo! Koo-koo!" went the clock, high on the cluttered wall.

"Ah, two o'clock," the old man said. "Shall we discuss this further over a hot cup of cocoa? Perhaps you could heat some milk for Pooky, my dear."

"Pooky?" Kelli asked.

"That's my little girl's name. My cat you were so interested in. . . ."

And with Kelli on his arm, Winston walked out of the den, patting the girl's hand soothingly, a bewildered Rick trailing behind. Kelli glanced over her shoulder and grinned at him like the cat that ate the canary.

The warm California breeze played with Kelli's long blonde hair, which shimmered in the brilliant sun like threads of finely spun gold. Stretched out in a lounge chair by the pool, she looked like a goddess in her white bathing suit and Ray-Ban sunglasses. Next to her on a wrought-iron table lay fruit, caviar and champagne. Her pouty-pink lips were fixed in a smug, satisfied smile. She was in heaven.

"More champagne, my dear?" asked Samuel Winston, who stood next to her in a terry-cloth robe worn loosely over swimming trunks.

"Yes, please!"

He filled the empty goblet she held in one hand.

"Another beer, Rick?" Samuel called out.

Rick, in a purple polo shirt, white Bermuda shorts and

wrap-around sunglasses, sat a few yards away, beneath the umbrella, a can of Bud Lite by his feet.

"No thanks, Sam . . . haven't finished this one."

Samuel returned to his chair, next to Kelli. He looked at her, studying her, and frowned. "You'd better put on more sunscreen, my dear," he advised.

"Am I red?"

Samuel nodded.

"Well, I don't feel it . . . Rick! Do I look red?"

"Not that I can see."

Samuel stood up. "Let me get your back for you," he said.

"Would you? I can't do it myself."

Samuel took the tube of sunscreen off her towel and squeezed some out on his hands. He spread it gently on her back. "Does that hurt?" he asked.

"Not a bit."

When Samuel had finished, he wiped his hands on the towel, then he went over to the cat, which lay on the patio in the shade of the umbrella, and picked it up. He went back to his chair, sat and stroked the animal's fur.

"Are you happy?" he asked it.

"Meow." Its tail swish, swished.

"Me, too, Pooky," Samuel said. He peered skyward. "Such a beautiful day. Don't you think?"

"I'll say!" the cat said.

"Oh, *yoo-hoo!*" came a grating voice from the gate.

Samuel looked sharply toward it. "Hell and damnation!" he said. "It's that woman next door. That housekeeper. And who's that with her?" He squinted to make out the forms. "Tweedledee and Tweedledum. Don't worry, my pets, I'll get rid of them."

He waved one hand half-heartedly.

The trio pushed through the gate, the housekeeper marching in the lead, the man and woman trailing timidly behind.

Samuel groaned behind his grin. He put down the cat and stood to greet them.

"Ah, madam," he said, "it's so nice to see you."

"I hope we're not interrupting anything," the house-keeper said with a silly little laugh.

"Not at all."

"I don't make a habit out of intruding . . ."

"Think nothing of it."

"But I'd like to introduce you to my niece Millie, and nephew Larry—Larry is your biggest fan."

Samuel smiled politely at the two. "It's a pleasure to meet you," he said.

The niece had a blank expression, but the nephew looked like an eager puppy-dog, beads of sweat forming on his brow. The boy rushed forward and grabbed one of Samuel's hands, pumping it vigorously.

"Mr. Winston," he gushed, "you don't know how much the 'Safari Sam and Pooky Show' meant to a little kid with asthma in Akron, Ohio!"

Now Samuel smiled genuinely. "Why, thank you," he said, "That's very gratifying."

Suddenly Larry clutched his heart, mouth gasping, eyes bugging.

"Is anything wrong?" Samuel asked, alarmed.

"Pooky!" Larry cried, pointing a wavering finger at the cat that lay a few yards away on the ground. "It's Pooky!"

The pudgy boy-man ran to it, and fell on his knees, palms outspread as if worshiping.

Reverently, he looked up at Samuel. "May I?" he asked. Samuel nodded.

Gingerly, tenderly, Larry picked up the cat. It lay limp in his hands. "It's so well preserved," he said in awe.

"I did it myself."

"Really!"

"Taxidermy has long been an avocation of mine. Have you ever been out to the Roy Rogers Museum?"

"You didn't do . . . *Trigger!*" Larry gasped.

Samuel merely smiled.

Larry seemed spellbound by Pooky. "There's a place for your hand . . . he's real *and* a puppet! So that's your secret!"

"One of them."

Larry gave his wife a withering look. "I told you he was a genius!"

The plump little wife, however, only looked sickened.

Larry handed the cat back to Samuel. "Could you have Pooky sing the 'Pooky Song'?" he asked.

"I'd rather not," the old man answered.

"Oh, please!" Larry pleaded, his chubby hands pressed together, prayerlike.

Samuel sighed. "Well, all right," he said, but irritated.

"And do the Pooky dance . . .?"

Samuel glared, then nodded, grudgingly.

". . . while you drink a glass of water?"

"I don't *have* a glass of water!"

"I could get you one," Larry offered.

"No!" Samuel snapped. "Never mind. Just hand me that champagne."

Samuel stuck his hand inside the cat, slung the bottle to his lips and drank it, while Pooky, his legs and tail flapping in a crazy jig, sang in a high-pitched voice.

"I'm Pooky, a little kooky, it's kind of spooky . . ."

Larry, with joy on his face and tears in his eyes, applauded wildly. So did the housekeeper. But the niece stood frozen, horrified.

"That was just like the show!" Larry exclaimed.

"Thank you," Samuel said tersely. "Now, if you don't mind, you must go . . . I need my rest."

The housekeeper stepped toward him. "We were just wondering," she said, "if you could join us for lunch."

"I've just had brunch, thank you."

"Well, what about your guests?" the housekeeper pressed.

"My guests?" Samuel asked, annoyed, frowning. He turned and looked at the lounging Kelli and Rick nearby; the two had their backs to Samuel's unwanted company.

"Oh, I've been rude," Samuel said. "I didn't introduce my son and daughter . . . they're on an extended visit . . ."

"We'd love to have all three of you for lunch," the stupid woman persisted.

"Well, I'll have to decline," he said, then added with a wicked little smile, "but of course, I shouldn't speak for Kelli and Rick . . ."

"Oh, I'm not hungry," Rick said.

Though the trio of intruders didn't notice, the lips of

Samuel's children didn't move when they spoke, nor did Samuel's—for he was no radio ventriloquist.

"Me neither," Kelli said. "We couldn't possibly eat. We're just stuffed!"

A Few Strokes for Mitzi

.

Herbert Resnicow

I have always wanted to own a Vermeer. An original, I mean. Copies I have plenty; walls covered. I made them all myself. First, from the Münchner Stadtmuseum, next the Rijksmuseum and the Mauritshuis, then the National Gallery and the Met, and now, of course, I have available to me the entire contents of the Fine Arts Museum of New York.

I am most careful, when I copy, to use modern canvas and modern pigments, so that if anyone should steal one of my paintings—I must live in a not-so-good neighborhood because the best pigments cost so much these days—he could not sell it as an original. Only I, and possibly Goldberger, could tell my work from the true Vermeers.

I had hoped to become a real artist, but it was not to be. Skill I have, great skill, and talent too, but not the spark. So be it. I am a very good copyist, possibly the best ever, and that will have to do. The copies I make are not for sale but for practice, so that before I die I will be able to paint the blue satin so that even I could not tell it from Vermeer's.

I follow every brushstroke, every build-up of pigment, the sequence of painting, exactly the way *he* did it. In my loft, on the big screen, is projected in great enlargement the Vermeer I am working on. It is not from a 35-mm slide, but from a large transparency made by myself using a big view camera with a very sharp Zeiss lens and an extra-fine-grain film. I project macrophotographs too, all made with a long-focus lens and contour lighting to emphasize the very fine brushstrokes around the eyes, the ears, and the lacework. It

20

was not easy to get permission to take the photographs, but once I became known, doors were opened to me.

I work like a miniaturist, microlenses clamped to my head like a neurosurgeon, strong spotlights focused on the work area. When my eyes get tired, as they do more and more often now, I flip up the lens assembly and do my eye exercises: a funny old woman with antennae, a modern witch muttering spells to her familiar. Without even a familiar anymore.

Mitzi used to lie, purring, on the table under a spot I put there especially for her. Her old bones needed the heat, and she knew better than to swish her tail over wet work. She was twenty-four when she died, equivalent to one hundred sixty-eight years in a human person.

I hope I am not so unlucky as to live that long. Money is not the problem. Not that I am rich, but Mitzi did not eat much, nor did I, and I was able to put away regularly much of my wages. Unfortunately, the price of Vermeers went up many times faster than my savings. I can live at this level for fifteen more years, if inflation remains constant, but it is clear to me—as it should have been long ago but was too bitter for me to face—that I will never be able to buy a Vermeer. And if I lose my job, if the director-general of the museum is able to force me out, as now seems likely . . . generous though this country's Social Security is, I will no longer be able to buy good pigments and canvas. Then what? Sit and look at my copies? Make more copies with cheap pigments? Better I should turn on the gas.

Unless . . .?

I had many offers, especially when I was young. They thought I could do a Vermeer so even *he* could not tell. Nonsense, of course. If *I* could tell, *he* could. Even more easily. I am not an angel, nor an innocent, but I came from the wrong place and the wrong time. There, in my day, the law was respected absolutely, and a uniform, even a streetcar conductor's, was holy. One did not break the law; one did what the uniform ordered. Even today, I cannot cross on red, I cannot take unearned coins from a telephone box, and, especially, I cannot kill Alford C. D. Charles, director-general of the museum.

It is not terribly important to me that he betrayed his

predecessor, the man who gave him his first opportunity; every executive I've met climbed over broken bodies. It was not all that unusual that he replaced almost all the curators and assistant curators with his own lackeys, although sudden, outright dismissal of the older ones was unnecessarily vicious. It is an open secret in the field that sales to the museum can be made only through one of the five galleries that split the commission with the director-general. I don't really care that before a living artist can be exhibited in the museum he must first sell six of his early paintings to Charles at a very low price. Or that for a female assistant curator to be hired, she must first have a highly personal, and fully satisfactory, interview with the director-general.

It doesn't bother me that there are a dozen lawsuits pending against the museum by the estates of people who left their collections to the museum on the promise that these paintings would never be sold. Charles, of course, promptly sold what he wanted when he wanted, usually to one of his favored five galleries, at suspiciously low prices, and used the money to buy from these same galleries paintings by big-name, popular artists, pushing prices to the point where even the rich Metropolitan complained. Charles then used these paintings to promote circus-type exhibitions featuring TV soap-opera ingenues, illiterate rock-music superstars, famous gangsters, and even politicians. The lines would stretch around the museum for weeks; Charles knew how to bring in crowds. Not necessarily crowds of people who understood or appreciated art, but crowds nevertheless.

I didn't want to kill the director-general for any, or even all, of these reasons. No, I wanted to kill Alford C. D. Charles because he murdered Mitzi. Not with a knife or a gun, but he killed her. Deliberately.

I work on the cleaning and restoration of the most costly paintings in the museum, so I am the only conservator who has her own room. This allowed me to take Mitzi to work with me. She lay on my table under a spot, just like at home, and we talked while I worked. Occasionally I would give her a few small strokes on the head and scratch behind the ears, her favorite place. She was a sweet and well-behaved cat and did not bother anyone. Anyone but Charles.

He kept trying to have me fired, naturally, since I was the only one who stood up to him. Most of the directors know me and respect me, especially Mr. Belmont, the chairman of the board, and it does not hurt that I sometimes clean their personal paintings free. Also, I am truly the best in the business. The museum would have trouble replacing me; could never *replace* me, actually. You have to be very careful whom you allow to work on your multimillion-dollar artworks, and I don't mean just spoiling a painting. There are more forgeries hanging in museums, all museums, than they would like anyone to know about. I could go to the Met tomorrow at a big increase in salary, but I am too old to change, and I am comfortable here, in my own room. I know where everything is and no one can tell me what to do.

Charles came into my room once, without my permission. Without even knocking. Mitzi knew him for what he was and properly scratched him. The next day he issued an order that no animals were allowed in the museum. I could have forced my way in, no guard would have dared touch me, but then Charles would have fired one as an example, and they are all poor people with families, so what could I do? Mitzi died exactly one week later, of loneliness, of a broken heart. Charles had killed her. Deliberately.

Everyone in the field knew the story, and I got offers from friends and strangers all around the world, but I decided to stay at the museum; it would make it easier to kill Director-General Alford C. D. Charles. Even though I could not do anything illegal, I would find a way.

One month ago, a wonderful thing happened: somewhere in Europe, the Third Vermeer was found. On May 16, 1696, the record shows—one of the few records about any Vermeer—that three works by Jan Vermeer were sold, listed collectively as Portraits in Antique Costume. It is believed that the tiny *Young Girl with a Flute* and the equally small *Girl with a Red Hat*, both on wood—the only times Vermeer used wood—were part of that group, but no one even knew the subject matter of the Third Vermeer. Until now.

At a huge press conference, Director-General Charles announced that he had contracted to buy, subject only to the approval of the board of directors of the museum, the newly discovered Third Vermeer painting, tentatively called *Girl in a Blue Kimono*, for $60 million, the highest price ever paid for any painting. Yes, on wood, slightly larger than the other two. In fact, everything was exactly like the other two: heads and busts of young women in costume rather than in Dutch clothes, seated in chairs with carved lion-head finials, wearing unusual hats, with—also unusual for Vermeer—relatively dark, figured backgrounds, and all probably made with the aid of a *camera obscura*. A perfect match and arguably Vermeer's greatest work. One of the rarest paintings in the world, and by one of the world's greatest artists; only thirty-seven fully authenticated Vermeers were known to exist. Until now. Yes, carbon dating and X-rays checked out and no, no provenance, the present owner insisted on remaining anonymous. He was represented by a well-known gallery, one of Charles' pets. Yes, definitely Jan Vermeer, authenticated by three of Europe's most respected experts. Charles named three well-known *patzers*.

My heart jumped at this. Not Goldberger? The only one who knew Vermeer, who loved Vermeer as well as I did? Almost? Goldberger who lived in Lucerne? Who would have gone to Antarctica at his own expense just to *see* the Third Vermeer? Goldberger the incorruptible? This had to mean that our well-beloved, crooked director-general was not quite sure of the authenticity of his little $60 million acquisition. I would check *Girl in a Blue Kimono* myself. If it was a forgery, I would know at once. In seconds; my heart would tell me. On copying Vermeer, I am *the* expert. And if it were indeed a forgery, I would let Charles buy it and, while cleaning it, I would find out it was a fake and Charles would hang.

I started calling my friends and colleagues. Holland first, then England, Germany, Italy, Switzerland, Austria, Hungary, last Yugoslavia. Each I asked only one or two questions; I didn't want anyone putting the whole story together the way I was doing. Each answer led eastward. Finally I had it, the whole picture. Mostly conjecture, of course, but everything fit perfectly.

The dirty little wooden portrait, less than eight inches

square, was stolen from some Dutch farmer's house in the first days of the Nazi invasion by a soldier who slipped it into his knapsack. When the soldier was killed, an ignorantly zealous SS man set the painting aside for Hermann Goering, who wanted to acquire personally all the artworks in Europe. The painting went into a packing crate of one of Goering's treasure caches, unnoticed among the bigger, more spectacular works. The Russians captured the warehouse and shipped the contents to the Hermitage. Since Stalin and Hitler between them had killed most of the competent curators in Europe, the little wooden plaque gathered dust in a storeroom in the museum's cellar.

Last year a young art lover, working as a janitor because the State had already enough curators of the right political persuasion, found the painting, recognized it for what it was and, trying to use it as a stepping stone to a better job, reported it, not to a curator but to a KGB officer. For the same reason, this officer bypassed his immediate superior and got the message to a KGB general. This general, recently widowed, saw the painting as a passport to a new life in the decadent West. After having the young art lover and the KGB officer carefully killed in accidents, the general took the painting personally to Split, where he arranged to have the little sealed package shipped by the usual routes to Zurich, via Budapest and Vienna. There it went to a Swiss bank, not the one he kept his mad money in.

An Italian expert was brought in to examine the painting in the bank's vault in the presence of a bank officer. Based on this limited inspection, the expert stated that the painting was almost certainly genuine, though more tests would be required before he would put his report in writing.

This was enough for the general. He decided that Alford C. D. Charles was the proper man to deal with, the director-general's reputation having by now reached the Urals. After the Italian expert had a fatal accident in Lugano, a sealed memo was presented to the London office of Charles' pet gallery for transmittal to New York by hand.

The deal was simple: The museum would place $15 million in the Swiss bank in escrow, in gold and gold-backed money: krugerrands, mapleleafs and Swiss francs. The painting could be examined in the bank's vault by any experts the museum chose. Scrapings of wood and flecks of paint could be taken for laboratory tests. Portable X-ray equipment could be used. If the painting were damaged in any way, or disappeared, the money would be transferred immediately to the painting's owner. Within thirty days, the museum had to decide whether to buy or not. If yes, the money would be transferred electronically, broken up, transferred again, and the general would disappear, presumably to South America. If no, the money would be returned to the bank, less bank fees, and the same deal would be offered to the Metropolitan or the Getty. A copy of all expert opinions and lab reports would be given to the Swiss bank for the owner.

There was only one trouble with this from Charles' point of view: he couldn't make any money for himself out of this kind of transaction.

The problem was easily solved. Charles would buy the painting himself and sell it to the museum, where he had almost complete control, for $60 million, even more than the Van Gogh *Sunflowers* had brought. Not under the same conditions as the general had set, but as a simple transaction between the museum and the gallery representing the owner, with a ninety-day money-back guarantee of the painting's authenticity. Acting through his Swiss bank and using the London branch of his tame gallery as his agent, Charles would become the new anonymous owner.

Charles did not have the $15 million in cash, but he knew the certain people who always had that much lying around and were looking for ways to turn it over. They were not true art lovers and would probably insist on half the profit, but it was a safe deal for all involved, since the money would be returned if Charles' experts said the painting was not genuine. The Swiss bank's fee would be negligible; Charles could handle that himself, as well as the fees to the experts. Charles had the authority to contract for the purchase by the museum, subject only to the approval of the board of directors, who always gave him his way. So if the authentication was positive, there was absolutely no risk.

The technical tests and Charles' three experts pronounced the painting genuine. The money was transferred and the painting now had a new secret owner, Charles. As director-general, Charles immediately bought the painting for the Museum, subject only to the approval of the board.

When *Girl in a Blue Kimono* arrived at the museum, I unpacked it in my room. Charles was furious. He wanted to unpack it himself in front of the TV cameras, but I had primed Mr. Belmont, and when the chairman of the board wants to be firm, he is immovable. All I did was point out how embarrassing it would be for the museum if its $60 million acquisition was damaged in the unpacking, or stolen by someone in the crowd, or proved to be a forgery. The museum would not lose any money if it was a forgery, since it had to pay only if the painting was a genuine Jan Vermeer—another little detail I had mentioned to Mr. Belmont when he asked my opinion about approving the acquisition—but no board of directors likes to be laughed at.

My heart leaped when I saw the painting. It was Vermeer, the lost Vermeer, positively Vermeer. I didn't need a loupe; I *knew*. Put Mitzi in a room with a hundred black cats, I would pick her out in one minute. Mitzi I knew only twenty-four years before Charles murdered her; Vermeer I knew all my life. My heart also fell; now I was unable to ruin Alford C. D. Charles.

Of course, I could have taken a month, even two, in the cleaning and restoration. During that time I could have made a forgery and substituted it for the real painting; an almost-perfect copy with just one anomaly ready to be found by any *patzer*. I had plenty of wood of the right age in the storeroom, plenty of Dutch junk of that day to grind pigments from. I could, but I couldn't. Not forgery. Not Vermeer. Better I should die first.

I examined the painting closely, with a twelve-power loupe, and then suddenly I knew how to kill Charles.

That night I called Goldberger. I told him to get ready to come to New York, what to bring with him, where to look (he got insulted at that), and how to make his announcement to the press most effectively.

The next day, I told Mr. Belmont that to authenticate the painting, we had to call in Goldberger. When he asked my opinion, I told him the truth: that it looked like a true

Vermeer, but I managed to sound a little hesitant. I also said that, since I wasn't a curator or a recognized expert, it would be improper of me to offer a professional opinion.

It made all the papers. Headlines. For $60 million, why not? Goldberger's enlarged sidelit photographs, especially around the eyes, the ears, and the lace, compared with authenticated Vermeers with unimpeachable provenance, showed a pattern of brushstrokes completely different from—opposite to—what Vermeer always used. Goldberger firmly and authoritatively pronounced the painting a forgery—a great forgery, but unquestionably a forgery. On being presented with Goldberger's evidence, Charles' three experts hemmed and hawed and pointed out that in the major areas of painting, the brushstrokes were unarguably in Vermeer's style, but they could no longer state with certainty that the painting was authentic. Not for $60 million worth of paint and wood; not for something insured for a million dollars a square inch.

The board of directors of the museum voted unanimously not to approve the contract the director-general had signed. Charles' pet gallery, ostensibly representing the owner, tried to sell it for $15 million. No one would touch it at any price; no rich man wants to be thought a fool.

Charles disappeared. I assume that the certain people who had advanced the $15 million the general took to South America were upset with Charles and, when he could not repay their money, the money he had assured them was absolutely safe, they decided to wipe the slate clean.

The gallery was unable to find the owner of the forgery, since Charles could not risk letting even his pets know about this deal. Not being burdened greatly by honesty, if they ever sold the fake they might spend as much as ten minutes trying to find their secret client before they pocketed the money. In trust for the owner, of course, should he ever be found. However little that money might be, it was better than nothing.

It really wasn't much trouble to put in the wrong brushstrokes around the eyes, ears, and lace. It didn't take long either; I had everything I needed available to me in the museum. It is illegal, a crime, to forge a painting; to make a false painting and represent it as authentic. It is not illegal to paint a few strokes on a dead artist's painting; I do it all the time in my restoration work. It is not illegal, when one paints those few brushstrokes, not to copy the original master's brushstrokes perfectly in every detail. It is, in fact, good practice, to show which is the master's work and which is the conservator's work. And if, when I paint these strokes, I cry, and I say out loud, "This is for Mitzi," well, crazy old women are allowed such fantasies.

And it is certainly not illegal to remove these false, ugly brushstrokes later, to restore a Vermeer to its own true perfection.

Next month, the lucky London branch of Charles' pet gallery will get an offer from a small European gallery. Lucky because the offer may be for as much as two thousand dollars. Cash. Tax-free. Found money. No questions asked.

I have always wanted to own a Vermeer. An original, I mean.

Next Year, Kankakee

·

Mark Richard Zubro

I dropped my luggage on the rotting boards of the pier and stared at the crumbling town in front of me. A few people muffled against the milky autumn sky hustled down the street and around corners. Several brick buildings, a couple of stucco structures, a taxi with a flat tire, a ten-year-old Toyota, and a fifteen-year-old Chevette all vied with each other for ugliness awards. No smiling street urchins greeted the boat to beg for a few coins.

Scott thumped his bags down next to mine. He took a deep satisfied breath. "Isn't this great?" he asked.

"Wonderful." I tried to keep the sarcasm out of my voice. He wouldn't have noticed. All the way down here in the plane, and then in the boat (rusted, rat-infested, plastic chairs from the fifties), he'd been ecstatic. "Tierra del Fuego," he said. "I've always wanted to be here, and it's at the end of the earth. Nobody will know me. I'll be able to have assured peace and quiet."

The problem was real. He's one of the highest paid pitchers in baseball and won more than a few World Series games. Made enough commercials to make a politician nauseous with envy. Here at one end of the earth, maybe he wouldn't be recognized.

We'd taken a plane to Rio Grande from Buenos Aires then the twenty-four-hour boat trip to Porvenir.

I gazed overhead. Clouds rushing east in the prevailing westerlies.

"We could walk to the hotel," Scott said. He held a guidebook in his hand, studying it carefully.

I looked back at our fellow passengers. One was a college kid from the States, with a backpack and wearing shorts, a T-shirt, and hiking boots. Said his name was Jack Hill. He brushed his long brown hair out of his eyes, peered out of his glasses, and shivered. I'd chatted with him on the boat. Majoring in engineering at MIT. He seemed quite bright, but he needed a bath.

A couple in their late seventies fussed happily at each other as they descended the gangplank. I'd eaten a snack with them in what the brochure claimed was a dining room on the boat. More like a cabin with some plastic-wrapped junk food. The couple had scrimped and saved for years in a small flat in Brighton, England, and now they liked to travel one place new and unusual every two years. Edith and Edward Blackwell had been to Tashkent, Timbuktu, Bombay, India, and the Arctic Circle. This elderly British couple power-walked around the deck of the upgraded garbage scow we sailed on. If they'd passed me one more time on their rounds, I'd have been tempted to shove them overboard. Talking to them was like being beaten to death with an all-day sucker.

An African-American man, who spoke with what I thought was a Jamaican accent, said he was scouting for locations for an oil company. His name was Alfred Jones.

Our last passenger was Margarete Villon, a down-and-out French actress, coming home to her husband, a sheep farmer near Porvenir.

The wind chilled me through my warmup jacket. I knew I should have brought my overcoat. Even in early autumn this far south it was cold.

I gazed at the skyline again. Nine at night and the sun barely beginning to set. Not a Hilton in sight. At the moment I'd take a Motel 6. The trip down had taken nearly three full days. I wanted a hot shower, a warm bed, and a night's sleep.

Scott said, "Let's stop in a cafe or bar and talk to the locals."

I didn't speak Spanish, neither did he, but I really didn't want to spoil the trip for him. I put as much cheer as I could in my voice and said, "What a great idea, but maybe we should put our luggage in the hotel first."

Thankfully he agreed to this.

It turned out we didn't have a choice about walking to the inn. There were no working taxis and neither Hertz nor Avis wanted any part of the local franchise.

As we walked to the end of the pier, an enormous black cat emerged from around the corner of a pile of odoriferous fish heads, entrails, and netting. It gazed from me to Scott and then stalked deliberately over to us. The cat sniffed at my ankles, then moved over to Scott, where the animal proceeded to rub his back against the leg of Scott's jeans.

Don't get me wrong. I like cats, all animals really, but I'm not good with them. Same with little kids. Put one of them in my arms and it squalls for its parent. I looked at Scott. He knelt down. The cat jumped into his arms and purred contentedly. Little kids love him too. I sighed.

Scott and the cat finished making friends and we proceeded up the street. Scott, guidebook open, claimed to know where we were going. We saw three more cats, these all sleek and well fed. A few natives peered out at us from grime-encrusted shop windows. The other passengers were all staying at the Tierra del Fuego Hacienda, described in their brochures as the place to stay in Porvenir. We had reservations at El Grande Palacio, which our travel agent claimed was heavenly bliss.

A group of youngsters rushed by us, flinging a brown-with-age basketball back and forth. It could have been keep away, or might have been simple fun, but none of them laughed or smiled.

Eight squalid blocks later we arrived at the edge of town, topped a rise, and looked down on what must have been the largest still-operating medieval castle outside of Europe. We crossed a drawbridge over a working moat probably filled with piranha and alligators.

Our lodgings, according to the tour book Scott read to me at extensive length on the flight from Miami, was run by the Sisters of Mercy of Tierra del Fuego.

The solid oak doors swung open on silent hinges. We stepped into an Italian baroque nightmare. The decor looked like a place where all the mad interior decorators in the world had been sent since the first ships came west over the Atlantic. Gargoyles glared from the vast number of niches and corners. The ugly figures often peeked around fans of enormous ostrich plumes. Five sets of Spanish conquistador armor had groups of black leather couches grouped around them. The vastness of the reception area dwarfed grand staircases rising to both left and right.

The door thudded shut behind us.

Straight ahead of us, fifty feet away, was a front desk. In front of it, a nun in a black-and-white floor-length habit smiled at us. Up close she was beautiful. As spiritual and otherworldly as you would expect a nun to look. She murmured welcomes and told us her name was Sister Constance.

I leaned an elbow against the desk and then jumped back, startled. A gray blur half an inch from my ear dissolved into a long-haired charcoal-colored cat. It turned its yellow eyes on me, sniffed, then padded over to Scott. He scratched the cat behind the ears before it made a stately pilgrimage to the far end of the marble-topped counter. It stretched itself majestically, lay down, and closed its eyes.

In her soft voice Sister Constance said, "Most of the sisters here speak numerous languages. We pride ourselves on our learning, but many of us have taken vows of silence. It would be best if you wait for them to speak to you before you approach them."

I nodded. I looked at Scott. He gazed eagerly at each piece of baroque trash around the room. He began asking questions about separate pieces that caught his fancy. He especially asked about one wall filled with weapons: scimitars, cutlasses, broadswords, Bowie knives, blunderbusses, elephant guns, muskets, rapiers, assorted daggers, battleaxes of various sizes, hatchets, and spears. Various torture devices from throughout the ages perched on a wide platform on the left side of the room.

Slits of windows high up in the masonry walls let in narrow shafts of dappled light from stained-glass windows. This softened and deepened the effect of the gloom below.

In all the time we'd been in this entrance, I hadn't heard a sound besides our own voices and our own breathing. Not the tick of a clock, the hum of a radio, the buzz of a neon light—total silence. The only movement besides ourselves were dust motes brushing against each other.

I listened to Scott's third tedious question and Sister Constance's interminable answer. Then he began to ask another. I drifted away. My eye caught a gleam of metal in a corner of the platform under the grand staircase on the left. The object was situated in such a way that a shaft of sunlight from a stained-glass window gleamed redly on its polished blade. A guillotine. I walked over to it slowly. I'd never been this close to one. I reached out to touch the side of the blade. An inch before my finger felt the metal, a soft hand on my shoulder startled me.

I whirled around. An elderly nun, her face tightly encased by her wimple, spoke soft, "Perhaps it would be better not to touch."

While my heart returned to its normal pulse rate, she introduced herself as the mother superior. I tried to smile and edged away. Finally turning around, I saw Scott waiting for me at the bottom of the staircase nearby. The gray cat, purring contentedly, rubbed its back against Scott's legs. Sister Constance floated noiselessly around the desk. The mother superior watched us climb the stairs.

Reading from a piece of paper, Scott muttered directions. We trudged down halls, around corners, and up narrow stairs all decorated in basic dungeon. A bit of gaslight at rare intervals showed stone-flagged passages stained with what could easily have been blood. I decided my overwrought imagination was getting the best of me. By the time we came to our hallway, I'd lost all sense of direction.

We had separate rooms with the bath down the hall. I opened my door and expected a bundle of straw on the floor for a bed and rats keeping house in the corners. Actually, except for the gruesome picture of a martyr being stoned to death above the bed, and the lack of a phone, it wasn't bad. Of course, who did I expect to call? My nearest relative was over a continent away.

The narrow twin bed had a soft mattress. I checked under it for vermin, but found it spotless. I dropped my suitcase on the bed. Next to a chest of drawers, french windows led out to a balcony. I stepped out and saw Scott gazing over the parapet. I joined him and looked over. The sun had set, and the galaxy blazed above us in a splendor I'd never seen before. Below us only a few flickering lights broke the spell of the velvet night. I thought I could hear faintly the distant sound of the ocean. A soft wind puffed against my left cheek. I glanced around. The balcony ran the entire length of this level of the castle.

I heard a soft thump. Another guest? One of the nuns? A cat? We'd seen no one but ourselves. "Did you hear that?" I asked.

"Hear what?" Scott asked.

"I'm not sure." I returned to my room, Scott following. At first glance everything looked the same, then I noticed my suitcase had been moved.

"Somebody's been in here," I said. "My suitcase isn't where I left it."

I opened it, but everything seemed to be in order.

"You memorized where you put your suitcase?" Scott asked.

I wasn't absolutely certain, and I was tired, so I didn't argue. He still wanted to go out on the town immediately. We compromised. I'd take a shower, but then accompany him to, according to the guidebook, an authentic Tierra Del Fuegan bistro.

I stifled a martyr's sigh. I took my shower, changed into comfortable clothes, and joined him in the lobby. Before we could leave, a small group bustled in through the wooden portal.

The college student, the English couple, the African-American, and a fifth man, I recognized as being our captain, all joined us. He had a thick black mustache and dark olive skin. Edith Blackwell told us she'd heard our captain had deserted from the Iraqi air force in the first days of the Persian Gulf War. She didn't know how he'd become captain of a cargo freighter in Tierra del Fuego.

It seems the Hacienda they were to stay in had a power failure. Our castle could accommodate a mob. Scott told them of our plans to see the town. The Blackwells and the captain decided to join us.

As we waited for them, I was drawn to the guillotine. I was startled to see that the blade was now all the way down. This couldn't have been the thump I heard. Much too far away. Then again maybe they had a guillotine room instead of a video arcade, where guests could be entertained. My imagination was getting the better of me, but I admit the place was spooky.

The captain returned wearing a white turtleneck sweater, jeans, and a beret. He smoked a cheroot. Sister Constance glided up to him. She informed him they had a no-smoking policy. He yielded the cigar up to her without a murmur of complaint. Edith and Edward joined us dressed for an evening out, he in blue blazer and gray pants, she in a fur jacket and a basic black dress with a string of pearls around her neck.

We walked back to town. Topping the rise, we saw our boat swaying peacefully at anchor in the harbor, starlight glittering on the sea, and near at hand the ghastly buildings of the rotting town.

Scott tried to direct us to our destination using the guidebook, but the captain smiled at us and told him he could find a much better place to eat. I'd heard tales of unwary travelers dragooned by evil locals, but Edith, Edward, and Scott all cheerfully followed the glow of the captain's newly lit cheroot to the water's edge. We hiked through deserted streets and along the quay for nearly half a mile, nearly to the other end of the city, when he led us into an unlit doorway.

Inside a fireplace blazed near the door. A row of bottles stacked against one wall declared this a bar. The smell of onions stated this could be a place for food.

An enormously fat man in a white suit, spangled with rhinestones, sat in a corner. The close-cut gray hair and sagging skin put him in his seventies. He raised his wine glass in greeting and lumbered over to our side of the room.

Before he could reach us a woman bustled out of a swinging door. I glimpsed stoves and a sink before the door shut. She gave us a thin smile. The captain spoke in Spanish. She nodded, pointed to a chalk board near a cash register, and hurried away.

"I'm Harry Jackson," the fat man said with a broad southern accent. "You order from that." He pointed where the woman had pointed. "Food won't kill you. A little tangy. Lot of cats around the streets." He laughed at the look on our faces. "Just a joke, folks."

Unbidden, he joined us. Harry and the captain translated

for us as we ordered. Harry claimed to be a rich American bum, former surfer, drummer in a rock band, and clam digger.

After the meal, over what was supposed to be coffee, I asked Harry, "Where are all the people?"

"Superstition," he said.

Our waitress came into the room and began clearing away our plates.

Harry said, "The locals think on this day, every year, evil spirits come and take away one of the locals. Supposedly a male virgin over the age of twenty-one. Silly superstition. Probably started by the local young bucks who couldn't get the girls to put out."

The waitress snarled. We all stared at her. She spoke in heavily accented English. "Is not superstition. Is true. One of us will die tonight. Has happened for many years, not only the young. Could be anyone. Best to be wary on streets."

For all of Harry's bluff joviality, the rest of dinner, already subdued, became nearly funereal. Edith, Edward, Scott, and I huddled together during the trek back to the castle. Each of us examined every blackened nook and cranny as we listened to our footsteps over the brick streets. The captain seemed amused with us and puffed contentedly on his cigar. I was glad to enter the castle, comforted to see Sister Constance at her post, and felt even better when I collapsed into bed. Worn out from nearly three days of travel, I fell asleep immediately.

I woke in darkness. I heard another soft thump. I gazed around the room. Moonlight streamed through the french windows, although the partition in the middle seemed much larger than I remembered. I heard a moan. The partition moved.

I jumped to the windows and yanked them open. Jack Hill slumped to the ground. I saw wetness flowing down his shirt. I rushed to flip on the light. I turned. Blood gurgled from a horrific gash in his throat. I leaned over him, realized I could do nothing to help. I ran to Scott's room. It was empty, the bed unslept in. I bellowed for help. No one came. I threw some pants on.

I ran down the maze of hallways, twisting and turning

through the narrow corridors. I continued shouting for help. Slowly I realized I was in a section of castle I hadn't seen before. I'd taken a wrong turn. I saw no one, heard nothing. Finally I hit the main entrance from the top of the grand staircase that led to the right. I pelted down the stairs, shouting frantically for assistance. No one was anywhere in the vastness. The long-haired gray cat sat on the marble-topped front desk and stared at me indifferently.

I glanced at the guillotine, now in the up position. I hurried over and felt the blade carefully, damp, but not bloody, as if someone had recently wiped it clean.

I heard a sound behind me. The aged mother superior glided toward me over the carpet.

"What is it, my child?" she asked.

I gasped out my story.

She pressed a silent button on top of the desk. Moments later two nuns appeared. The mother superior spoke softly in Spanish. I hurried after the two sisters up the grand staircase on the left. In minutes we arrived at my room. Inside I gave a startled gasp. The body was gone.

For a moment I had the feeling I was in a Stephen King novel. I discover a dead body and now it's gone, in a strange country, in a bleak castle, with no help for miles.

I led the two nuns to the still-open french doors. I felt nausea and relief when I saw the copious quantities of drying blood. We followed the trail along the balcony to an old stone door, where it abruptly ended. I twisted the knob. Locked. I shoved at the door. Wouldn't budge. I looked at the sisters. They joined my ramming at the door. They grunted softly but did not speak during their exertions.

I heard voices from the other end of the balcony. I looked back. Streaming from my room were the mother superior, Scott, most of the rest of the guests, and a man who looked to be a local. His shirt was out of his pants, his hair uncombed, and he yawned widely. He looked about thirty and was introduced to us as the chief of police.

After several minutes' debate, translated for us by Edith Blackwell, I came to the conclusion that the cop was less bright than the most dimwitted village inspector in Sherlock Holmes. We tried a few more futile shoves at the door. Finally a nun showed up with a person introduced to us as a caretaker. He smelt of rotting dog fur and rancid outhouses. His hands shook as he detached a large metal circle of keys from his belt. Ten minutes of trying one key after another, then suddenly we heard a click. The door swung open.

Moonlight shone on an ancient shrine. Jack Hill's head stared at us from the top of an altar. The body lay on the floor directly in front of it.

I hate to admit that my first thought was now Scott will know I was right, and we shouldn't have come to Tierra del Fuego.

A babble of Spanish and English burst forth mixed with the sound of three people retching over the side of the parapet.

We endured hours of waiting, translating, sorting out events.

I found out that earlier Scott had gone down the hall for a late-night visit to the john. He'd run into Ed Blackwell, who'd invited Scott to join Ed and his wife for a cup of tea in the castle kitchen.

Eventually they put the body on a stretcher, covered it up, and carried it out. Back in my room, unable to imagine sleep, I sat on the bed. Glancing toward the dresser near the french windows, I saw an object under it. Two yellow spots blinked at me. For a moment they moved closer, then a gray body flowed from underneath. I opened the french windows to let the cat out. I glanced underneath the dresser. Something else without eyes lay underneath. I prodded it with the toe of my shoe. No reaction. Couldn't be some lethal critter. I knelt down for a closer look. The french doors swung open. I leapt up and whirled around. It was Scott.

He smiled at me. "Come and see the dawn." he said.

I said yes, but first stooped down and felt under the dresser. I grasped the object with my hand and dragged it out from its hiding place. I held up a jammed-full billfold. He ignored it and beckoned me outside. I trudged after him.

It is still the most glorious sunrise I've ever seen in my life. Hot pinks, deep reds, brilliant oranges, slashed by muted gray clouds.

I watched in awe until a tinkling noise drew my attention below. I gazed into the castle garden. I saw rows of bean and tomato plants strung on wooden slats. A stand of corn stood furthest east. The tassels caught the golden light of the morning. The whole scene was lush and green, sheltered by the castle walls from the biting winds, and a few weeks yet from the first killing frosts. It was more gorgeous than any garden from a public-television program.

To one side in a shadow of the castle, at a row of at least twenty small bowls, a dozen cats ate and drank. A nun with a large gray apron over her habit was pouring milk into the last few bowls.

"The nun probably uses dead bodies for fertilizer," I said. I regretted this the minute I said it, because Scott gave me a woebegone look.

Avoiding the reproach in his eyes, I fumbled with the billfold. I found Jack Hill's passport and driver's license, along with three other sets of identification, all with different names, but with the unmistakable photo of the person I knew as Jack Hill on them. Who was this guy?

I showed it to Scott. "We need to give this to the cops," I said. I thought they might still be hunting through Jack Hill's room. We got the number and location from a new nun at the front desk. Five minutes through the castle maze and we arrived at his room. I heard voices inside it. I knocked at the door. Immediate silence from the people inside.

Again I rapped on the portal.

The door opened a crack. I saw one eye and a portion of the blue-rinsed hair of Edith Blackwell.

"What?" she asked.

I held up the billfold. "I found this in my room," I said. Her hand snaked out to snatch it from me. I yanked it back.

"What is this?" I asked. I pushed at the door. The little old woman, a foot shorter than I, held it firm against my strongest shove.

She turned her head back to whomever else was in the room. I watched her ear as seconds ticked by. Finally the door swung open. The small chamber seemed quite crowded with: the boat captain, Ed and Edith Blackwell, Alfred Jones, Margarete Villon, not to mention Scott and me. Several of them sported vicious-looking firearms.

40

I held up the billfold and repeated my question, adding another. "What is this? And why are you all here?"

They all looked at Margarete. On the boat she'd given us a soft French accent and blonde-haired, blue-eyed vacuity. When she spoke now, it was with a harsh Brooklyn accent.

"You can't be part of this," she said. "Give us the billfold. We are more than capable of seizing it from you."

I eyed the menacing group warily and edged toward the door as they closed in on me.

Alfred Jones, the African-American man with the Jamaican accent, said, "Everybody hold it."

We all looked at him.

Margarete glared at him. "I'm in charge here," she said.

"No more killing of innocents," Jones said. "Remember what happened in Lisbon."

Margarete's stare wavered.

"This group has made mistakes," Jones continued. "We cannot afford to fail. The two of them are in danger. We must find a way to do our jobs and not strew victims in our path."

"What's going on?" I said.

Margarete sighed. "We are a team of international agents formed from around the world. We are on the track of one of the most vile terrorists of the past ten years. We have excellent reason to believe she is in Tierra del Fuego."

"Is this the reason the local people were so frightened?" Scott asked.

"If the inhabitants are afraid, it isn't because of us. As far as we know, no group of terrorists has any reason to harm people here," Margarete said.

"That Jack Hill was executed here indicates that the killer could be hiding among the sisters," Edith Blackwell said, "and if she is, that presents us with a nasty problem. It could mean the nuns are in on a terrorist's plotting."

Ed Blackwell said, "What better cover? A convent at the end of the world."

"Are you people nuts?" I asked.

"You saw the dead body," Margarete said. "It was a message for all of us. You two should leave on the first boat out of here."

"That's not for two days," I said.

"Then you'll have to stick it out," Margarete said. "We can't provide protection for you. You'll have to be careful on your own."

Fifteen minutes later, stunned and still only half-believing them, we left the room.

"I'm hungry," Scott said.

"You can eat at a time like this?" I asked.

He shrugged. "I get hungry when I get nervous. Let's find the kitchen and see if we can get anything to eat."

In a sun-filled dining room, rows of nuns sat at tables with starched linen tablecloths. One of their number stood at a podium reading, I presumed from some religious text. We found the gray-walled and ill-lit kitchen further down the same corridor. A nun pointed us to a rank-smelling five-by-five room on the far side of a wood-burning stove. We sat at a table that wobbled, one leg shorter than the other three. Behind my chair a warped wooden door, half-open and hanging by one hinge, led into depths I didn't want to explore.

They brought us toast and runny eggs.

"I don't buy nuns as international terrorists," Scott said. "And hiding in Tierra del Fuego?"

"I'm with you on that," I said, "and I also don't picture that group of losers in Jack Hill's room as crack agents from some secret police force."

"I believed their guns," Scott said. "Do you really think they would have let us go if they weren't cops?"

"I don't know," I said.

The gray-haired, yellow-eyed cat jumped up on the table. Scott began to scratch it behind the ears. The cat closed its eyes and purred.

"I really don't appreciate cats on the dining table," I said.

Scott gathered the cat in his arms. He murmured endearing names to it while I shoved eggs around on my plate. The cat rubbed its head under Scott's chin.

"I want to get out of here," I said. "There must be a place we can charter a boat, rent one, something. I'm willing to try swimming if we have to."

The cat jumped down from Scott's arms and streaked through the door behind me. Silence followed for thirty seconds, then we heard a loud crash followed by an angry feline shriek.

Scott leapt to his feet and tore through the door. The remaining hinge snapped and the door smashed to the ground. Scott ignored it and disappeared down the flight of stairs.

I followed carefully. About twenty feet down, the stairs turned left. I looked back up. Two nuns, one the mother superior, stood in the doorway.

"Here kitty," I heard Scott say.

I tried to follow his voice as he stalked the cat. Aged oaken beams crisscrossed overhead. Water dripped from hidden outlets. Bare light bulbs hung at intervals of twenty feet. They might have been all of five watts for what little good they did at pushing back the darkness. The passageway twisted and turned. I couldn't see Scott, so I continued to follow his cries of "Here kitty." Occasional doorways led off to the side, but I didn't want to chance what might be behind them. After what seemed like miles and hours, I came upon him standing at a pool of water that stretched across the path.

The lights flicked out.

"Great," I said, "and where's the cat?"

"I can see his eyes," Scott said. "We'll follow them. We'll be all right."

Two pinpricks of light bobbed and weaved in the distance.

"I hate to bring this up, but I'm frightened out of my mind," I said. "Why don't we retrace our steps?"

"Just a little further," he said.

"Are you nuts?" I said. "Don't you remember Jack Hill? His head was no longer attached to his body. There are lunatic killers around here."

I heard the murmur of voices. I put my hand out for Scott. He squeaked when I touched him.

"Don't do that," we both said at the same time.

We heard a pounding and a rumbling. Suddenly a door on our right burst open. Daylight flooded the corridor. I saw Edith Blackwell with a crowbar in her hand and a triumphant smile on her face. The other passengers crowded behind her.

The light gleamed on the pool of water. I looked into its depths. A face, deeply scared with eyes boring into mine, stared back at me.

I pointed to it and said, "We are vacationing in Kankakee next year."

The local police arrived. More hours of waiting, explaining, and translating followed.

It turned out there was more than one body in the pool. Two days later on the boat out Edith Blackwell filled us in. Edith told us that the international terrorist had hidden in the castle, murdered Jack Hill, and been caught by the nuns. They'd subdued her and killed her. They hadn't reported this to the police because, as the other bodies in the pit revealed, the nuns had been kidnapping the locals and murdering them. The sisters were going broke with nothing but the ratty old castle and its few visitors and the garden to support them. The nun who ran the garden was crazy. She put mounds of cat fertilizer on her plants, which was why they were so lush, but she found that feeding humans to her cats is what kept them so well fed and productive of what she needed. Only the mother superior and Sister Constance had been in on the scheme with her. It was the terrorist's misfortune that she trusted the nuns, when she should have run as fast as she could from their innocent countenances.

Where's Mittens?

.

Matthew J. Costello

I didn't do it.

But I guess you hear a lot of that. Sure, I understand your quite reasonable skepticism. In my case, though, it happens to be the unvarnished truth. I *didn't* do it and I have something to offer you—I know who did.

Now, wait a minute. *Listen*—surely you heard that wailing sound just now, that mocking, mewling noise? *There!*—no, it's gone now.

You see, there's quite a bit of evidence that you've overlooked. You haven't even heard my story. I'll tell it to you, I'll tell you everything. Then you'll see—

That sound, again! Just outside the window. It must have made that sound that night, sounding so much like a siren . . .

I get ahead of myself. Mustn't rush, must we? Hear my whole story, how cleverly it was all arranged and how I fell into the trap so neatly . . .

It began when she walked into my Scarsdale office one rainy April afternoon. I remember the rain, an incessant New York rain, gray clouds sending down a waterfall that made my office window glass look bevelled. The trees were still winter-bare outside. The day was so damp and cold.

And that miserable chill was matched by the sorry state of my economic affairs. A bad economy touches everyone and everything, and therapy is one of the first frills to be jettisoned by the well-heeled.

I had resorted to taking ads out in the Pennysaver, a ragtag collection of classified ads that arrived in suburban mailboxes like clockwork every Monday. The Pennysaver offered half-price meals at bad restaurants, out-of-date computers that misguided owners thought still had some value, and motorboats that threatened to sink a tapped-out owner.

It was a distressing journal but I thought that I might find some lost souls whose medical coverage still condoned psychological counseling. I advertised for the overweight, for those struggling with demon nicotine, for the lonely and depressed.

And almost by accident I discovered a unique specialty . . . something to set me apart from my fellow counselors.

It happened almost by accident. A woman came to me, middle-aged with silver hair. She held a tissue in her hands that was twisted, laced into her fingers. She had been vague about her problem on the phone. "A family matter," she had said. "Perhaps you could help . . ."

Her dog was depressed. I listened attentively. Her dog was moping around the house. I learned that her husband had passed away a few months earlier and old Fido was taking it hard. (Though the woman didn't seem terribly troubled by her husband's passing.)

Did I have any suggestions?

Thus was born my specialty. I asked the woman about the dog's habits before, what she liked to do with the dearly departed and—after a good number of sessions—I parceled out a regimen that restored a few of the dog's favorite activities, such as long walks, playing catch with a Frisbee, and long drives in the car with his gooey snout poked out the window, sniffing the air.

So then I added—cautiously—"Pet Counseling" to my ad. Certainly there might be other people out there with similarly troubled pets?

And people showed up—not in droves but a steady stream of people came who, for one reason or another, were having difficulty with their pets. Apparently even when the economy turns most dire, people continue pumping money into their pets. Such attachment was charming. And more, it helped ease the pressure on my monthly cash flow.

Here we come to the crux of the matter. I'm trying to

hurry my story. But I don't want to leave out anything, no detail of how I came to meet Mrs. Elaine Randall and learn of the terrible difficulty between her husband . . . and the calico cat she called Mittens.

Elaine Randall had made an appointment without giving the reason she wanted to see me. That wasn't uncommon—people are often reluctant to discuss their problems with the receptionist. Everyone always thinks that their problem is special.

So Mrs. Elaine Randall walked into my office, attractive, wearing an elegant suit, her brown hair pulled back off her face. She sat down in the comfortable chair that faces my desk with an imperial air and the confidence that only money could bring.

Already I was interested in her case.

Whatever it might turn out to be.

Though I must admit to some surprise when she pulled out a little color photograph of a calico tabby.

"This," she told me after the briefest of formalities, "is my cat. His name is Mittens," she said, as if that was an important fact. "I've had him for over ten years."

I nodded. Obviously there was a deep and serious bond between the two.

"I saw your ad . . . about pet counseling . . ." On cue, I looked up, my face a mask of understanding and concern. Lately, I had begun to feel that my acting skills were being called on more and more. And—

Damn! There's that yowl again. You heard it that time, didn't you? Let me get up to the window and I'm sure we'll find it, just outside. If you'll let—

But no. I'm in *media res* here, aren't I? And I haven't gotten to the strange part. Onward, then . . .

I handed the photo back to Mrs. Randall. I studied her face. She was quite beautiful, reminding me of my first wife who had since married her divorce lawyer—though I suspect that she was involved with the shrewd bastard before any proceedings began against me.

"Nice-looking cat," I said. "What seems to be the problem . . . depression . . . loss of appetite . . . confusion . . . bumping into things?"

Cats seemed prey to their own particular kind of Alzheimer's. An old cat could get positively dotty, or so I've been told. But this one, this Mittens, was at most merely middle-aged.

Mrs. Randall shook her head. She took out a cigarette and, in the fashion of the time, looked at me for approval to light it ... though I had a sign on my desk that said Thank You for Not Smoking. It seemed that people with problems also had a predilection for polluting the air.

I smiled and said, "Certainly."

My fee structure was set up to accommodate suffering through such unpleasantness.

"As I said, I've had Mittens for ten years. He's been my friend for all that time. But now—"

The cat's turning on his owner? I thought. There was a dramatic pause.

"Now he and Ralph just don't get along."

My eyes widened. A new character just entered the clinical situation. "Ralph?" I said.

Mrs. Randall nodded, as if admitting a terrible secret. "Yes, my new husband. He didn't particularly like Mittens. That didn't bother me. It wasn't *his* cat."

So, I was thinking, where's the problem?

"But Mittens took an instantaneous dislike to Ralph."

Ah, a family dispute. Perhaps a love triangle. I nodded thoughtfully.

"He leaps out and scratches at Ralph. Mittens actually hisses when Ralph walks by ... and now—" Mrs. Randall looked away and tears seemed very close—"Ralph wants me to get rid of Mittens."

I was tempted to say, "And you'd rather get rid of Ralph?"

Instead, I said, "I guess that Mittens is jealous of your new husband. And that's a natural thing, Mrs. Randall. There are things you could do, though, to—"

Mrs. Randall stood up, again giving me a chance to appreciate how well her suit was tailored, how nicely it showed off what was a very nice shape. My own divorce, I must admit, had certainly put me in that group of therapists who were not above dallying with the more attractive clients.

She came close to me and I smelled a wondrous perfume that certainly helped fuel the fantasy dancing through my head.

"I can't stay now." She looked to the window melodramatically. Were there more problems between Ralph and his wife than a mere cat? "But could you come to the house? Meet—"

The disgruntled spouse himself?

"—Mittens. Perhaps you'll have some ideas."

"And Mr. Randall?" I asked.

She shook her head violently. "No, he mustn't know anything about this. He'll think it so stupid." She grabbed my arm. "Promise me."

I nodded. She smiled and with the legerdemain of a Vegas magician, Mrs. Randall produced a check that more than covered my fee. There was also a slip of paper with an address. "Next Tuesday," she said. "Ralph will be out of town."

I nodded. And she left my office, even as her perfume lingered. I walked to the window and watched her get into a black Town Car illegally parked in front of my office. She pulled away quickly. I turned from the window . . . but not before I saw another car pulling away, a rumpled compact that sported rusty bruises.

I had some time before my next session . . . so I sat behind my desk and I thought of the well-heeled Mrs. Randall.

Tuesday next seemed to take an inordinate amount of time arriving—an indication, no doubt, of the state of my client schedule and, to be sure, my interest in again seeing Mrs. Randall.

I arrived promptly at her house, which was clearly more a mansion. The house was set back from the tree-lined street, girded by a neatly trimmed wall of twelve-foot bushes. The lawn, still brown and shriveled from winter, was nonetheless dotted with fresh grass seed. I rang the bell.

When Elaine Randall appeared she was dressed in tennis whites. I smiled, briefly admiring her appearance that, though functional, was still fetching and revealing.

"Oh, thank you for coming," she said breathlessly, as if she had just dashed off the tennis court.

I smiled. "You have a lovely house," I said, entering. She smiled.

"Would you like something cold to drink?"

"Sure."

She led me in to an all-white living room—meticulous, spotless, with couches and chairs covered with white linen and a thick white rug that I was afraid to walk on. But Mrs. Randall pointed at the couch.

"Please sit down," she ordered. "Some seltzer—or something stronger?"

"Seltzer's fine."

And when Mrs. Randall left—I resisted the temptation to watch her move out of the room, her little tennis skirt bouncing this way and that. I looked around for the object of this house call.

Here, kitty, I thought. Where's the cat? I always assumed that pets wasted no time in checking out new arrivals to their domain. Dogs barked and jumped on people, while cats prowled around, circling closer, suspicious, cautious . . .

I searched the white room but there was no sign of Mittens, whose calico blotchiness would certainly stand out in this pristine environment.

Elaine Randall returned with two glasses. She sat next to me on the couch, and again there was that perfume, now laced with something a bit tangy, the sweat of her tennis game.

And please believe me, it didn't occur to me to wonder who she was playing with that morning. Later I had questions. Later I had lots of questions.

I complimented her on her house. She again thanked me for coming. Then, after a pause, I asked:

"Where is Mittens hiding this morning?"

Mrs. Randall looked out to the hallway, to the staircase.

"He's upstairs. I didn't want him getting loose. So he's in the guest room."

I made an *O* with my mouth, meaning *certainly*. That makes sense. Mrs. Randall grabbed my hand. "Come, I'll take you to him."

The patient awaits, I thought, and I followed Mrs. Randall upstairs—when halfway up, an odd thing happened.

She slipped. She started to stumble backwards, and I quite suddenly found her in my arms—threatening to tumble me backwards, down the dozen or so steps we had just climbed. I might have enjoyed the moment, her slight weight falling into me, her slim body pressing against me. It wouldn't have been unpleasant.

But her sudden move threatened to knock me backwards, perhaps to hit my head on the marble steps.

So I reached out to the handrail for support, stopping both of our precipitous falls. She clutched me tightly—and again, my fantasies had clearly taken over.

"I'm sorry. All the stress, the problem between Mittens and Ralph. I get dizzy."

"That's okay," I said, trying not to hurry the moment. But she stood up and we continued to the guest room.

Now here was shock. No, more than that, here was a *warning*. It should have tipped me off. But I'm no detective. My mysteries are in the mind, not in the small, out-of-place details of everyday life.

The guest room was *dark*. And the smell when Mrs. Randall opened the door was overpowering. There's something about a litter box that's been let go that creates a toxic weapon of immense power. I closed my mouth and breathed shallowly.

I imagine that Mittens had been exiled here as long as the disagreement with Ralph continued.

I walked into the room. Mrs. Randall—no fool—stayed at the doorway. I bent down. I couldn't see any cat. In fact, I could barely make out the litter tray, and the small flecks of litter that dotted the floor, a constellation of litter. There were also some ominous-looking asteroids and meteors floating in that dark space.

"Mittens." I said. "Here, Mittens, kitty, kitty . . ."

Now we all know that cats don't come when you call them. They leave *that* obsequious trick for dogs. But on cue, this Mittens did appear from nowhere, landing in front of me. The animal hissed and followed it by a low, guttural mewl, very unattractive.

I rolled backwards, onto the bird-cage-like gravel. I think I landed on something smooshy.

Naturally Mrs. Randall said, "You scared him."

Right. I scared him. I eased back off my haunches and into a crouch. I risked sticking my hand out.

"Is there a light?" I said. The gloom didn't seem appropriate to conducting a psychological evaluation of the animal. Any creature would be angry in this dingy room.

Elaine Randall turned on a light which only highlighted the disarray.

But Mittens—at least—seemed to have accepted my presence. I stuck out my hand and the calico cat came forward and ducked his head. I scratched him behind his ears. He looked starved for affection.

"Hey, fella," I said. "There, I'm not so bad . . ."

"I'll leave you with him," Mrs. Randall said. "So you two can get to know each other."

Then, unfortunately, she shut the door. The short-haired cat crept closer.

On little cat feet, as Frost put it.

While I kept breathing from my nose.

Later, back in the white living room, the smell of cat and litter still clinging to me, I discussed a suggested course of action.

Get Mittens outside. Make a little fenced-in area that Mittens could explore, get fresh air—and keep away from Mr. Randall. Be sure to scratch behind those ears daily. Buy some special foods for the animal, maybe some chunk light tuna—dolphin-safe, of course.

Mrs. Randall nodded as if hearing the words of an oracle.

"But what about my husband?"

I could have almost given her the same advice. Scratch him in those special places. Feed him some of his special foods. But I said, "I think if Mr. Randall sees less of Mittens, it will be better. And if Mittens is feeling friendlier, your husband may not have any problem with him."

Mrs. Randall smiled. She stood up and another check magically appeared.

And so ended—I thought—another successful session of pet counseling.

Until a week later.

And no, I didn't see that car again, the one with the rusty spots. I told you that, didn't I? I didn't *see* it. But somehow I felt it. I felt that the car was just around the corner, or down a few blocks. I thought of that car, of Mrs. Randall in her tennis whites, and of Mittens, eating better thanks to my intervention.

When I got a call from Elaine Randall.

It threatened to rain again. A clear, warmish spring day gave way to dark clouds. The temperature dropped and in my apartment I could hear the rumblings of a distant storm barreling down the Hudson Valley.

The professional phone—only for emergencies—rang at home. A late-night ring on that phone was a rare occurrence. My answering service was instructed to be very resistant to patient's pleas.

But the woman from the service told me that a Mrs. Elaine Randall had called, insisting that she had an emergency.

There was another rumble, the storm creeping closer.

I called Mrs. Randall. She was crying.

"Mittens attacked Ralph. He scratched him. My husband says he's going to *kill* him."

Domestic violence, I thought . . . perhaps this is a job for the police.

"Put your husband on," I said. "Let me talk to him." *Mano a mano,* I thought, I could calm down the excited Mr. Randall. And I had to wonder why he wasn't enjoying Mrs. Randall instead of becoming so preoccupied with a harmless cat.

"No. He's upstairs in our bedroom. He says he's taking Mittens to a shelter in the morning. Please—come and talk to him."

Ah, another house call. Well, I was sure that Mrs. Randall would reward me for my efforts—even if I didn't dissuade Ralph from dispatching Mittens to kitty heaven.

I assured Mrs. Randall that I'd be right there. I slipped on some clothes, pulled a brush through my hair, and then ran down to my car. The first drop of rain splattered against my forehead. Another hit my back as I got into the car.

By the time I got to the Randall manse, it was a downpour, accompanied by great claps of thunder and flashes of lightning.

I was soaked by the time I got to the front door. And—thoughtfully—it was open. I ran into the hallway.

"Mrs. Randall . . . Mrs. Randall!" There was no answer. Then I called out "Mr. Randall?" feeling peculiar since I didn't know the man.

There was no answer.

I sniffed the air, smelling my own wet clothes, but also Mrs. Randall's perfume. I took a step and it was stronger, an aromatic trail leading me forward.

Perhaps they're upstairs, I thought. She said that her husband was in the bedroom. I knew where Mittens would be. I started up the staircase.

Thinking sure, they're upstairs . . .

I took the steps slowly at first—after all, I had just barged into the house unannounced. But then my pace quickened, hurried no doubt by my curiosity and apprehension.

Still, at the top of the stairs I heard nothing—except for another clap of thunder. It occurred to me that there were few lights on. None downstairs and now—only a single light at the other end of the second floor hall.

I called out again, "Mrs. Randall, Mr. Randall—"

Ralph . . .

My wet Rockports squeaked as I walked down the hall. Past the closed door to Mittens' room, I hesitated, thinking I should check that the cat was still alive. But it seemed likely that the husband and wife were in the bedroom, involved in some tête-à-tête about the fate of Mittens.

I walked to the bedroom, calling their names.

There was another clap of thunder. I heard rain splattering noisily against a window as I passed a dark room. Then another sound, a wail, almost catlike—

I reached the bedroom.

It was empty.

I looked down. No, it wasn't empty. A rather large man

was on the floor, face down. What hair he had was silvery white, thin.

He had had a heart attack, I thought. The stress of the family situation was too much for the old boy.

There was a wail again, now clear, resolving itself into—

Another step and I looked down, and Mr. Randall, if that's who it was, had a rope around his neck. I bent down close. The rope was pulled tight. I saw his face turned to one side. His eyes were wide open. But nobody was home.

His tongue lolled out, nearly touching the plush carpet.

This, I thought belatedly, is bad. This is very bad. I stood up.

Hearing the wail, hearing the *siren*, screaming through the night, closer, closer, accompanied by the cannon blasts of the thunder.

And even then I didn't realize what had happened, what—in fact—was still happening.

There was a scream from downstairs and I thought—at last—there's Mrs. Randall. She screamed. Why is she screaming? I wondered. And the sirens, there were two of them, were outside. Quickly there were voices downstairs. I stood up and started to move out of the room.

Of course, I'd have to tell the police everything that I knew. It wouldn't be good for business. No, this wasn't a very successful therapy.

The police ran upstairs. They had their guns out. They were pointed at me.

"I was too late," I said.

I gestured back at Mr. Randall.

But by the time I turned back to the cops, they already had the handcuffs on me.

So now you know what really happened. And sure, you hear lots of people say they're innocent. But now you understand how my fingerprints got in the house, on the glass, on the handrail.

I never had an affair with Mrs. Randall. I was simply trying to help. It was a set-up. If you find who's in that rusty car, that's your real killer . . . Mrs. Randall's tennis partner, her lover.

Not me. You can't believe her.

And I know ... you didn't find the cat. There was no cat, Mrs. Randall said. The guest room was empty, spotless. But I *saw* the cat, I touched it. This whole thing started with that cat and—

Wait a second. Listen. Hear that? Doesn't that sound like a cat to you? *Listen* ... Yes, *you* tell me what's that sound. Wait a minute. Don't just walk away. That's a cat, isn't it?

Find the cat, find Mittens, and you'll find whoever did this.

Like I said from the start ...

I didn't do it.

No Hard Feelings

•

Larry Segriff

God, I hate cats. Kind of a funny view for a cat burglar, I guess, but it was a cat that got me into this mess. All my life they've fouled me up, and now this.

It started off as a regular job. A three-story Victorian-style house, with an immense snow-covered lawn and a three-car garage. I'd never been inside the place, of course, but it just smelled of money. I watched it for a long while before I felt ready to do the job.

It was a family that lived there, an older couple and a girl that I figured was back from college. She was young enough, and had that attitude about her, like there were no such things as jobs in life. Plus, it was Christmastime, and she was never home. She had to be back from college, or someplace like that, more concerned about her friends than her family.

Why is it that the more a kid's got, the more ungrateful she is?

Midnight brings out the philosopher in most people, and I'm no exception. Even cold, cloudy nights like this one. Not much else to do, I guess, except think and freeze.

I saw the college girl get home around ten and thought that was decent of her, tomorrow being Christmas and all. She had a kitten with her when she went into the house, and I shuddered at the sight. I was allergic to cats, which was why I decided to go ahead and do the job that night. I didn't want the place to get filled up with cat hair.

I went in at 2:15. That's always been my favorite time for working. Late enough so that everyone's sound asleep;

early enough that the older folks probably won't be up going to the bathroom; and, just in case I slip up, the cops are busy rousting drunks.

Besides, I just like that time of night.

I went in a window. In all the time I'd been watching the house, I hadn't seen any activity at all on the third floor, so that's where I slipped in. The climb was a bitch, but I'd done this enough to know to be careful, and one good thing about a new cat in the house: I was pretty sure there wasn't a dog.

The window went up quietly, and I was glad to see there wasn't any alarm system. Those things are a joke, really, but they do take a few minutes to deal with, and I didn't like to waste time.

There were six rooms on the top floor, and none of them looked to be used for anything. At a guess, I would have said they'd belonged to the kids when they were growing up, except that I hadn't seen anyone besides the college girl. Maybe the house had been in the family for generations. I didn't know.

There wasn't anything worth taking up there, which was all I cared about.

The second floor was more rewarding. I cleaned out the old couple while they slept. Got some cash and a lot of jewelry, and they never roused up at all. They never do. Sometimes I'd leave a little rose on their pillow, but not in December.

Their room was at one end of the house. Hers was at the other. In between were two guest rooms, a sewing room, and a large bath. I took nothing from any of those.

As soon as I opened her door I knew I'd found the cat. I could smell it, and my nose started to itch. Psychosomatic, I knew—even if the place had been lousy with cats it was too early for any symptoms to show up—but there it was.

Her bed was beneath the window, the curtains open to the cloudy night. The room was cool, and she was bundled up beneath a thick blanket. I could see the kitten curled up beside her head, and I cautioned myself to greater silence. I didn't know much about cats, other than that I didn't like them, and I didn't know how it would react to strange noises.

I found her purse by the door, but there wasn't much in it, just a few lousy dollars and a college I.D. card. The state university, which surprised me. I'd have guessed Ivy League, but maybe that wasn't important to her. Then I checked her dresser and got a couple of small jewelry boxes. I didn't open them for fear they were musical.

That was it. The job was over. I'd learned long ago not to be greedy, and it was time to get out. I was turning to leave, quite happy with my haul, when it happened.

I sneezed.

I got most of it muffled, but not enough. Spinning back towards the bed, I saw two eyes glaring at me. Not hers. The cat's.

I freaked. When I was a kid, I once saw a cat that had cornered a rat and was playing with it. The rat was as big as the cat, maybe bigger, but that didn't seem to matter. The cat was quicker, and while watching their little game there was no doubt in my mind who was in control. They played for about ten minutes, the cat batting the rat every so often, avoiding the lunging bites easily and flipping these lightninglike paw shots in return. Finally the cat got tired of it and started to turn away. I figured the rat was so mad it would jump on it from behind, but it was smarter than I was; it bolted for a trash can.

It never made it.

I heard its claws click once on the bricks, and then the cat had spun back towards it, pinned it, and disemboweled it, all in the time it took me to blink. It didn't even eat the rat; just batted it a few more times until it finally died, and then it walked away. As near as I could tell, all it had gained from the encounter was a drop or two of blood on its paws.

I never forgot that scene. It was only a month or two later that I developed my allergy. And now this little kitten was looking at me in the same way the other cat had eyed that rat.

I knew I had to get out of there. The college girl was still asleep, which was a lucky break, but one that couldn't last long. My eyes were burning, my nose was running, and

I could hear my breath whistling in my lungs. Besides, I wanted away from that cat.

I got out of there, heading back up to the third floor. I knew better than to use the front door. People who wouldn't think to put an alarm on a third-floor window often put one on the door. No sense giving Fate another chance to screw me over.

I got to the window and threw a leg over the sill. Turning to go out butt-first, I saw that damned cat had followed me. God, but things were not going right for me. At least there wasn't any sign of the college girl.

Catching the sill with my hands, I started lowering myself down slowly. The old couple's window was directly beneath this one, and the decorative molding around it was a perfect place to put my feet. After that, I could easily reach over and grab the same downspout I'd shinnied up on my way in.

That was my plan, anyway.

Going down was trickier than going up because I couldn't see my feet. Normally I tried to find a better route out, but this time I was too anxious. I hadn't wanted to take the time to look for alarms, not when I could start sneezing and wheezing and wake up the whole house.

I was hanging by my fingers, trying to remember just how far beneath me the top of that window was, when I felt something sharp prick my skin. The cat had found my fingers and was playing with them.

I thought of that alley, and had a sudden vision of those sharp claws slicing open my hands, and instinctively I let go.

I was closer to the window beneath me than I'd thought and my feet struck it before I was ready. My knees knocked against the siding of the house, and the next thing I knew I was falling.

Two stories straight down, and I landed on my back. I remember looking up as I fell and seeing that kitten framed in the window, watching me.

I survived, but I broke my back. The doctors say that I'll probably be paralyzed for the rest of my life. The family decided not to press charges, figuring that I'll suffer enough as it is, and they're probably right. The college girl, a sociology major, is taking it a step further. She wants to show that there are no hard feelings or something. And she wants me to have some company in the dark times ahead.

She's sending me a pet, a kitten, to sit on my chest and keep me warm. I can hardly wait.

Cat Burglar

·

Bill Crider

*I hate to mention this but ... I'm getting pretty darn
sick of cutesy cats all over the place. One cat per
book is enough,* but cats don't talk, cats don't think
and cats don't detect!

—Ellen Nehr,
"The Apron String Affair" #81

Benny decided to hit the house as soon as he saw the Kitty
Kare van parked in front. It was a dead giveaway.

He'd been keeping an eye on the neighborhood for a day
and a half. It was pretty easy to do.

In the morning, he was the jogger with the visor pulled
down low over his forehead. You could cover a lot of ter-
ritory that way, jogging slow, up one side of the street and
down the other.

In the late afternoon, he was out walking the dog, a greyhound that he'd picked up for free after it got too old to
race. He wore a safari hat that shaded his face and hid his
eyes.

But his favorite ploy was the one he used during the
middle of the day. He carried a handful of flyers that he'd
made himself at a coin-operated copier. They had a hole cut
in the middle at the top so he could slip them over door-
knobs.

The best thing about it was that the ad was legit. Benny
had asked a couple of boys for one when he was out jogging one day and saw the kids hanging them on doors. He
figured that he and the kids would both benefit if he used

the ad himself. They'd get free advertising, and he'd get a reason to be walking through the neighborhoods and right up to everyone's front door. If anyone ever called the numbers, they'd get a genuine lawn-mowing service, and if anyone asked him what he was doing, he'd say, "Just helping out my nephews."

LAWNS MOWED AND EDGED

SUMMERTIME

SCHOOLTIME

ANYTIME

$20–$25

We can save you $$$$$$! ! !

Call Robbie at 555–8989

Or Tommie at 555–7546

But no one had ever asked him, and he'd gone happily on his way, blanketing a lot of neighborhoods and peeking into a lot of front rooms when nobody was watching him.

He'd even thought at one time about advertising for Kitty Kare, since the business was such a big help to him. The Kitty Kare people were cat-sitters. If you were on vacation, you could call them up and they'd come to your house while you were gone and look after your cat. Feed it, water it, empty the litter box, whatever you needed along those lines. Maybe they'd even sit down with the cat and

63

rub its belly. He didn't know or care. He was a dog lover himself.

Benny loved those Kitty Kare vans, though. Wherever they were parked, a family was gone. It was a virtual certainty, even if the newspapers weren't stacking up, even if the mailbox wasn't full, and even if the yard looked as if it had been mowed yesterday. (Maybe it had. Maybe the homeowners had called Tommie or Robbie.)

When he passed the house and saw the van, he was walking his greyhound. The van driver, a pretty young blonde, was just getting out, and she glanced back at him and his dog.

"Good afternoon," he said brightly and brought his hand to the brim of his safari hat as if to tip it, though his real interest was in concealing his face a little better.

"Hi," the girl answered, then turned to the house.

Benny walked on by, knowing that sometime after midnight he'd be back.

Benny had his first problem just before he got back to his car that afternoon. He always parked on the edge of the neighborhood, preferably in a grocery-store lot, and walked from there.

There wasn't a grocery store nearby this time, but there was a strip mall with a lot of little shops, a bookstore, and a couple of fast-food restaurants.

He didn't know where the cat came from. Probably from behind one of the restaurants, where it had been digging in the trash, not that it mattered. It was moving slowly, not bothered a bit by the traffic in the parking lot. The drivers all stopped for it, tolerant smiles on their faces.

The cat was inky black, and for a second Benny was tempted to turn back. He wasn't superstitious. He just didn't like the idea of a black cat walking across his path when he was leading a greyhound.

Then it was too late. The greyhound, trained to chase the rabbit at the track, sighted the cat and took off.

Benny was taken by surprise, but his reflexes were good and he tightened his grip on the leash just in time—just in time to prevent the dog's escape, and just in time to get himself jerked off his feet.

He landed hard, but he held onto the leash. The cat bounded onto the hood of a Honda Accord, where it stood arching its back, writhing its puffed tail, and hissing at the greyhound, which, straining every muscle, was dragging Benny inch by inch across the hot asphalt.

Benny managed to get to his feet and pull the dog back just before it reached the Honda. The cat gave one last hiss and disappeared over the top of the car.

Someone applauded, and Benny was sorry to see that he and his dog had gathered a small crowd composed mostly of cat lovers. Not a one of them seemed to have a shred of sympathy for Benny, whose pants were ripped at both knees and whose palms were bloody from sliding on the asphalt.

Benny didn't care. All he wanted to do was get out of there before anyone got a good look at his face. But he didn't want anyone to see his car, so he had to walk away with as much dignity as he could muster, pretending to have business elsewhere. It was fifteen minutes before he came back to the parking lot, put the dog in the back seat of his nondescript navy blue Chevy Nova, and drove away, cursing the black cat all the way home.

He'd forgotten all about the cat by midnight. He spent the evening thinking about the house.

He'd looked it over carefully, and he'd been glad to see that it had a seven-foot wooden fence around the back yard. Even a locked gate wasn't much of a deterrent to Benny, who, given a little running room, could plant a foot in the middle of the fence, grab the top, and be over into the back yard in the space of an instant.

There was a streetlight at the end of the block, but it wouldn't bother Benny much. It was too far away. He hadn't seen any security lights on the house itself, so he could park in the driveway and load his car out of the garage door. There was a new moon, and it would be plenty dark enough.

He didn't think the house had an alarm system. There hadn't been any indication that there was one, and these days everyone who had an alarm put a sign in the yard and stickers on the windows. Even a lot of people who *didn't* have alarms put up signs and plastered their windows, just to make people like Benny think the house was protected.

He didn't worry about getting into the house from the back yard. There was always a way.

He shined the thin beam of the Black Max flashlight around the back yard. There was a glass-enclosed roofed patio, and beside the door there were two huge bowls, one of them half full of dog food, the other half full of water. The name *Killer* was painted on both bowls with red fingernail polish.

Benny chuckled. It was the oldest trick in the book. Because there was no giant dog in the back yard, he was supposed to retreat in fear of the monster that must be lurking inside the door.

But there was no monster. There was just a cat that the Kitty Kare people were looking after. He pushed the bowls aside with his foot and looked at the door. It was made mostly of glass panels, so he covered one with tape and gave it a little tap with the ballpeen hammer he carried in his back pocket.

When he had cleared the glass away, he reached inside and unlocked the door.

Walking across the enclosed patio, he shook his head ruefully at the sight of a sliding glass door. This was almost too easy.

There was a broomstick in the track on which the door slid, and that would certainly have prevented it from opening if Benny had intended to slide it.

He didn't intend to open it at all, however. He took a screwdriver from his pocket, and in less than a minute he had jacked up the sliding part of the door, which had simply been set in the track by the builder, and removed it. He set it aside, pushed aside the curtain, and entered the kitchen.

The owners of the house had thoughtfully left a fluorescent light on in the den, so Benny could see well enough to put away his flashlight. He glanced around the partially darkened kitchen. The first thing he noticed was a wooden sign hanging on the wall: THIS HOUSE IS PROTECTED BY A TRAINED ATTACK CAT!

"How corny can you get?" Benny muttered to himself.

On the other hand, he thought, it wouldn't hurt to locate the cat after he'd opened the door leading to the garage.

Oddly enough, however, he couldn't find the cat. He found its food bowl and its litter box (which seemed fairly clean; the Kitty Kare people did good work), but there was no sign of the cat itself. He didn't really care. He wasn't there to steal the cat.

Instead he took the VCR (four-head stereo), the color TV (picture-in-picture; he might keep it for himself), the stereo (a Bose acoustic wave machine; these people knew good stuff), the baseball card collection (lots of 'fifties cards, both Bowman and Topps, probably worth 'more than the TV), the jewelry (nothing classy; mostly stuff you could buy from the home shopping channels), the computer and monitor (a real IBM, not a clone), the answering machine (it wasn't worth a lot, but it was small), the good silver, and the hunting rifles.

He worked fast, putting everything in the garage. When it was all stacked, he was ready to bypass the automatic opener and swing up the door. He'd been in the house maybe fifteen minutes. A little long, but not too bad. He looked through the glass in the garage door. There was no sign that anyone was interested in the house.

He decided that he had time to wash his hands and get a drink of water. There was a small bathroom right by the door from the house to the garage, which Benny thought was a real convenience for someone coming in from working in the yard if he wanted to clean up without getting the house dirty.

The bathroom was a long way from the den and therefore quite dark, but Benny didn't need a light to wash his hands. He felt for the faucet handle and discovered it was one of the kind that you controlled by pulling straight out.

He pulled it.

Water shot from the faucet.

The cat that Benny had been unable to find, who had been sleeping in the basin, shot up in the air, or about as far up in the air as an eighteen-pound neutered male could shoot from a slick ceramic spot where its back claws couldn't really get much of a purchase.

"Miaor-r-r-r!" the cat yowled.

Angry at being so suddenly drenched, or fearful at being disturbed by a prowler, or perhaps catching a whiff of Benny's greyhound, the trained attack cat tried to escape by climbing over Benny, who was taken by complete surprise and was frozen in his tracks in front of the basin, not having any idea of what might be happening to him.

He got a much better idea when the cat's claws dug into his chest and face and then into the top of his head, right where Benny's hair was the thinnest.

The cat jumped from the top of Benny's head to the floor and charged off down the hall toward the kitchen.

"You son of a bitch!" Benny yelled, not being an expert on feline ancestry. He wheeled around and lunged after the cat.

There was no sign of the cat in the kitchen, so Benny went into the den.

"You might as well come out," Benny said. "I'm going to find you sooner or later."

The cat didn't say anything, and Benny suddenly realized how ridiculous the situation was. He was talking to a cat, and of course the stupid cat couldn't talk back.

He put a hand to the top of his head and felt gingerly at the spots where the cat's claws had sunk in. His fingers came away slightly damp with blood, and he wiped them on his pants leg.

It wasn't really the cat's fault, he decided. After all, cats can't think. It was just scared of him, and he didn't really blame it. How would he feel it someone came sneaking into his bedroom and threw water on him? He'd probably do something about like the cat had done.

What he needed to do now, though, was to get out of the house. He'd been there too long as it was.

He turned and started for the kitchen and stepped right into the middle of the cat, which had slipped up behind him while he stood there.

"Miaor-r-r-r!" the cat howled, somehow twisting around and sinking its claws into Benny's right calf.

"Son of a bitch!" Benny yelled, reaching down for the cat, another mistake, for the cat released his calf and lacerated his hand.

"Ga-r-r-r-r!" Benny said. He raised up and tried to kick the cat, but the cat was now merely a fleeing dark gray blur.

Benny started after it, but he managed to swallow his rage and stop himself. He had to get out of there. He limped toward the garage, sucking first one wound and then another on his hand.

The Nova started very quietly, out of its principal virtues, and Benny drove out of the driveway. There was a light on in the house next door now, and Benny wondered if he'd been spotted. He hoped not, but he couldn't let the possibility worry him. He drove slowly and carefully, careful not to break any traffic laws. Every now and then he would look at the long scratches that crossed the back of his hand and curse the cat.

But that was all behind him now. He'd gotten away free and clear, and all in all he'd made a pretty good haul. The TV was especially nice, and he was thinking again that he'd like to keep it for himself when he saw the police car speeding toward him.

There were no other cars on the street at that time of morning, and Benny prayed silently that the cops would just pass him by. He was several blocks away from the house now; maybe they wouldn't notice him.

They did, though. When it was about a block away, the police car slowed noticeably.

Benny kept on driving at a steady pace, not too fast, not too slow. His eyes looked straight ahead, past the police car and down the street. He tried to appear completely relaxed, and he hoped that it was too dark for the cops to see his cat-scratched face. He hoped they didn't spotlight him.

If he hadn't been thinking so much about the cops, he might have seen the orange tabby that was slashing into the plastic garbage bag sitting by the curb awaiting an early-morning pickup. And he might even have seen the black-and-white tom that came slinking out of the shadows of a hedge when the tabby opened the bag and dragged out a piece of a paper plate to which a half-slice of rancid bacon adhered.

He did hear the squalling that ensued when the tom

jumped the tabby, and he jerked his head to the right just in time to see the tom pursue the tabby into the street directly in front of his car, though he didn't notice the small strip of bacon dangling from a corner of the tabby's mouth.

He had two choices.

He could throw on his brakes, or he could kill the cats.

He didn't really think about it, however; no one in his situation would.

He threw on his brakes and pulled the car wheel hard to the right, swerving into the curb and jumping it. The bumper of the Nova hit the plastic bag, bursting it and sending garbage flying.

It didn't take long after that.

The cops stopped, of course. They took one look at Benny's face and knew that he hadn't gotten those scratches in the accident. That gave them plenty of reason to look in the back seat and trunk of the Nova, and what they found there gave them plenty of reason to haul Benny down to the substation and book him.

He sat there in the back seat of the police car while they called the station to say that they were bringing him in. He was thinking about cats: about a black cat that crossed his path, about a trained attack cat that had delayed him a little too long, about the two cats that had dashed into the street in front of his car. He knew that cats couldn't think, but it was enough to make you wonder.

He looked out the back window of the police car as the driver started it. The orange tabby and the black-and-white tom were sitting in the yard, as happy together as if they were the best of friends. The tom was licking a paper plate, while the tabby was looking back at Benny with eyes that shone red in the streetlight.

"Goddamn cats," Benny said. Maybe they could think after all.

"What's that you said?" one of the cops asked.

The orange tabby looked down and started biting at a flea on his back leg. It looked ridiculous. No way such a stupid-looking animal could think.

"Nothing," he said. "I didn't say a thing."

The police car rolled away.

Fat Cat

·

Nancy Pickard

"**Z**eke, have a heart. How would it *look*?"

My friend, the Mt. Floresta chief of police, Jamison Grant, screwed up his face into what he apparently thought was a pleading expression. The effect produced among the deep, tanned wrinkles of his fifty-six years was unnervingly grotesque.

"So that's how you get criminals to confess." I grimaced back at him. Not the same effect, though, me being thirty years younger. "No need to beat it out of them. Just pull a face like that and they'll say anything."

Having thrown himself on my mercy and found it wanting, Jamison resorted to his own particular brand of subtlety. "Now listen, you harebrain." He sucked in his stomach behind his massive brass belt buckle and pulled his gargantuan frame upward until his face hovered several inches above my own six feet. From up there, like a great blue bald-headed eagle, he loomed. I was not intimidated. Insulted, maybe, but not intimidated. The legal eagle squawked: "Now this may be a small town, and we may not get reams of rapes and murders to keep us busy, but that does not mean I am free to go chasing some old lady's damn cat!"

"It's more than one cat and more than one old lady," I informed him. "And they're not all old. The ladies, I mean. I can name you at least one who's young and pretty."

"Do not interrupt me when I am being officious," Jamison said sternly. He grabbed a sheaf of paperwork from the in-basket on his desk and fanned the air in front of my nose with it. "Do you see these papers? *All* these papers? If you were to examine them closely, you would see there are blanks on them. I have to fill out those blanks, Zeke. And I have two thefts to investigate, one mayor to meet, the owner of a health spa to placate, three trials to attend in Gunnison, and a hell of a lot of other *important* work to do."

"The cats are important to their owners," I protested.

As owner, manager and general runabout for our town's animal shelter, I know a priority when I see one. It was quickly evident, however, that my priorities were not necessarily those of the Mt. Floresta, Colorado, police force.

"I don't even *like* cats," the bald eagle reminded me. Under the fluorescent light, his shiny pate gleamed. "Cats are sneaky, like thieves in the night and some young friends I could mention."

I decided it was the better part of caution not to argue with him. When you're an animal freak, as I am, sometimes you forget all the world does not love a cat. So I said in my best martyr's tone, "Okay, okay. I don't know what's become of the police in this town. Used to be they'd come help you get a kitten out of a tree, just one little kitten—"

"That was the firemen, Ezekiel."

"But now—" I waved my arms to encompass the entire one-room police station. "But now, I can't even get your attention when fifteen cats vanish."

"You exaggerate."

"No way, Jamison. I swear to God, fifteen cats have disappeared from this town in the last two months. And there may be more, for all I know."

"They got run over."

"Nope. No bodies, no squashed cat bodies lying around the streets. And don't tell me they ran away from home. These are pets, gorgeous cats, mama's little darlings."

"Zeke." Jamison's voice dripped compassion. "Old pal, friend of my own son, I would love to help you. You know I'd do anything if I could—"

"Yeah, right!"

"—but you are a fanatic when it comes to animals. And fanatics cannot see the forest for the aspens, the glacier for the ice. Just trust me on this one. There is no mystery.

There is no problem. Cats come, cats go. Like tourists. And, like tourists, not soon enough, in my opinion."

I squinted my eyes like an angry tom. "You forgetting the cat lobby, Jamison?"

"The what?" He looked suspiciously on the verge of laughing.

I yelled at my friend the political appointee, "Cat owners vote, you know!" I let the door slam behind me when I stomped out of the station.

Outside, the crisp mountain air cooled me off as it always does. There's something about living in the mountains, at 10,000 feet above sea level, that puts things in perspective, or so the tourists say. I wouldn't know. Having lived in Mt. Floresta all my life, I have no perspective on that. Maybe Jamison was right, I thought, maybe I have blown this out of proportion. I snapped my ski vest shut against the fall wind and hiked up my jeans. Worry makes me lose weight, and I'd been getting real concerned about the increasing number of lost-cat reports coming into my office from distraught cat owners.

"Mr. Ezekiel Leonard?" That's how many of the calls began. The really older ladies called me by my full name and mister. It made me feel older than my twenty-six years, and smarter, which is possibly what they hoped I was. Like most of the cat owners, they sounded nervous, timorous, hesitant to bother me, and sad. "Mr. Leonard," they'd say, "my Snowflake has disappeared." Or Big Boy or Thomasina or Annabelle. "He's (she's) never done this before, and I just don't know what to think. I've looked everywhere, and I've asked everybody I know. But nobody has seen my Big Boy (or Thomasina or Snowflake) since Tuesday."

At first, I didn't attach any significance to the calls. I just searched our pens for a feline of the right description and then assured the caller I'd keep an eye out for kitty. Then I'd add kitty's name and phone number to my "missing" list.

It took me a while to notice how long that list was getting. And how few names I was crossing off. Oh, I found Mrs. McCarty's Siamese and returned him. And I had to break the news to Bobby Henderson after I saw his calico lying by the side of the highway. But by the end of September, the obvious was becoming just that: seventeen pet cats had been declared missing since August and I'd found only two of them. I was sure somebody was stealing them. But what the hell would somebody want with fifteen very spoiled cats? There wasn't any animal experimentation lab in the county, or anywhere else nearby that I knew of. And I made it my business to know such things. I just couldn't figure it out.

I broke off my reverie on the steps of the police station and headed down Silverado Street toward the office of the *Lode*, which passes for a newspaper in our town. "Get a Lode of This!" is their motto, which actually appears above the masthead. I guess everything's a lot more casual up here in the mountains, where everybody wears blue jeans and nobody ever wears a suit, except maybe visiting bank examiners.

Mt. Floresta is an old mining center turned chic: we're about as "in" as a ski resort can get and still stand itself. We have your restored Victorian buildings, we have your ugly new condos, we have your charming gas streetlights and your café au laits, we have your lift tickets and your gourmet restaurants, we have your drunk tourists and your inflated prices. We also have a lot of great big dogs—Malamutes, Samoyeds, huskies, and the like—that people who move here think they just have to have along with a nice cat to sit by the fire at their rental hearth. And then, when they move out after getting a taste of one whole cold long snowy winter season, they sometimes abandon those poor creatures, and that's where I come in, at the Mt. Floresta Animal Shelter located on the edge of town just around the corner of the closest mountain.

As I walked, I ducked my head, but not against the wind or the tourists. The longer I went without finding those cats, the harder it was to face the cat lovers in town. I knew if I encountered the lugubrious eyes of Miss Emily Parson one more time I'd go jump in Spirit Lake. Miss Parson's great black Angora, Puddy, was among the missing.

I was so intent on making like a turtle that I nearly collided with the current love of my life.

"Hello, Atlas," she said. "World a little heavy on those shoulders?"

"Hi, Abby." I leaned down and kissed her cheek, which was soft and downy and well shaped like the rest of her. Abigail Frances, late of New York, was by far the best of the current crop of easterners to have fallen in love with our town and decided to grace us with their permanent presence. If I sound cynical, it's because in a resort town, *permanent* has a shelf life of about nine months. I've gotten leery of making new friends and weary of farewell parties.

"No luck with the police?"

There was sympathy in her soft voice, but I thought I detected an edge to it that had nothing to do with her New York accent. If I was a fanatic, Abby was a flaming zealot when it came to cats and, as I knew only too well, she was one of the grieving and aggrieved cat owners whose baby was missing. In fact, she and I had met over the report of her lost cat, a magnificent—to judge by the pictures she showed me—Himalayan, name of Fantasia.

Like Atlas, I shrugged. But I didn't feel any burdens roll off.

I took Abby's arm and turned her around.

"Come spend your lunch hour with me," I said. Abby, who didn't need the money, worked hard at the gift shop she bought when she moved to Mt. Floresta. "We're going to give the *Lode* a front-page story."

"Classifieds, Zeke, that's where missing cats go."

"But, Ginny," I protested to my friend, the editor of the *Lode*, "that's where they've been going for two months! Aren't your classifieds getting a little full by now? I'll bet you've got more missing cats than you do skis for sale—"

"I doubt *that*."

"Well, I'm telling you this is a bona-fide front-page story, a *scoop*."

Ginny Pursell cast her navy-blue eyes skyward. "Dear Ezekiel, darling Zeke, whom I have loved more or less like a brother since grade school, in your business you may know all there is to know about *scoops*. But let me tell you a thing or two about front-page stories."

By my side, Abby cracked a knuckle ominously. It's a

disgusting habit she likes to indulge in when she really wants to annoy somebody—like a local who makes it clear who is the newcomer to town and who is not. I did think Ginny's comment about grade school was a shade gratuitous.

"A front-page story," she lectured us, "is our cretinous mayor making an ass of himself in front of the White House in a protest against oil-shale development. No," Ginny held up a forestalling hand, "we shall not argue politics. I have my editorial stance and I shall keep it. What's good for oil-shale development is good for Mt. Floresta."

More knuckles. Mine. I am about as much in favor of digging into our mountains as I am of vivisection. Besides, the mayor's also a friend of mine. But Ginny's an anomaly—a conservative Republican journalist in a liberal Democratic county. As a newspaper editor and publisher, she's the only game in town, however, so we have to swallow her opinions along with the news.

"A front-page story is the hassle I'm getting from Larry Fremont—"

"You too?" I recalled the chief's gripe about having to "placate" the owner of a health spa. "Hell, I never thought ol' Larry would give this town anything, not even so much as a hassle or a hard time."

"What do you mean, 'you too'?"

"I think he's bugging Jamison Grant about something."

"Oh, lord." Ginny groaned. "He'll try anything to keep my story out of print." Like Jamison before her, she picked up some papers and waved them at me. I was rapidly tiring of the gesture. "I had this article practically written. All about trash disposal and what we're going to do about it in the future. It's a major problem, you know, because we need places to toss our garbage and the environmentalists won't let us put a dump near any place that's practical or economical."

"Like right beside Spirit Lake? Good for them."

"Who's Larry Fremont?" Abby asked, bravely asserting her ignorance.

Ginny threw me a knowing look, local-to-local, as it were, whereupon Abby's knuckles cracked resoundingly. I hurried to explain. Larry, I told her, was a local boy made good. So good he wouldn't have anything to do with us anymore. He was the founder of La Floresta, the combination health spa/dude ranch down in the valley. It was one of those resorts where rich ladies paid thousands of dollars to get a few pounds beaten and starved out of them.

"They all look the same to me when they come out," said Ginny, who has nothing to worry about herself when it comes to the slim-and-trim department. She also has lots of curly black hair—like a standard poodle, I tell her, which always makes her reach for a comb immediately, to my regret—and one of those tanned mountain faces in which blue eyes stand out like beacons. "Except they look like they go in fat and unhappy and they come out fat and happy."

At first *everybody* was happy about Larry's success, I told Abby, particularly since he was generous with jobs. But in the last year he'd started firing everybody from around here. Not that he made it so obvious; it happened little by little, person by person. Before we knew it, there wasn't one person from Mt. Floresta left on his payroll. Instead, he was hiring folks from further down the valley. And he took on a lot of college kids looking for resort work.

"Since then," I said, "nobody from Mt. Floresta cares much for Larry Fremont. We call him Fremont the Freeloader. He trades on our famous name without giving anything back to our economy. The S.O.B. even banks in Denver." I turned to Ginny. Her office cat, a stray she'd picked up from my shelter, jumped on her desk and made pet-me sounds. "What if Tiger was one of the cats that was missing?" I reached over to stroke his ugly yellow head. "Then how would you feel?"

"Why is Fremont hassling you about trash dumps?" Abby asked. She sticks to a subject better than I do.

"Because La Floresta sits on a landfill," Ginny told her. "Remember, Zeke? That was the old county dump for fifty years. God knows how many secrets are buried there. They filled it in just before Larry bought the land and built his spa.

"And he doesn't want me to say so in my article," she went on. "I have to mention it because it's such a good example of a landfill. Shows how the land can be reclaimed successfully. But he's afraid for his image. Can you believe it? He doesn't want his precious customers to know La Floresta sits on a trash heap!" Ginny shook her head in apparent dismay over the sorry state of progressive conservatives in the United States. "So I can't help you, Zeke. I've got more on my mind than cats. If you want a front-page story, give me something with blood and guts. Like a good juicy murder."

She smirked. We left.

Knowing Ginny, I'm sure she regretted that smirk the next day when she had to write the story of Rooney Bowers' death. OIL SHALE ENGINEER VICTIM OF HIT AND RUN, her headline told me. The story said that Rooney Bowers, associate professor of petroleum engineering at the university, had been bowled down in front of his house in the frosty hours of the morning. Whatever hit him threw him fifty feet across Mabel Langdon's holly hedge and into her front yard. Mabel found him a few hours later when she went out to get the paper.

"It was awful," she allowed herself to be quoted as saying. "There he was dead as a smelt and him such a nice quiet neighbor and all." Mabel sometimes has a colorful way of putting things.

I called Chief Jamison Grant immediately.

"It's Zeke." I got right to the point. "Where is Rooney Bowers' cat?"

"Honest to God, Ezekiel, you have the most one-track mind of anyone I ever knew." Jamison sounded harried. "The man gets killed and all you can think of is his damn cat. I don't know where it is. Maybe the neighbors have it, maybe—"

"It's a long-haired silver tabby. It wasn't in the house when you got there?"

"No, it wasn't in the house or around the house and I didn't even know Rooney had a cat and will you please stop bugging me about cats? Look, we'll get the cat to you. You know we will. Nobody's going to let the darned thing starve. But I got a hit-and-run to solve, Zeke. The cat's got to wait."

"Wait, Jamison, listen to me. I know Rooney pretty well, I mean, I knew him. We used to get together for a beer, he and the mayor and I, and we'd argue about oil shale."

"Zeke, please—"

"But the last time we didn't talk about oil, Jamison. We talked about cats. I told them all about the missing cats and how I thought somebody was stealing them."

"So?"

"So Rooney always gets—got—up real early to start his research. About four in the morning. And that's when he let his cat out, Jamison. He used to joke about it. Said his Tom was the only one he ever knew who liked it better in the morning than at night. Like some women he knew, he said."

"I repeat: so?"

"So . . ." Suddenly I knew how foolish I sounded. "So maybe it's got something to do with his death, that's all. I mean maybe all the missing cats are some kind of clue or something." It has been pointed out to me more than once that the less I know the more inarticulate I get.

"Thank you so much, Zeke," Jamison said heavily. "I'll certainly think on it."

I hung up quickly while we were still friends.

Abby thought I was crazy, too.

"But what if somebody was stealing Rooney's cat and Rooney saw him do it?" I said, expressing my theory in the sparsity of its fullness.

"Well, I seriously doubt they'd kill him over it," she said. We were sitting in my office trying to talk over the cacophony coming from the pens. I'd just put a new dog out there and he was getting quite a greeting. "I mean, don't you think you're being just a bit melodramatic? I'm as upset as you about the cats, but still—murder?"

She took a careful sip of the truly awful coffee I had brewed in my brand-new machine. "You know, if you put a lot of sugar in this, you might cover the taste of the plastic."

"Sugar rots teeth," I said righteously.

"These missing cats are rotting your brain. Zeke, I've shown cats before. I know that competition at cat shows is killing, and there are a few cat owners I could easily have murdered when their mangy beasts placed higher than my own Fantasia. But that's all hyperbole. We wouldn't really kill each other. We love our cats, but not that much."

"So?" I demanded in good cop form.

"So I can't believe anybody wants these cats badly enough to kill for them."

She had me there. I love cats, too, but murder?

I tried it from another angle: "Okay, then where is Rooney's cat? What if it doesn't show up? Will you say that's just coincidence, just another missing cat?"

"It'll show up," my lady love assured me. When she thought I wasn't looking, she poured her coffee into the litter box I keep in the corner.

It didn't show up, not hide nor long hair of it.

Abby drove out to my office on the Saturday morning after the hit-and-run, which was still unsolved.

"Wake up, Zeke!" She lifted one cat off my stomach, pushed another aside and sat down beside my sleeping body on the overstuffed couch I keep for the convenience of visitors, human and un-. *"I believe!"* she said, like one born again. "Rooney's missing cat is one too many coincidences, I agree. Let's talk." She tickled my ear with a strand of her long silky blonde hair. I loved the hair, hated the technique. Like a cranky old dog, I barked at her: "Dammit, Abigail, don't do that! Can't a man get a little catnap?"

Her lovely gray eyes widened. Her delicate jaw dropped. She looked like a woman who's seen the truth. I panicked, shot up in bed, grabbed and hugged her. "Abby! I'm sorry! I'm a grouch in the—"

"Catnap," she said breathily into my left ear, so that it sent nice little electric shivers down my side, and I didn't for a moment catch on that she wasn't whispering sweet nothings to me. "That's it, Zeke! Catnap, catnip, *kidnap*— that's how we need to think about this business. Like a kidnapping!"

Distracted as I was by kissing her neck, I said, "What?"

She pushed me away. "What if it weren't cats that were

missing?" she enunciated with a clarity that was just this side of insulting. "What if they were *people*?"

I leaned toward her. "Um?"

"Well, how would the police investigate their disappearances? However *they'd* do it, that's how *we* should do it."

"How would they do it?"

"Oh, honestly, Zeke. Well, let's think about it. I mean, wouldn't they want to figure out why these particular people were kidnapped?"

"Yeah." Finally, I got excited about something besides her proximity. "What do these people—cats—have in common that might attract a kidnapper?"

"Good, Zeke!" She was no longer condescending. Unfortunately, she was also no longer within reach, having stood up and started to pace. "Maybe they'd look at the times and days the kidnappings took place."

"And where, to see if that had anything to do with it."

"And method."

"And motive." I picked up a cat and tucked him under my arm. "Come on, Abs, let's look at my list of missing cats."

We looked.

"So what *do* they have in common?" Abby demanded. "I don't know them, and you do."

I squinted at the list until something hit me.

"Geez, Abby, they're all long-hairs."

"Really?" She was excited, too. "What does that mean?"

"I don't know," I confessed.

We stared at each other in frustration.

"Find me another clue," she demanded.

I did, but it took a while. First we considered the ages of the cats, but that was no good because they ranged from a few months to seventeen years. Sex was no good, either, so to speak, as they were males, females and "other." Nor could we find any common denominators in their owners, other than the fact that they all lived around Mt. Floresta and they were mighty upset with my lack of efficiency. But then Abby raised the question of breeds. And it turned out that all but two were purebreds—Angora, Himalayan, Persian and other classy cats. There were two mixed breeds, which stumped us until Abby asked me if they *looked* like purebreds.

"Yes," I decided. "If you didn't know cats, you'd think they were Persians."

"So maybe our catnapper doesn't know cats?"

"Maybe." I was doubtful. "But he knows them well enough to know he wants only long-haired cats that are purebreds or look as if they are."

As I summed up, Abby jotted down key words on the chalk board I use for messages. She scrawled *long hair* and *purebred*. Then she added *elegant* and *beautiful*.

"Maybe that doesn't have anything to do with it," she said defensively in the face of my skepticism. "But those are other qualities all the cats share. What if a lot of women were kidnapped, and they all happened to be young and beautiful? Don't you think the police would call that a clue?"

I guessed so. But then we ran up against the problem of motive. People kidnap other people for money, sex, revenge, power or leverage. Why cats? It obviously wasn't for ransom, since none had been demanded. And Abby didn't think the catnapper was selling them, because if he were he'd have snatched some valuable short-hairs, as well. I'd already eliminated lab experiments, I told Abby, unless she wanted to consider the possibility of a mad scientist working in a secret mountain cave, conducting weird tests on long cat hair. She thought we were pretty safe in eliminating that.

"Maybe the tourists are taking them," I offered.

"Have you ever tried to get a cat in a suitcase?" But then, as though inspired, she pronounced: "Oil shale! Maybe they didn't kill Rooney because he saw them take the cat. Maybe they killed him and took the cats because of something to do with the oil-shale controversy."

"Come on, Abby." I felt tired and crabby again. "What do you think, that they've discovered a way to get oil out of cats?"

She withdrew into a dignified and injured silence to my coffee pot. I knew she must be really mad if she was going to drink that stuff, but I was too frustrated to be contrite.

"Maybe we're getting the wrong answers because we're asking the wrong questions," I said into the chilly silence.

Being of a basically forgiving nature, she looked at me with interest.

"Maybe we're getting too fancy by asking what's the motive," I suggested. "Maybe the question is real simple. Like, what's a cat for?"

"Rats!" said my lady love, and I knew it wasn't because she'd spilled the coffee. "*Rats*, Zeke!"

My legs being longer than hers, by all rights I should have beat her to the car. But she was already in the driver's seat by the time I got in and slammed the door.

"So sorry, but only guests are admitted to La Floresta."

We got that maddening response at two out of the three gates of the walled compound of the health spa. Having raced five miles as fast as Abby's specially-calibrated-for-high-altitude Jag would scream, and gotten ourselves wound to a fever pitch of resolve, it was infuriating to be so easily halted by an upturned hand.

A snooty upturned hand.

"Maybe it's me," I suggested, humbly, after the second rejection. "Maybe I don't look the part. You try it alone next time. You look like trust funds."

"So kind," she said through gritted teeth. She didn't like to be reminded of her inherited wealth. I always told her if she felt so guilty about it, she could assuage that guilt by sharing the loot with poor folks like me. "The only reason you don't look the part is because you've let yourself get so skinny. On the other hand, as it were, if you let your fingernails grow, maybe they'd think you were Howard Hughes."

"Touché," I said, wounded. I'm told I can dish it out, but I can't take it, a piece of criticism I resent very much. "I mean it, though. I'll stay back in the bushes, and you try the next gate by yourself."

It didn't work. Abby's name wasn't on their list and she didn't have the gold membership card they so tactfully demanded. Perhaps the young lady would like to call and make a reservation? Perhaps they'd like to go to hell, the young lady said to me upon arriving back at my bush.

* * *

We thought it best to wait until dark before launching our assault on the elegant buff walls. When we left Mt. Floresta the second time, we packed a ladder into Abby's precious Jaguar. "You scratch that paint and I'll kill you," she said sweetly. I'd heard that Jags get something like seventeen hundred coats of hand-rubbed lacquer on them. I told her she would never miss one little coat of paint in one little spot. "I won't miss *you*, either," she said. I took the hint and stowed the ladder without damage to the car or the relationship.

So getting in was no problem.

"It's awfully dark," she said, as we crouched on our respective haunches in the well-pruned shrubbery. In the dark, the bushes looked like fat ladies squatting.

"It's awfully big," I rejoined. Across a lawn like a cemetery, the administration building rose white against the night. All around in the darkness we could hear the sounds of guests moving from their cabins to other parts of the compound. A splash to the right alerted us to the location of one of the swimming pools, presumably heated for cold fall nights like this one. Like spies in a B movie, we scuttled across the grass to the shelter of an enormous fir tree.

"Zeke, I just thought of something." Abby sounded less sure of herself than usual.

"I wish you wouldn't say things like that at a time like this," I whined.

"No, listen," she whispered. "I've been thinking about how Rooney Bowers died. If you're letting your cat out of the house, all you do is open the door, right? And the same thing when you let him in. I mean, you don't have to step outside with him. You don't *walk* a cat."

"Few do."

"Yes, well, how come Rooney was out there in the street where he could get hit? Zeke, I think he opened the door to call his cat in, and that's when he saw somebody grab the cat. If it were you, what would you do?"

"I'd go chasing and yelling after the son of a—"

"Right, and that would put you in the street. But, Ezekiel, if somebody were stealing a cat, they'd have to slow down to do it. So when Rooney saw them, they couldn't have been going fast enough to hit him as hard as they did."

"Oh, God." Gooseflesh crawled down my arms.

"Yes," Abby whispered in a curiously vibrating voice. "And that means they saw *him* when he saw *them*. So they came back around to kill him. They had to speed up to do it."

We stared at each other.

Premeditated murder? Even if it was only premeditated by a few seconds?

We stared at Larry Fremont's million-dollar administration building.

"What is important enough for premeditated murder?" I asked, appalled at the idea we had formed. A hit-and-run was one thing, and plenty bad enough, but this . . . "Abby, we should go back out the way we came in. We should drive back to town and call Jamison."

She told me what she thought of those cowardly ideas by scooting across the lawn to a stand of pines further inside the compound. I thought of all the times my mother told me not to cross the street without looking both ways, and I ran after her. She had slipped into the shadows, so I couldn't see her, when she suddenly called my name. Just as I was ready to shush her, she grasped my elbow. Or, at least I thought she did. I was certainly surprised when the person attached to that grasp turned out to be good ol' Larry Fremont himself.

"Zeke Leonard," he said in a less-than-welcoming tone of voice. In the years since the high school football team, Larry had not lost muscle, he'd added it—on his fancy spa weight-lifting equipment, no doubt. If he'd looked then like he looked now, we'd have won every game for the Mt. Floresta Mountain Lions. "And friend."

"Long time no see, Larry," I babbled. "I'd like you to meet my good friend Tanya Smith. Tanya is staying up at Mt. Floresta and she indicated an interest in your beautiful place, so I said, well, Tanya, I'll take you down and introduce you to ol' Larry himself."

Ol' Larry himself proved there is such a thing as a cold smile.

Abby moved out of the shadows and looked at me as if I were the resident fool of the mountains.

"That's thoughtful of you, Zeke," he said. "And I'd show your friend, uh, Tanya, around, but as you can see, it's rather dark for show and tell. So I think I'll just escort you to the gate."

Instead of releasing my elbow, he added another to his collection. From Abby's wince, I could tell his grip of her was every bit as firm as the one he had on me. But it wasn't so strong I couldn't break away when I saw a black cat stroll by about three steps ahead of me.

"Zeke, it's Fantas—" Abby cried.

I didn't look to find out why her last syllables were cut off. I just threw myself on the bundle of soft fur as if it were an opposing lineman, and held on for dear life. The cat, unclear as to my intentions, returned my embrace—with claws. I swore loudly. Which is probably why I didn't know Larry had come up behind me until his head hit me in the middle of the small of my back. In high school, he and I had played on the same team, so I never knew how much damage he could do with his famous illegal tackles. As I collapsed, the cat jumped over my shoulder, landing with all four clawed paws on Larry's head. His attention having been thus nicely distracted, I turned and threw a tackle of my own. I didn't grieve when his head hit an imitation Greek sculpture like a football hitting a goal post.

Fremont the Freeloader lay on the ground, out cold.

But the hollering from cats and people had switched on a lot of lights in the compound. I sat on Larry and took the petrified cat in my arms. He held still, probably paralyzed by fright, like me.

"Zeke, Zeke, are you okay?" Abby ran up out of the dark where Larry had thrown her into the bushes in his chase after me. "Zeke, is it Fantasia? Is it my Fantasia?"

Her voice was full of tears and hope.

"No," I said gently. "It's not."

She sank to her knees. I saw the light go out of her face.

"It's not Fantasia," I said quickly. "It's Puddy! It's Miss Emily Parson's cat, Puddy."

Hope returned to Abby's eyes just as the guests and employees merged on our mangled scene.

"Call the police!" someone yelled.

"Yes," I agreed, "do that. Ask for the chief. Tell him I told him so."

"We smell more than a rat," Jamison told us the next day in his office. "Larry confessed to Rooney's hit-and-run. When Rooney saw him grab the cat, he went racing out to Larry's car, accusing him of stealing all those other cats. And that was enough to panic Larry. He knew if that got out, everything else would too."

"*What* else?" Abby looked up from a chair in the corner where her hands were occupied in petting Fantasia. The Himalayan purred and blinked smugly at me as if to re-establish squatter's rights to that lovely blue-jeaned lap.

"Fraud," Jamison announced. "All kinds of consumer fraud." He glanced at the intrepid editor busily scribbling notes. "Ready, Ginny?"

"Go," she commanded, pencil poised.

"It's almost funny." Jamison was seated on a corner of his desk, and now he folded his arms over his stomach. "It seems that Larry got himself financially overextended, so he started cutting corners to save money. For one thing, the food at La Floresta is not exactly what their menus say it is. They've been altering the recipes with cheaper, more fattening ingredients—using starches for fillers and sugar for taste, for instance, instead of all those expensive herbs and spices they advertise."

"But don't the guests get weighed?" I asked.

"They fixed the scales!" Jamison hooted with laughter. "And they made sure the guests got plenty of exercise to burn up some of those calories they didn't know they were eating. Plus, nobody stayed long enough to gain much. Most of them just went out weighing the same as when they went in. Gives a whole new meaning to the phrase, 'fat farm,' wouldn't you say?"

"But they'd find out the truth when they got home," Ginny said.

"Nope." The bald eagle preened on his exclusive information. "Larry told them they could expect to gain back some water weight as soon as they started to eat regularly again."

"Diabolical," Abby hissed. "Not to mention mean and lousy."

Jamison said, "It wasn't just the food, either. The doctor was a quack, the physical therapists were phonies, the dietitian was just an amateur cook, and the European chefs were ordinary restaurant cooks from Denver; not even the aerobics instructors had the experience the advertising says they did. Almost nobody was quite what they claimed to be, and so they could be paid a lot less. It was all a joke to most of them, but it meant serious money in the bank to Larry. Now we know why he fired everybody from Mt. Floresta. His original employees from up here knew how things were supposed to be. They wouldn't have stood for his cheating."

"He didn't want any of us to know." I shook my head over the greed of my old teammate. "I bet that's why he took all his business away. It was safer to deal with out-of-town banks and suppliers. They weren't close enough to catch him at his shell game."

"But the cats," Ginny interrupted. "Why the cats?"

Abby and I traded supercilious smiles.

"Remember your story about landfills?" I asked Ginny. "The one Larry didn't want you to run? That was our best clue. We thought of all the reasons somebody might want a cat and came up with the oldest reason of all: to kill rats. And where in this wide valley might there be a problem with rats?"

"At a landfill over a garbage dump!" Ginny exclaimed.

"Right. Larry saw big fat ugly rats invading his precious gold mine. He had to get rid of them. Poison was dangerous because some of the guests bring their dogs to stay with them. And dead dogs are bad for business. Live cats was the answer."

"But not just any cats." Abby giggled and held Fantasia aloft. "They had to fit the 'ambiance.' They had to be beautiful, elegant cats, so the guests would not object."

"And they had to be long-haired," I added. "Because Larry wasn't going to feed them much. He wanted them hungry so they'd kill rats. And a long-haired cat always looks fatter than a short-hair. So nobody would notice if the cats lost weight."

"But why so many?" Ginny persisted.

"It's a big place," was my simple explanation.

"Beast," Abby said, and she didn't mean cats.

"It was all a matter of appearances," I continued, taking the opportunity to philosophize grandly. The others exchanged tolerant glances, but I ignored them. "That's what La Floresta was all about anyway, wasn't it? Appearances. Larry stole the cats and killed Rooney to keep up appearances."

I stood up and stretched carefully. My kidneys still hurt where Larry's head had dented them. "Glad to be of help, Jamison," I said graciously. "But Abby and I must be off. Miss Emily Parson is serving tea in our honor."

I looked into his amused, craggy face.

"You wanna come, too?"

"A cop having tea?" He recoiled in mock horror. "Have a heart, Zeke. How would it *look*?"

Kitty

.

John Lutz

Why not love at first sight? Especially if that sight was Katherine Prim?

William had never regarded himself as the sort to conduct a whirlwind courtship and marriage, but when he'd met Katherine at the sales convention in Cleveland, somehow he'd embarked on that road. And here was where it had led him, to a secluded honeymoon cottage in the Ozark Mountains.

William was from New Jersey and had never been to this part of the country. It was green and beautiful. The mountains weren't really mountains but gently rolling hills of pine and cedar trees that were high enough to be fogged with webs of mist each morning just after sunrise. But then little in this country was what it seemed. It had taken William only a few days to realize the eerie and ancient ritual and superstition that thrived in the area. Katherine seemed not to be surprised when the old woman five miles away at the market had mentioned being hump-backed because her mother had been gored by a bull when pregnant with her. Nor did she bat a beautiful green eye when the acne-pitted boy servicing their rented Jeep at the gas station talked of snake worship as casually as if he were referring to conventional church canon.

Maybe it was that kind of local talk and superstition that had prompted the peculiar dreams.

William had experienced the first one the night of their arrival. It hadn't been particularly frightening, and he hadn't thought much of it at the time. He'd been sitting in a cramped, dark place, watching a small black cat preen and watch him. The cat stared at him in the unfathomable manner of cats, but with something in the way of amusement; William was sure of it. Not the classic Cheshire cat sort of feline amusement, but something more subtle, more curious.

When he'd told Katherine about it over breakfast on the screened back porch, she'd smiled and told him there was no telling what dreams meant, and maybe in a previous life he'd been a cat.

He pointed to the eight-inch square door, hinged at the top and set near the base of the closed cabin door of thick oak—the pet door—and said, "A cat might find its way in here that way."

Still smiling, she said, "That's why the door is there."

"Only we don't have a cat."

"Why don't you block the pet door if you think that's how your dream cat got in?"

He suddenly felt foolish, being afraid of a small cat. It wasn't how husbands were supposed to feel, to act. Husbands were the protectors in nature and in society. "I don't think it'll be necessary," he said, and sipped his coffee with exaggerated unconcern.

But he was miffed for a while that she hadn't taken his dream seriously.

Then he had to admit to himself that he couldn't blame her for how she felt. There was no reason for seriousness. Dreams and reality were two different things entirely, and it was reality where William and Katherine lived, where they were beginning their lives together.

She was, in fact, the most real creature he'd ever seen. Small, dark, vivid, with those striking green eyes that had weakened his knees with a glance. Though he'd pursued her over the next six weeks, he knew she had, in her own fashion, been luring him, almost toying with him in a way he found incredibly sensuous.

His anticipation had been agonizing; she had to have known that. It was, he was sure, the object of her measured enticement. Had her anticipation been the same?

That insane and raucous night in his bedroom had been her idea as much as his. It was clear to him then that from the beginning she'd wanted him. It had been in the silent message of her glances, of her elegant body language. She'd been a dancer at some point in her life, she'd told him, and she moved with an almost liquid grace. How long ago she had danced he didn't know.

From time to time he realized with momentary alarm that he didn't know much about Katherine at all, other than that he loved her. But that was enough. He'd never even asked her age, though he estimated she was in her early thirties. Not too young for William's forty-seven. And what did age matter anyway? He'd always scoffed at the idea that love could overcome all obstacles, but now that he'd found love for the first time in his life, he couldn't believe otherwise.

At breakfast the second morning of their stay in the cabin, he told Katherine about having the dream again. This time the cat was perched on the dresser near the bed, simply sitting very still and staring at him intently.

She said, "Someday I'll tell you about my dreams, William. Pass the cream."

He watched her add cream to her coffee, waiting for her to comment further, but she didn't.

The third night he opened his eyes—or dreamed he opened them—and there was the cat on his pillow, only inches from his face, calmly appraising him.

He yelped and sat straight up. Leaped from the bed.

On the other side of the room, he turned and saw that the cat was gone. That there had never been a cat. Katherine was sitting up, rubbing her eyes and staring curiously at him.

"What on earth's the matter, William?"

"The dream again." He was surprised that his voice quavered.

"Dream?"

"The one about the cat staring at me while I sleep. Only this time it was curled up right there on my pillow."

She laughed. "Careful or it might steal your breath."

"What?"

"That's the old wives' tale: cats will creep into an infant's cradle and suck the breath from its body."

"They probably believe it around here," William said,

wiping his forehead with his palm and finding that he was perspiring even though the night was cool.

"Well, it isn't true, no matter how hard they believe. Come back to bed, William."

He did, and they made love. Katherine moaned into his ear and dug her fingernails into his back with passion. The dream seemed less real. Distant. By morning it was only a fogged memory, like the mist that lay in soft shreds on the hilltops.

The fourth night he awoke without apparent reason. He was cold but he was perspiring, and it took him a few seconds to realize he was afraid.

He had no idea why.

The softest of sounds, like velvet on velvet, came from the shadowed corner of the bedroom. Then a slightly louder, gently rasping sound. Rhythmic. Familiar.

William's bowels turned to ice as he realized what it was he heard.

Something breathing!

Something large!

Within the dark shadows, a darker shadow moved.

A panther stepped out into the dim light, graceful despite its bulk. Its eyes, luminous and knowing, were fixed on William.

He tried to scream but the sound lodged painfully in his throat. He was awake! He was sure he was awake! The panther was real!

His gaze locked with the panther's in a horrible hypnosis, he stretched out an arm and probed with his hand to wake Katherine.

His fingers found cool linen. The other side of the bed was empty.

He slid from the mattress and backed slowly toward the door. His heart was hammering and his own ragged breathing fell into rhythm with the panther's. In a fascinating and primal way, they were for a moment as one creature with one inevitable fate.

The panther took a slow, stalking step toward him, as if toying with him.

William's gasp was almost a shriek as he leaped to the

bedroom doorway and hurled himself through it, slamming the door behind him.

He stood shaking for an instant only. Then he was out on the plank porch, in the cool starlit night. The gentle hills seemed ominous now, a benign facade masking an ancient evil.

So isolated was the cabin that he'd fallen into the habit of leaving the keys in the rented Jeep. He ran to the vehicle, ignoring the sharp stones that gouged his bare soles, and clambered inside.

He twisted the key and the starter ground.

The engine sputtered but didn't turn over.

He tried again.

Again.

The starter ground more slowly, like something groaning in agony. Finally, when he desperately twisted the ignition key the only sound he heard was a futile clicking from beneath the hood.

"William."

The voice, so near, startled him and he jerked violently and struck his head on the Jeep's roof.

Katherine, wearing only her nightgown, was standing alongside the Jeep and had spoken to him through its cranked-down window.

When he stuttered and couldn't reply, she smiled and said, "Where on earth were you going at this time of night?"

"The panther!" he managed to blurt out.

She looked puzzled for a moment, then nodded. "I see. Another dream."

"The cat was larger this time. Huge. A black panther."

"I was in the bathroom and thought I heard a commotion in the bedroom. When I went back to return to bed, you were gone. I, uh, didn't notice a panther, William, and I think I would have if there'd been one in the room."

"It was real, I tell you!"

"A dream, William. They seem real sometimes, but they never are. Come back in the cabin. Come to bed."

He sat still for a moment, trying to gain control of himself.

She stroked his bare arm. "You have goose pimples. You *must* have had a fright. A terrible nightmare."

"It was."

"Come back to bed, poor baby. I promise there'll be no more dreams tonight."

He could believe that, looking into her eyes. "I don't know if I can."

"You flooded the Jeep's engine, then ran down the battery trying to start it. Can't you smell the gasoline?"

He sniffed. She was right. In his desperation he'd pumped the accelerator too hard and too often. That was why the Jeep wouldn't start.

She leaned forward and kissed his ear, whispered, "Come with me, William." Probed his ear with a warm, skillful flick of her tongue. "Come back to bed with me. We can talk about this in the morning."

There was, after all, nowhere else to go. Like an automaton, he climbed from the Jeep and followed her into the cabin, then into the bedroom.

He insisted on switching on the bedside lamp and leaving it burning. She told him that was okay with her, if it would make him feel safe. She wanted him to feel secure. Then she curled up next to him and began enticing him.

He was surprised to feel himself respond. Then it was as if his fear somehow heightened his desire as well as hers, and they made love with a new and violent passion.

In the morning, when he showered, he could feel but not see the deep scratches in his back.

He did feel slightly foolish about last night. After breakfast, during which he didn't mention the dream, Katherine said, "If it would make you feel better, why don't you seal the pet door? That's the only possible way a cat could get inside the cabin."

"The pet door's too small for a cat the size of the one in last night's dream to enter. A panther."

Katherine shrugged. "Well, I guess you're right, if you want to mix dreams with the real world. Doesn't that strike you as kind of a silly thing to do, match the size of a cat in a dream with the size of a pet door that's real?"

"Silly?" He felt a momentary anger. Then he sighed. She

was right. Anyone sane listening in on their conversation would agree she was right. "Yeah, it's silly," he admitted, and said nothing else while he finished breakfast.

Later that morning, while Katherine fished for bass and sunfish down at the small lake, William tried again to get the Jeep started. The battery was still dead. He opened the hood and peered into the engine compartment. He was no mechanic. Maybe there was a loose battery cable. Maybe someone had sabotaged the Jeep. It was possible.

In this land of hills and mist, anything was possible, wasn't it?

"I caught a fish," Katherine said proudly behind him. She was holding up a medium-sized bass in triumph, grinning. "We'll eat him for lunch."

"Fine," William said, and followed her into the cabin.

He thought about striking out on foot through the woods without telling Katherine. But he felt dumb even considering such a strategy. If there really was a reason to run, he'd be less safe in the forest, in the unfamiliar wild, than in the cabin. And surely there was no valid reason for such drastic action. His intellect told him that, while his instincts persistently whispered otherwise.

William was a man of intellect, and he was determined that intellect would resolve this matter.

That night he only pretended to sleep.

When Katherine's breathing had leveled out and deepened beside him, he eased off the mattress and left the bedroom, softly closing the door. He lifted one side of the massive oak breakfront and silently moved the heavy piece of furniture over in front of the door, blocking access from the bedroom except for its open window that led out into the night.

William then made a quick tour of the tiny cabin, making sure all other windows and doors were firmly locked. Then he got the long-handled axe used for splitting firewood, slid a chair over near the front door, and sat down.

He leaned the axe against the chair and sat motionless with his hands on his knees, staring at the small square outline of the pet door.

The solution to the problem, he'd decided, was actually simple.

He would sit awake in the chair until morning. His apprehension wouldn't let him sleep anyway. In all probability nothing would happen; the cat wouldn't make its appearance. It was absurd to suspect his new wife was some supernatural creature that could turn itself into a cat. But if it just happened to be true, and it occurred tonight, this would certainly resolve the matter.

She might be able to become a panther, but not one that would fit through the pet door.

Only a small and manageable kitty could do that. And if one did, William would be ready to strike and kill it with the axe before it could possibly become the huge and fearsome thing he'd seen last night. Or thought he'd seen.

The nightmare world he was enduring awake or asleep would be ended, for that night, or forever.

Around midnight he thought he heard a soft stirring inside the bedroom, and he sat rigidly and attentively, gripping the wooden axe handle. Ready.

Murder? Was he resolved to do murder? No, he told himself. Under the circumstances it could hardly be called murder. He knew so little about Katherine, really, who she was . . . what she was. And here in the Ozarks it didn't seem so unlikely that . . . Well, nothing seemed unlikely.

He sat that way for almost half an hour, but no more sounds came either from behind the blocked bedroom door or from outside the cabin.

Finally William allowed himself to relax, resting the long axe handle against the chair arm again, settling back.

At one-thirty he came awake with a start, frightened that he'd dozed off and left himself vulnerable. Katherine might have had time to enter as a small cat, then become the panther. And something told William she was finished playing with him and would mean business tonight.

But the opening and closing of the pet door would have alerted him, he was sure. The cat hadn't entered.

Around two o'clock, fatigue overcame fear. William's eyes closed. His head bowed. And his muscles relaxed in sleep.

The reverberating opening and closing of the pet door jolted him awake. He knew immediately what had made the sound. This was it! It was happening! His heart leaped crazily in his chest as he reached for the axe.

Something was wrong.

Very wrong!

His arm wasn't responding. He tried to stand up but every fiber of his body felt strange, unresponsive to what his mind willed.

Then he heard the massive breathing. The feral scent of the cat filled his nostrils, causing his nose to twitch. He tried to scream but could only squeal. Frantically he scampered around on the chair and fell off onto the floor. He scrambled to his feet and darted about, seeking shelter.

Understanding!

Oh God, understanding!

He hadn't fully comprehended the extent of Katherine's powers. His heart crashed with panic and his body sang with dreadful and desperate energy as he realized the horrible thing she had done.

The beast that had entered through the pet door was a normal-sized cat, exactly as he'd anticipated.

But William was now a mouse!

He sensed it before he saw it, a low dark sanctuary beneath the sofa on the opposite wall. So far away! Yet it was his only chance! He scampered toward the sheltering recess in fright and hope, only vaguely aware of his terrified squeals, his tiny claws scratching for traction on the rough plank floor.

Halfway across the room he knew it was useless. Katherine had merely let him think he might escape. Allowed him his momentary wild hope. She was toying with him the way a—

No! He couldn't bear to let himself think it!

He ran harder. What else could he do? Quivering in terror, he strained every springlike muscle in his narrow body for speed. For survival. Aware of the feral stench and the huge and effortless padded footfalls behind him.

Gaining on him.

The Wall

·

Lisa Angowski Rogak

Mrs. Whitmore set the vase of daisies on top of two stacked cartons and brushed her white-gloved hands before placing them on her hips. She took a step back to admire her handiwork and patted her pinned and sprayed jet-black hair that bore a faint resemblance to a gladiator's helmet.

"There now," she said. "Home sweet home."

Sandy and Bill Pickard glanced at each other long enough to roll their eyes without having the realtor see. "I guess we spent too much time in Cambridge," Bill said to Sandy with his eyes. Sandy shrugged her agreement.

"I couldn't think of another couple that I'd rather see get the old LaCroix place," Mrs. Whitmore exclaimed. "Did I tell you that lots of these old houses have hidden alcoves and root cellars? Some, I believe, were even stations on the Underground Railroad. But of course there's no proof." She sighed deeply, still staring at the flowers. "You know," she said, lowering her voice, a conspiratorial air entering it as soon as the fake cheerfulness had left, "it's not easy being sole watchdog of the historical integrity of these old Vermont towns. Or these houses, for that matter. But *some*one's got to do it." Her body suddenly hunched over; her gaze went from the flowers to the floor.

This time, she was facing Sandy and Bill directly, so they couldn't for the moment communicate their mirth to each other.

Sandy and Bill had only signed the papers on the 150-year-old farmhouse the day before, and had just gotten back from returning the U-Haul when Mrs. Whitmore stopped by. The move was pretty streamlined. After all, it wasn't as though their Cambridge one-bedroom warranted the hiring of a moving company, or even a man-with-van. They had driven up to Clinton yesterday for the closing and spent the night in the empty house in a double sleeping bag, too nervous to sleep or make love. They picked up the U-Haul that morning at 6 A.M. in nearby Barre and headed south. Once they got to Cambridge, they loaded the truck and were on the road back to Vermont by noon.

Timmons—their black-and-white tuxedo cat—was the only member of the family who didn't care whether or not the move went off without a hitch: he hated riding in his cat carrier in the truck. Sandy compensated by buying the cat a whole cooked chicken at a deli in southern New Hampshire and letting him out of the carrier, but it didn't help. The cat was so freaked out by watching the world go by at sixty-five miles an hour that instead of attacking the chicken with his teeth he sat on top of it, leaning against Bill as he drove.

"There, there," he had crooned above the noise of the loud diesel engine. "Soon you'll be in the country in our new house with all the mice, birds and squirrels you want."

"Bill, that's gross," Sandy blurted out.

"Sandy, that's the country," Bill replied and started peeling strips of chicken off the carcass to hand-feed Timmons, which the cat scarfed down despite his nervousness.

They had been thinking about moving out of the city for years. Then one Sunday six months ago, after one too many dents in their Honda and too many weekend mornings of sleeping-in interrupted by piercing car alarms, Bill threw back the covers, jumped out of bed and said, "That's it." He quickly dressed, ran out to the newsstand kiosk in Harvard Square that carried out-of-town newspapers, grabbed the Burlington *Free Press* and the Rutland *Herald*, and rifled through the real estate pages back at the apartment in a frenzy while Sandy looked on, a mixture of fear and amusement on her face and Timmons in her lap.

After an hour with the paper and a few phone calls, they got in the car and began what would become a flurry of trips that put at least six hundred additional miles on the Honda every weekend. After initially deciding on central

Vermont for its proximity to Montpelier, Burlington, and the interstate, they discovered the town of Clinton after about a month of househunting. A month later, they made an offer on the LaCroix house on the far edge of the main village.

Bill and Sandy were both graphic artists. After they made up their minds to move to the country, they proceeded to set up enough work in Boston to keep the mortgage paid and the cat fed for years. Bill had spent summers in Vermont at his grandparents' while Sandy was strictly a product of the suburbs. She figured it was about time for her to discover what it was like to live in another category: first suburb, then city, and now the country. Her sense of calm about the impending move unnerved her.

Mrs. Whitmore was still standing before the couple with the weight of the world on her shoulders while she waited for one of them to take pity on her. Sandy nudged Bill with her elbow.

"Mrs. Whitmore, you mentioned you were a member of the Clinton Historical Society," he said.

Yeah, only about fifty times, Sandy thought to herself.

Mrs. Whitmore's head bobbed up suddenly. "Why yes, I *am*," she gushed. She walked over to the big bay window. The sunlight streamed across her face and made her look almost ghostly, Sandy thought. "I did tell you, for instance, that this very house was the birthplace of Aldus LaCroix the Third, who sold you the house and who—"

"Yes, I believe you have," Bill quickly interjected. "But you never told us about *that* house across the way."

Bill walked over to the window and pointed to a grayish old Cape with a chimney that had a few bricks missing, peeling paint, shutters hanging from one hinge, and grass that looked like it threatened to overtake the house, as this was the beginning of July. He saw a white streak flash across the window to the right of the front door.

Sandy joined the other two at the window and squinted into the light. She thought she saw parts of the grass move—only parts, and there was no perceptible breeze this afternoon.

"Oh, *that* one," Mrs. Whitmore replied, a distinct look of unease crossing her face. She turned away from the window and walked back over to the daisies. "That's old Lily Cole—grew up in this town, and has always lived in that house. Her husband died years ago and, well, she's just getting on in years. You know how that is." She turned to face Sandy and Bill still at the window. "Poor soul can't keep up the house. Not that it ever was looked after properly, and she drives away anybody who goes over there."

Just then a rustling sound came from the corner of the living room, followed by what sounded like the scraping of metal. Mrs. Whitmore's penciled-in eyebrows rose up on her forehead almost an inch.

"What's *that*?" she squeaked.

Sandy walked over to a pile of boxes. "That's Timmons. He thinks we're ignoring him and he's probably hungry." She reached back for the cat carrier. She held it up in front of her face. "And he's probably sick of living in a box." She put the cage on the floor and unlatched the door. First to emerge from the cage were an indistinguishable number of quivering whiskers, then a black head with a white beard popped out. Finally, the entire cat stepped tentatively onto the parquet floor and slowly crept towards the window where Bill and Mrs. Whitmore were standing.

Many tuxedo cats have a white *M* imprinted on their foreheads. When Bill first went to the pound, they picked Timmons out because he had not an *M* but what looked like an upside-down *J* on his forehead. "Almost looks like a gallows," Bill had observed out loud.

"Oh yes, I forgot to tell you, Mrs. Cole is notorious for her cats," added Mrs. Whitmore, grimacing and taking a step away from Timmons. "*That's* why no one goes over there. There are all these furry, writhing bodies all over the place." She shuddered. "You hardly know where to walk."

She glanced down at her wrist, which Sandy noticed was bare, and then sneezed. "*Well,*" she said, straightening up as the false chipperness entered her voice again. "*Have* to run. Enjoy unpacking and I'll probably bump into you at the store or town meeting one of these days." Before she opened the front door, she threw back one last long admiring glance at the flowers. "Toodle-oo," she said, then was gone.

Sandy and Bill looked at each other and rolled their eyes exaggeratedly. Then they burst out laughing.

"So what do you say we enjoy unpacking?" asked Bill.

"Sounds fine to me," said Sandy, as they attacked the pile of cartons in the corner.

Later, as they were eating cold pizza and warm beer over a carton with a flashlight spreading its beam across the ceiling—the power wasn't scheduled to be turned on until tomorrow—Bill suddenly looked up and said, "Hey, where's Timmons?"

Sandy stopped chewing. "You're right, I haven't seen him since Mrs. Whitmore left."

Bill grabbed the flashlight and swung it from one corner to another as they made their way through each room of the darkened house, calling out, "Timmons!" But no cat responded.

As they headed up to the second floor, Sandy said, "Hey, wait a minute," and led Bill back into the kitchen to look for a manual can opener to shake. But they couldn't find the box it was buried in, so Sandy grabbed an envelope of Tender Vittles instead.

They made their way back up the stairs, Bill lighting the way and Sandy shaking the bag of cat food through the upstairs rooms. Still no cat.

When they got to the attic stairs, Sandy stopped. "What's the matter, honey?" Bill asked.

Sandy swallowed loudly. "I don't do attics. Remember?"

Bill recalled that when they first met, Sandy refused to go into the attic of his parents' house, preferring instead to remain in the purgatory of sheetrocked rooms, as he put it. Basements were almost as bad, but attics were absolutely out of the question. She thrust the bag of cat food into his hands and he creaked up the stairs solo.

A few minutes later, he creaked back down, his mouth set in a rigid line. "No Timmons." When they got to the basement, Sandy ripped open the envelope of cat food and passed it to Bill, thinking maybe if Timmons could smell the food, his hunger would get the better of him and he'd come running.

She gave Bill a gentle push as he descended into the basement, a flashlight in one hand, an open pouch of Tender Vittles in the other. "Here, Timmons honey. I know it's not Cambridge, but I'm sure we can get moo-shoo pork for you somewhere within a hundred-mile radius of here," his voice echoed.

He wandered around the basement, examining all the places he thought a cat would love to hide. He flashed the light across all four walls. Three looked like they were part of a traditional fieldstone foundation, while one was constructed of cinder blocks. Funny, he had missed this detail during their earlier inspections of the house. Bill ran the light down a distinct streak of black coursing down the wall. Water damage. He'd take care of it later.

This time, when Bill emerged from the basement—still with no cat—the tears that Sandy had been holding back came out in a flood. Timmons was like a baby to her—Bill had given her the kitten a few months after they met and when they moved in together six months later, the two of them proceeded to spoil that cat like any only child. Bill put down the cat food and put an arm around Sandy as they walked back into the living room. "He's just scared, honey. Look at all the excitement he's seen in the last couple of days. Once he checks out all the smells in this old falling-down farmhouse, then he'll be ready for us again."

Sandy sniffled, then smiled behind her tears. "I guess you're right," she said. "He'll come out in the morning." She suddenly felt very tired. "Let's go to bed now."

The next morning, Bill got up before Sandy. The light woke him up; Sandy could sleep through anything. He began to comb the house again, starting in the attic and painstakingly going through every room in the house.

He hesitated before the door to the basement, and then opened it and turned on the flashlight. He stepped more gingerly on each tread than the night before. There was a little bit of light coming through the six basement windows, but he still needed the flashlight to see. He headed over to look behind the furnace when, out of the corner of his eye, he saw something quiver. He swung the flashlight over in that direction and saw a sodden ball of black fur, shivering, wet and dirty. At first, Bill wasn't sure it was Timmons, because the cat's white bib and paws were so dingy.

But it *was* Timmons. Bill reached for the cat, who

looked like he wanted to bolt, but was too scared to move. He picked it up and made a hammock with his sweatshirt, enveloping the cat. It continued to shake uncontrollably, purring that crazy purr all the while.

"Boy, is Sandy going to be glad to see you," he informed the cat as he made his way up the stairs, thinking, I looked for you everywhere last night. And how can you be wet? There's no water in the basement.

Bill stood at the foot of the sleeping bag where Sandy still slept. "Hey," he said, nudging her foot. "Look what I found," he said, holding out the cat. Sandy opened her eyes and smiled briefly before a look of concern came over her eyes.

"What happened to him?" she asked, peeling off the sleeping bag and sitting upright. She cradled the still-shivering cat in her arms.

"The hot water heater has a leak in it," he said unconvincingly. "Timmons must have gotten stuck behind it. I'll keep the basement door closed until I can get it fixed."

Sandy fussed over the cat for a while longer and then got dressed. After some more cold pizza, which they shared with Timmons, who hungrily devoured all stray slices of pepperoni, they resumed unpacking. In the middle of washing the kitchen cabinets, Sandy said, "Hey, I've got an idea. What do you say we go over and introduce ourselves to Mrs. Cole?" She wiped her hands on her jeans. "Anyone who can spook Whitmore is certainly someone I want to get to know in this town."

Bill, who was in the living room, hesitated before he answered. "Okay, but let's stop at the store to bring her a pie or something."

Their intended quick dash in and out of the general store turned into a twenty-minute-long introduction to all three aisles of the store by the owners, Jim and Rita Griswold, a stocky, boisterous couple who felt compelled to speak in voices a few notches too loud. After the tour, Jim disappeared out back while Rita invited Bill and Sandy to run a tab anytime they wanted. "We don't do that for just anyone," Rita said to Sandy in a loud whisper as she rang up the fresh-baked apple pie wrapped in cellophane. "Melba Hart makes these three times a week for us, and especially in the summer we can't keep 'em in stock." She lowered her eyes and batted them gently in Bill's direction. "But you're not summer people. You want me to save one of Melba's pies for you just like some people reserve the Boston *Globe*, you call me and I'll tell the from-away people that we're all sold out." She winked at Sandy.

"I know your power isn't turned on yet, so I'll heat this up here now if you'd like and you can eat it warm for lunch."

Sandy wondered how the woman she had just met knew they were still without electricity. Small-town life. She had been warned.

Bill grabbed the pie. "No need, Mrs. Griswold, we're taking this over to Mrs. Cole to introduce ourselves."

In less than one second, Rita's chubby face washed over with white, her hospitable smile replaced with a grim line. "You hear this, Jim?" she boomed. "Mrs. *Cole*?" Rita whispered to Sandy and Jim as best she could. "Have you been over there yet?"

"No, but why is everyone around here afraid of her? What does she do, kidnap and eat little children?" he asked, chuckling.

Mrs. Griswold pulled the pie back across the counter. "Don't laugh about what you don't know. I'm deadly serious. All those *cats* and all! Yeeck!"

Jim ambled up to the register, shaking his head. "Waste of time," he said, forming the words around what appeared to be a toothpick that was permanently embedded between his teeth. "Wouldn't if I were you."

Bill pulled the pie back and this time picked it up off the counter. "Timmons—our cat—will probably welcome the company. Besides," he said as he started to walk towards the door, grabbing Sandy's elbow, "we like cats. It seems like you do, too," nodding towards the large gray tabby sunning itself in the store window that faced out onto the street. "See you later," he added as he let the screen door slam behind them.

They were two blocks away from the store when Sandy finally spoke. "Wow, what do you make of it, honey? How much damage could an old woman have done in this town in her life?"

"I bet not much. She's probably eccentric and a border-line Alzheimer's to boot. My grandmother Esther was the same way. I bet Mrs. Cole and I will get along fine."

They walked in silence for the five minutes it took to reach the front walk of the old woman's house. "Oh, wait," said Sandy. "I want to get my mother's pie server. Wait here," she said as she ran across the street.

Bill watched after her, then looked up at the old woman's house. "Boy," he thought, looking at the peeling paint and unkempt lawn, "I should help her out here." He thought fondly of Esther. Even when he was a boy, he helped her mow her lawn and took her trash to the dump once a week. He saw something wiggle in the tall grass alongside the Cole house and then watched a ghostly face pass in front of one of the downstairs windows, stop, stare at him for a moment, and then disappear.

He was still staring at the empty window so he didn't hear Sandy sneak up on him.

"Boo!" she said, sticking the dull edge of the pie server into his back. He let out a yell and dropped the pie. He turned to look at her, his eyes wide.

"Don't do that!"

"What's the matter? I was only playing."

He took a deep breath. "Sorry," he said. "Okay. Let's go," he said, leaving the pie where it fell.

A machete would have been useful as they made their way through the tall grass to Mrs. Cole's front door.

Sandy knocked loudly on the splintering door.

After a moment, a raspy voice said, "Go away," from the other side of the door.

"Mrs. Cole, we're your new neighbors," said Sandy. "As long as we're going to be living next—"

"I *have* no neighbors," the voice hissed, louder this time, booming almost. "I *want* no neighbors." The door opened a crack, and the overwhelming stench of wet cat fur and wet cat box instantly permeated the air. Sandy and Bill recoiled as if they had been slapped. An eye completely surrounded by wrinkles and a nose covered with moles appeared in the space while a tiny liver-spotted hand gripped the edge of the door.

"You don't exist for me," she hissed before closing the door. Another white flash flew across the window.

They looked at each other. "Well, we tried," said Sandy, clutching her pie server. On the way back to the house, Bill picked up the smashed pie as best he could.

As they reached the front door of their house, they heard the muffled sounds of Timmons' crying. "Did you leave the basement door open?" Sandy asked.

"No."

Bill grabbed the flashlight from the kitchen counter and opened the basement door. The cat's frightened mews pierced the air. Bill started down the stairs, this time with Sandy tightly holding on to his jacket as she followed him. They heard claws scrabbling on the cinder-block wall. Bill shone his flashlight on the wall and saw two paws in an opening. All of a sudden, the two glowing green orbs of Timmons' eyes appeared at a space about two-thirds of the way up the cinder-block wall. Neither Bill nor Sandy was aware of the space in the wall before—Sandy because she hated basements and Bill because he didn't notice it.

Bill suddenly stopped in his tracks. "What is it?" Sandy tugged on his sleeve.

"Look at the pattern on the wall. Does it remind you of anything?"

Sandy squinted at the wall, then gasped. What Bill had thought were watermarks was an upside-down *J*, exactly matching the markings on Timmons' forehead. But now, at this distance and this size, it looked exactly like a gallows.

Timmons squeezed through the crevice, paused on top of a shaky cinder block, then leapt onto the dirt floor and ran up the stairs, leaving a trail of water behind him.

Bill walked towards the wall. Sandy clutched tighter. He took the loosened cinder block and placed it on its end on the floor. The damp smell of rot quickly permeated the room. There was the faint sound of a faucet left running. Bill stood on the block and shone the flashlight through the opening. He angled the light and pointed it towards the floor of the enclosure. He froze.

"Oh my God," he finally managed.

"What is it?" Sandy asked in a trembling voice. She

grabbed an old wooden crate lying nearby, dragged it over to the wall and stood on it next to Bill. She gasped.

Fifty, maybe as many as one hundred cat skeletons covered the floor of the space, which measured about four by six feet. But atop the pile of cat skeletons was a human skeleton draped in a matted flannel shirt and workpants. Bill swung the flashlight around the space. A thin pipe stuck out from the wall, a slow drip of water collecting in a drainpipe. Bill suddenly felt the urge to pee.

"We figured you'd find out about the Coles sooner or later. Not that it would've scared you off or anything." Jim Griswold took the John Deere cap off his head, scratched his balding pate, then replaced it as he watched the workmen chip away at the mortar in the wall and remove the cinder blocks one by one. Rita stood beside him.

The bright lights he brought in to illuminate the room threw off eerie shadows on the walls. The power still wasn't on, so Jim had to speak louder than normal in order to be heard above the drone of the generator outside the basement window.

"Anyway, Harry—the guy in the wall—was Mrs. Cole's ex-husband. They owned both houses; they rented out your house, sometimes for the summer, sometimes to newcomers for the year. But people never stayed longer than a year, complaining the house creaked too much and was haunted.

"Harry was always jealous of the attention that Lily gave to the cats. He used to come into the store, drunk as a skunk and rant about the damn cats. 'I'll get them,' he'd say, 'I'll get them for all of their fucking nine lives!'

"We never paid much attention to him—there are a lot of people in town who use the store as their soapbox. But one day, about fifteen years ago, Harry got fed up with the cats and killed one right in front of her. She kicked him out and he moved in across the street. Luckily it was vacant at the time. She thought that they owned both houses jointly, but from the beginning Harry fixed it so that they were really just in his name. Then, when he moved out, he changed his will, leaving everything to his nephew Aldus LaCroix—that's who you bought the house from."

"Yeah," Rita added. "Right after Harry moved out, the

rest of Lily's cats began to disappear. She had so many cats that at first she didn't notice one or two missing. She thought that one of her toms had just wandered off in the woods for a few days. It turned out that he lured the cats over to his house and killed them. We could never figure out where all the cat carcasses went. You can see the yard from the road, and I never saw it dug up. And Rankin, the chief of police, had old Murphy down at the dump go through Harry's garbage for a while, and he never saw any dead cats in there."

"Then Lily found out about Harry changing the will," Rita interjected. "*That's* when things got interesting. She went over there, had a huge fight with Harry and she killed him. Not right away, mind you, but it was rumored that she slowly poisoned him with some kind of flea dip for the cats just to get even.

"After he died, she never rented it out. She cleaned it and kept it heated in the winters, but she always had someone else go over there. She never set foot in that house again."

"Where did she find the money for that?" asked Sandy.

Jim shrugged. "Oh, she got some money from Harry's insurance settlement and pensions and from other money she had stashed away over the years, I suppose."

"How do you know so much about this and how did she manage to get away with it?"

"Oh, it's come out in dribs and drabs and in idle gossip over the years. Everybody knew she did it, too, but the local authorities had sympathy for her because Harry was such a bastard that they let the case fall through the cracks. Oh, and one more thing. Harry's body was never found—before now, that is. And there are just as many cats at her house now as there were back when Harry first moved out. Maybe more."

The workmen had removed ten of the blocks and placed them on the floor. Jim walked over to the wall. He chuckled.

"Looks like he was determined to torture them," he said. "He probably lured them over here and then threw them behind the fake wall. Then, for spite, since most cats hate the water, he rigged up the water and a drain." He got down on his haunches to inspect the water and the copper tubing. "He did a good job, too. He cared more about the house than anything else. Old Harry designed the drainage so well that it never affected how the house sat. Most old houses with poor drainage sag and sink after a while.

"After a couple of weeks stuck back there, the poor cats died. He never completely mortared the blocks together, because he probably wanted to keep his options open. Lily in her day was a strapping woman. She was able to remove some of the blocks and somehow get Harry's body over the wall. Gave him a taste of his own medicine," said Jim, shaking his head.

Bill started up the stairs just as the workmen began to transfer the cat carcasses to a wheelbarrow. He sat beside Sandy, who was staring out the bay window, looking at Mrs. Cole's house. Timmons sat in her lap, purring. He could hear the purring even above the din of the generator.

He stared out the window.

"I was wondering why the basement seemed a couple of feet too short," he said. Suddenly, he saw something—a white streak—flash across the window of the old Cole house across the way.

Constant Companion

·

Peter Crowther

There's something about the Gulf Coast in the summer.
I think the word is *heat*.

I've always been a sucker for the white sands of the
American Riviera so long as I don't have to sit out there
and bake. I love the food—the seemingly endless supply of
shrimps and oysters—and I enjoy the simple, sun-slowed
conversation that drifts languidly around and across the im-
possibly blue water of the Gulf Stream.

It's a far cry from New York and its sticky humidity, the
dopplered cry of lonesome police cruisers searching the
streets and the crazy-eyed stares of the down-and-outs sheltering in the relative cool of the subway stations. Just being
a few miles from all that was all the tonic I needed. And
here I was several hundred miles away.

But I was working.

I had gone down to Sanford, about fifty miles inland
from Florida's Daytona Beach, to spend some time with
Jeff Sandusky. It had been booked since early spring and
the arrangement was I just go down and turn up at the door,
obligatory case of beer firmly packed with the shorts that
got tighter each year I pulled them out of the dresser. There
was no need to phone or write, Jeff had told me repeatedly.
Just come.

I came.

But when I got there, things were not so casual. In fact,
they were downright tense. You can recognize it most any
time, but when you're geared up for sun and fun and days
filled with the promise of shooting the breeze and pulling

up ring-tabs, you notice it more than ever. Jeff had even forgotten I was coming. He didn't say so, but I could see it in his face.

People wear worries like ill-fitting clothes. You notice them straight away. Three beers in—and two of those mine—he told me about it. It was his sister. She was missing.

Jeff's sister, Irma, had married some guy over in Mobile and they'd gone to live in a little Mississippi backwater name of Greenville, situated just inland—but still only a good spit from the sea—between Bay St. Louis and Picayune and close enough to Lake Pontchartrain not to wear shoes if you went walking.

It sounded good to me, I told him. He brightened up and we cracked a few more cans and hit the sack before the alcohol made the walls creep. We were on the road before sun-up next morning.

We came off U.S. 31 at Gulfport at around eight P.M., having ridden the late afternoon blacktop through Escambia and Baldwin counties, taking in some of the finest examples of blue-highway, small-town Americana you could find, our bellies filled with catfish nuggets, taco salad and Lone Star beer and eyelids reaching for our jawbones with a strength and a determination you just wouldn't credit.

Irma's house was modest.

The mailbox displayed one scrawled word—*Wilberton*—and defied gravity reaching for a clump of nettles and crabgrass littered with potato chip bags and beer cans. The dirt path led to a two-step walk-up. Standing in the shadow of the swing door was a man who could make a couch potato seem anorexic. I heard Jeff mutter "Son of a bitch!" as I pulled the car off the road and switched off the engine.

I leaned back in the seat and stretched, more to give Jeff the opportunity to get out first and start the introductions. Those introductions were like Central Park in January—bone-numbing cold and overcast with the constant threat of bad weather.

Jeff stood out of the car and nodded. "Beauregarde," he said.

The man returned the nod. "Sandusky."

I got out into the cool of the conversation. It was too stuffy in the car.

Jeff pointed to me. "Koko Tate, a friend of mine." He turned to me. "Koko, this is Beauregarde Wilberton. The man Irma married."

"Bo," said the man. "B-O. Bo."

"Bo," I said, holding out my hand. "Good to see you." He grunted. "You want to wash up?"

The hand was like baking dough, the vaguest hint of warmth amidst a clammy coolness. Like something that was alive a while back but wasn't any more. I turned to Jeff.

"Where is she?" Jeff said.

"She's gone, Sandusky," Bo Wilberton replied coolly. Was that a hint of pleasure in his face or just the sun pulling facial shadows into a rictus grin?

"Gone where?"

"If I knew that, now, would I be here?"

Jeff didn't answer.

"You coming in to wash up or you going to stand out there all night? Gets cold when the sun goes down."

"Come on, Jeff. Help me get the things."

We went around to the trunk and pulled out a couple of overnights. Just fresh shirts, clean denims, couple pairs of socks and shorts and my trusty .38. Grizzly Adams backed into the house and let the screen door slam, the small flap cut into the mesh squeaking to a stop. For a second I thought I'd been shot.

We ate in silence.

Wienies and stale rolls. But there were lots of them, and after the endless road, they tasted like haute cuisine.

Washing down my fourth dog with the first slug out of my third Bud, I felt almost human. It helped looking across at Bo Wilberton. He'd make grazing cattle feel like aristocracy.

"So?" Jeff wiped his mouth and reached for another can.

"So she's gone. What's to say?" Wilberton tucked his collection of chins into what passed for neck—or badly squeezed-up belly—and let out a loud belch.

"She leave a note?" I said, joining in with the after-dinner repartee.

Wilberton shook his head. He reached into his pants pocket, fumbled for a few seconds and pulled out a ring. "This is all she wrote," he said, holding the ring high for us to see. "Left it on a dinner plate over there on the table and split for parts unknown." He lifted his beer to just in front of his mouth and added, "And good riddance is what I say."

I ignored the crackling electricity coming from Jeff Sandusky and leaned over the table, frowning like I was thinking. I wasn't. I was just trying to avoid a brawl. "You and her have a fight?"

Wilberton laughed and shook his head. It was a forced laugh. "Hell, no. Nobody in his right mind would take on Irma. She makes me look slim!" He patted his gut for effect.

It was hard to believe. Only a scale model of the State of Texas could have made Bo Wilberton look slim. I let it ride.

But Jeff didn't. Hell, he couldn't. "And you made her that way, Beauregarde," he said. "It was you drove her to eating."

Wilberton sniggered again. "Ain't a truck big enough to drive Irma anywhere," he said.

"She take anything with her?" I asked him, swigging beer and watching Jeff out of the corner of my eye. "Like clothes and things?"

"Few things." Wilberton nodded. *All* of him nodded. "And that fucking cat. Took that, too."

"She took her cat?"

Wilberton looked suddenly defensive. "Fucking cat," he said again while he thought of what to say next. "Fucking constant companion . . . crawling 'round the place, scratching and mewling, smelling the place out, shitting and farting all the time. Bringing in those damned carcasses."

"Carcasses?"

He looked over at Jeff through piggy eyes encased in thick folds of face. "Yeah, carcasses. Birds and mice and things, all chewed up and stiff-legged." He was starting to motor on this one, enjoying himself. "Wandered in through the goddamn door and dropped the things right down on the carpet in front of Irma like they was fucking trophies," he said, misting the air in front of his mouth with spittle-spray.

Jeff stood up. "I'm getting some air," he said and he stalked to the door and left us there, watching each other and measuring up what we saw.

I spoke first. I'd run out of measure. "Did the cat have a leash?"

"A leash?" His face folded in on the question.

"Yeah, you know . . . a leash for Irma to keep it by her while she traveled."

Wilberton shrugged.

I sipped my beer. Looking through the window, I could see Jeff throwing stones across the road at the bushes.

"You can sleep on the sofa and the floor," Bo Wilberton said around a gassy emission. He crunched his empty can and tossed it towards the trash container over beside the oven. In a cleanliness competition the trash container would have won hands down.

I walked outside to catch the end of the day.

"He's an asshole," Jeff said when he saw it was me.

"He's an asshole but maybe that's all," I said.

Jeff stared at the thin line of orange squeezed down onto the treetops over on the horizon. The clouds bunched together slickly, like dirty taffeta, and promised a storm. "Maybe," he said.

I didn't believe it either.

The storm was up before us.

Bo Wilberton's living room smelled like a bunkhouse on Sunday morning. Which was pretty much the way it smelled when we came in.

Outside, rain swirled and wind buffeted the wooden walls and set the cat flap to squeaking in the screen door. That was all there was between us and the elements—if there had ever been an inside door, there wasn't one now. It was like we were lost at the end of the earth. Lost and very much alone.

Wilberton hadn't shown by the time we'd washed up and dressed so we just left to get some decent breakfast.

If Greenville was a one-horse town, then the horse was lame.

The road that Wilberton's house sat upon continued about a half a mile and wound up at a filling station, a general store and a truck-stop cafe. Beyond that, the bushes started again and the road wound on to U.S. 51 and Jackson. It might not be Louisiana officially—though it was only a tired man's spit away—but it was bayou country nevertheless.

As we'd walked through the stinging rain we'd been able to hear the slopping of the waters in the wetlands behind the trees and the undergrowth. It wasn't a place to take a late-night walk after a few beers. At least not in this weather.

Inside the truck-stop the smell of cigarette smoke, frying bacon and fresh coffee seemed like the purest country air. We sat at the counter on a couple of riveted stools that may have been there since Huey Long's day and ordered. I looked around for a Wurlitzer but the only entertainment was a high-mounted television showing a heady mixture of Hanna-Barbera cartoons and static. Pity about the cartoons.

Jeff spoke to the waitress, a woman in her mid-thirties who looked twice that age—Rosie, her name was—and asked if she knew Irma. Yes, she did, Rosie told him. Did she have any idea where she'd gone? No, she didn't. He said he'd thought she might have come in here the day she left, looking to catch a ride someplace. No, not that either, she said, and did we want any more coffee.

I spoke to a fat man in a plaid shirt and a Dodgers baseball cap—he obviously worshiped them from afar—about Irma. He looked at me suspiciously. Kept himself to himself, he said. The underlying message was *I don't want no trouble, mister*. A couple of other guys finished their coffee and left, which left only a single truck driver sitting at a window table thumbing through the *Enquirer* and nodding vacantly to something on a personal stereo. Rosie was the only female representative.

After a large helping of scrambled eggs and bacon, plus a side order of flapjacks and maple syrup, we were just about ready to hit downtown Greenville to ask a few more questions when the screen door blew inward with a flurry of rain and movement. I looked around from behind the Dodgers fan at the same time Jeff turned around on his bar stool.

"Jesus H. Christ, what a day," a voice boomed over the canned laughter of "The Jetsons." "Rosie, pot of coffee and a double chocolate when you're ready."

"Coming right up, Ted," Rosie answered with a smile and wandered off through the waist-high saloon doors into the cooking area.

Ted was in his early forties, a tall man dressed in full-length oilskin britches and wading boots. He sported a thick beard, a thick head of hair tied back in a ponytail and slicked down with rain, and a wild, disarming smile. He nodded to everyone who was paying him any attention, set down a large bag of fishing tackle and proceeded to unzip his waterproof jacket.

"Great weather for fishing," I shouted over to him.

He opened the door and lifted in three rods and a holding net, all bound together with twine, and stood them against the comic-book stand just inside the door. "If the fish can stand it then I guess we should be able to," he replied. "A day's about as much as I can take in a sitting, though," he added. "Weather report says it's set in for more than that."

Ted walked over to the bar, sat on a stool next to Jeff. I wandered over with my coffee and sat on Jeff's other side. "You do this for a living?" I asked him, leaning over.

"I do it," he said with a laugh, "and I live . . . barely. I doubt I'll ever make a million, though." He looked over our faces, took in Jeff's expression and held out his hand. "Ted Chambers," he announced.

We took the hand in turn, returned the firm shake and gave our names.

"Where you guys from?"

"Daytona," Jeff said, picking up the lead. "He's a New Yorker." He indicated me with his thumb. "So you can't tell him nothing about weather."

"Guess not," Ted said. "What you doing in these parts?"

Jeff told him as Rosie placed a cup of fresh, steaming coffee on the counter alongside a plate containing the biggest and gooiest chocolate doughnut I've ever seen. Ted became suddenly animated.

"Yeah, Irma. I know her," he said, spraying crumbs on Jeff. "Nice lady. Nice lady. She married to that dork B-O Wilberton?"

Jeff nodded and motioned for Rosie to fill up his mug.

"Yeah. Now that's an aptly named man if ever there was one," Ted said with a shake of his head. "B-O." He laughed. "I met skunks that smelled a sight sweeter than that feller. Got a temperament to match, too. Don't blame Irma for finally getting up the courage to leave him to it."

"You didn't realize she'd left?" I asked.

Ted shook his head and took a drink of coffee. "Nope. I don't see her all that regular, mind. Just now and again. She's a sad lady, though, I could see that. Sad in spite of all that eating—if you'll pardon me for saying."

"No offence taken," Jeff said. "She ate for comfort."

"That's a fact," Ted agreed. "Seemed she didn't get any other kind at home. She had put on the pounds, though."

"At least she had her cat," I said.

Ted threw his head back and laughed loudly. "Yeah, that cat! Jesus H. Christ, but that damned cat followed her everywhere. It was a real hard-eyed feller, too. Could catch a rat or a bird quick as that." He snapped his fingers in the air. I watched him enviously—it was something I'd always wanted to do but had never been able to perfect. What good's a private investigator who can't snap his fingers?

We took up the next half hour or so talking about the fishing scene, wondering how long the rain would stay set in this way and about what it was like to live in New York. He listened like a small boy while I told him all about Central Park and the subways, about the Empire State Building and Radio City. Then he zipped himself up, picked up his belongings and made set to hit the weather.

"You could ask around the houses down the road, see if anybody's seen your sister. Most folks'll know who you're talking about. You get up a mile or so further and you're about ready to hit Route Eleven, up there to Hattiesburg, and Fifty-one, which goes all the way to Jackson. Could be somebody saw her trying to hitch a ride." He shrugged as if to say he didn't expect we'd have much luck and walked off into the storm.

Jeff paid up and we followed him a few minutes later. We weren't optimistic.

The day wore on the way it had started out. Wet.

We ran back to Wilberton's house and got a couple of zippered jackets out of my trunk. Jeff went inside the house to tell Wilberton where we were but he still wasn't out of bed. It was a little after eleven by that time. Then we set out for the intersection with Route 11 and a house-to-house search for anyone who might have seen Irma Wilberton on the day she left her husband.

It was hopeless.

Wet and hopeless.

The weather reflected our feelings of despair. But as we checked house after ramshackle wooden house, it somehow strengthened Jeff's resolve. He didn't believe Irma had wandered up the road to stand with a suitcase and her cat trying to hitch a ride with some sticky-fingered truck driver bound for God knows where. I didn't believe it either.

But though most of the folks we asked knew Irma at least by sight, not a single person recalled seeing her on the day she left.

It was with empty bellies and soaked to the skin that we finally decided to head back. Dusk had fallen early with the rain, and though it was only a little after eight o'clock, nighttime lay heavy on the land. I knew it lay even heavier on Jeff's heart. We had made up our minds to leave Greenville, drive back to Gulfport and make some inquiries there. Jeff figured that if she *had* left, Irma would head back towards him and not in the opposite direction. The first town of any real size was Gulfport.

Walking back, dodging puddles on the uneven road, we spoke little, preferring to listen to the sound of the night wind blowing squalls of rain through the trees. The first crack of thunder sounded from over New Orleans way just as Beauregarde Wilberton's well-lit house came into view.

He was watching a "Honeymooners" rerun, sitting with his feet propped against the table, swigging Miller from a can and working his way through a bag of bagel chips.

We stood just inside the door and dripped on his floor.

He didn't look away from the television when he said, "Had a good day?"

Another crack of thunder sounded—nearer this time—and a flash of lightning lit up the outside, letting us see the rain for a brief moment. Jeff walked over to the sofa and shuffled his clothes into his bag.

"You changing?" I said.

He shook his head.

"What you fellas been doing, anyway?" said Bo Wilberton. "The Honeymooners" had finished and he sat up and turned off the set.

"Looking for Irma," Jeff said.

Thunder rattled the house and set the cat flap to swinging. I could hear it squeaking and catching the mesh of the screen door. I was looking at Jeff and trying to decide whether to change clothes but it was Wilberton's face that made me turn to look at the door.

It was a cat.

Irma's cat.

It had come home.

It stood there, soaked and muddy—dirty, filthy, muddy . . . the stuff was caked onto its fur—and its eyes were gleaming like they were on fire. Just for a second it stood there, with me and Bo Wilberton staring at it, and then it walked slowly and stealthily past me and past Jeff over to Wilberton's chair where it stopped. It sat down right next to him, leaned forward and dropped what looked like a thick piece of twig onto the carpet.

Wilberton's eyes were open wide, wide like they were going to fall right out of his head and land next to the piece of twig. Only it wasn't a piece of twig at all. It was a finger. A very fat finger . . . with a very large knuckle. I think we all realized at the same time what it meant.

Jeff looked at the ragged fray of skin and then stared at Wilberton. He looked up at Jeff and seemed to gulp. Then he looked at me. And then he looked past me. That's when I realized his eyes hadn't been open wide at all. *Now* they were wide. And his face was white. His eyes rolled up and he slumped back into the chair.

I turned around and looked at the door just in time to see another flash of lightning illuminate the path to the door. To see the figure walking stiffly up towards the house, straining through the rain and the wind. To hear the labored sound of feet schlepping through the water and the mud.

The thunder rolled like someone banging a tire iron on a metal sheet. The screen door opened slowly.

"Jesus Christ," I said quietly.

Jeff shook his head.

"Been out in the creek," Ted Chambers announced proudly, shifting the dripping, canvas-wrapped bundle in his arms. A hint of pale-colored skin could be seen through a rip around the middle . . . a rip just about big enough for a small animal to get through. "You wanna see what the cat dragged in?"

Dumb Animals

·

DeLoris Stanton Forbes

"**D**umb's a sly dog."

That's a quote from an Englishman named Colley Cibber who lived from 1671 to 1757, serving as poet laureate from 1730 to 1757 and earning the title of worst poet to hold the office. I know this because Richard said so and Richard should know because Richard is very erudite, intrigued by history, particularly history of the theater, and this same Colley Cibber was not only poet but dramatist and actor.

Furthermore Richard is given to expounding on his specialized (if not rarefied) knowledge at the droop of a mascaraed lash. Not only is Richard keen on history but assorted young ladies constitute an ongoing preoccupation; in this regard I've heard him say, "A lifetime. It will take a lifetime to complete my research on the female of the species." He said this to Dumb, if you can imagine. I gather he thought he'd understand it but would be unable to pass it on. Me he doesn't trust. "I know you," he's told me upon occasion. "You're a treacherous soul from some ancient civilization." Richard also believes in reincarnation. When he makes these untoward accusations I simply smile and let the moment pass. He doesn't mean it. I am his best friend. And intend to remain so.

In pursuit of his studies he's said at least a dozen times to as many young ladies, "Dumb's a sly dog, that's why I named him Dumb. He's a sly dog. See, he even has a tag that says so. Dumb—a sly dog. In old English letters. To go with his breed." Not exactly brilliant repartee but his audience either giggled or smirked or—in one memorable case—pushed him onto the down-cushioned Oriental-style sofa, scattering pillows all the way. I can't say what happened after that, I left for my quarters, for peace and quiet and the sanctity of my bed. Raw sex doesn't turn me on.

Slyness quite aside, Dumb was aptly named. He was a thoroughbred English bulldog, pure white with pale eyes and that stupid flat broad face so typical of the breed. I say typical because Richard researched various canine strains before settling on Dumb (formal title: Peerless Prince Colley's Folly—where do they get these dog names? Still, the Folly applies). Dumb had all the physical attributes necessary for dog-show stardom except for brains. In truth, his name should have been Sly, a dumb dog.

I'm not quite sure when I began to detest him—bad toilet habits, bad breath, atrocious manners at the food bowl, and noisy! The barking could drive one mad. But maybe he was sly, he didn't bark when Richard was around, only in his absence. And, I concluded, primarily for my benefit.

At any rate, in retrospect I've decided it must have been hate at first sight. Not only did Dumb create an unsanitary, Dempsey-Dumpster-like atmosphere but he got a good deal of unwarranted attention. It did put me off to see Richard permit Dumb to slather a wet dog tongue across his face. I simply couldn't imagine what he saw in Dumb, not for the life of me.

But I didn't let on, oh no. Richard was the breadwinner, the master of all he surveyed and why not, with his looks, his charm, his intellect, his far-above-averageness. I knew which side my bread was buttered on, it's by his grace that I share this elegant apartment overlooking Central Park and all the *hoi polloi* a dozen floors below. I kept my opinion to myself and went about my business as though nothing whatever had changed since the arrival of Dumb—a sly dog.

In the beginning I thought that Dumb, being brainless, couldn't help behaving like an animal. The nature of the beast, so to speak. But after I got to spend more time with him, to know him better, I decided that much of his misbehavior was purposeful. The messings on the off-white, deep pile wall-to-wall carpeting, for instance. He was walked three times a day by Fritz, the apartment house elevator man; there was no reason for such grossness, none at all. But it got Richard's attention, didn't it? He'd fuss at Dumb, he'd talk to Dumb explaining about good hygiene, he'd threaten Dumb with "Next time . . ." but then he'd let him kiss him with that ghastly tongue that had been working on Dumb's own rear but moments before . . . ugh, I can't go on. Too terrible!

The only remedy I could think of was to stay away from Dumb and I did that, emerging from my private hideaway only when Richard came home. Even so, I got blamed upon occasion for some of Dumb's actions. The broken lamp episode, for instance. An authentic Tiffany table lamp (Richard also collects Art Deco and turn-of-the-century objets d'art) had been knocked off a table and its shade was found in pieces. Richard dared to look at me and I wasn't quite sure he believed me when I assured him, "Never! I'm very careful with all your belongings." I was hurt.

The obvious culprit lolled that tongue and wagged a piglike tail, did contortions with his hips and looked even more idiotic than usual. "You?" Richard. "Dumb, you didn't!" Dumb pranced around his feet, then lowered the front half of his body into a doglike bow, put his head on his paws, *mea culpa*. God! How sickening.

Richard sighed and I knew the moment of retribution had passed. "What's done is done," said Richard. "After all, you didn't mean to break it. We'll just have to put certain things away, won't we, Lewie?" addressing me. And he reached down and patted the flat bony head. "All right, Dumb. I know you're sorry."

Sorry, hell! I was mad enough to spit. Obviously Dumb could do no wrong, at least no wrong bad enough to warrant his ouster. I gave serious thought as to whether I could continue to live with this uncouth creature the rest of my days and decided I could not. Not even the rest of Dumb's days, presumably shorter in length than mine.

Presumably shorter. Of course. Definitely shorter. It was up to me to get rid of—I refused to call him my rival—this low-life nuisance. That's what he was, an unnecessary nuisance. To do or not to do, that was no question, the question was how and when.

Once I make up my mind, I concentrate completely. The

problem at hand? The disposal of one white, approximately sixty-five-pound English bulldog, age almost one year. Let's see, one could sprinkle his food with any manner of deadly substances. I happened to know that the medicine cabinet held powders of all descriptions that could indeed be injurious to a dog's health. With some planning, it would be possible to add same to Dumb's food—and believe me, he ate like a glutton. A strange taste wouldn't put Dumb off his food at all, he'd probably like it. So . . . possible. Yes, possible. But . . .

There was a big *but*. Dumb's demise must look like an accident. All the way. To protect my status quo. Furthermore, it should be sudden and final, if Richard suspected for one moment that Dumb was seriously ill, he'd have him off to the vet's in two shakes of a Dumb's tail—no, it had to look like an accident (where no suspicion should fall on me, no way!) and it should be definitive. Sudden and final. No use, Dr. Cruise! (Dr. Cruise being the vet.) The elimination of Dumb must be the literal living end.

So . . . I had to bide my time while I considered and discarded, considered and discarded. How was I going to do that damn Dumb to death?

I began to pay attention to the plots on the mystery stories on TV. I pretended I was Columbo and examined every single idea with an eye to possible failure. I tried to put myself in Jessica Fletcher's shoes but that didn't help much either. I was thinking like a detective, that was the problem, when I needed to think like a killer. A clever killer.

About this time Richard acquired a new consuming interest. The interest's name was Marsha. I hadn't paid much attention to Marsha, she was just another of the seemingly endless supply of nubile young ladies Richard brought home, but then Marsha came a second time and a third and it finally dawned on me that Marsha might become some sort of permanent fixture in Richard's scheme of things. I watched warily, would Marsha's coming mean my going? Did she represent a threat worse than Dumb?

But, no, au contraire. Marsha took a liking to me, heaven be praised, and, heaven be praised even more, a dislike to Dumb. "Look at him, Richard," she'd say. "Look at what he's trying to do to my leg. That dog is obnoxious!"

Richard chuckled. "He's just horny, that's all. He's a gay young dog in his prime with no lady friends. I'll have to talk to Dr. Cruise about that." And he'd pulled the beast away, patted the flat head. "Poor old Dumb. Come on, boy, you're banished to the kitchen."

"He needs to be fixed, that's what he needs." Marsha made a face for me and I nodded, we were in accord, Marsha and I. Only my idea of fixed was not quite the same as hers. Still, something could be made of Dumb's problem. I put it on my list of Dumb weak points, when you're going in for the kill always seek out the weak points, yes? Yes.

Marsha was given a key so she'd show up now even when Richard wasn't at home. Usually she was bent on domestic errands, new sheets for his king-sized throne-bed or groceries for a gourmet dinner she'd prepare later. If she had time she'd stop and chat, we became quite chummy. She went so far as to ask my opinion—did I think Richard would ask her to move in? Even, fingers crossed, to marry? I hadn't the least idea, this was his first venture into any kind of a lasting relationship so I had no past performances to go on. I reassured her the best I could, I rather liked the lady. She was bright and pretty (short shining brown hair and sparkly hazel eyes) and neat and easy to be with ... what more could he desire? That's the way I felt about it but with Richard you never knew. His attention span woman-wise, well, there used to be an old joke that ended up with 'Wham, bam, thank you, ma'am.' A joke about rabbits, I believe. That was Richard—until Marsha.

Richard's affair of the heart was diverting my attention from Dumb to Marsha. If she did manage to trap him, to actually move in, how would that be? Would my future be truly threatened if she were a permanent (more or less) feature? I didn't think so, as I've said she actually seemed to like me, sometimes she'd even pat the sofa cushion for me to sit by her side and if I did Richard didn't seem to resent it, probably there wasn't a jealous bone in the man's body. He was so very sure of himself.

Lewie likewise. Some of Richard's self-confidence must have rubbed off on me because I decided that Marsha was an ally, not an enemy, and went back to the Dumb problem. Weak points, Dumb's weak points. His Achilles heel.

He often drank out of the toilet. It annoyed Richard and Marsha, it drove me wild. Slopping toilet water (and I don't mean the good-smelling kind) all over the floors, he drooled a great deal and always there were droplets of moisture from that obscene pink tongue. To say nothing of the drops of moisture from that other obscene pink append-age that Richard referred to as the "flower of Dumb's man-hood." Revolting! Absolutely revolting.

So, could I introduce anything into the toilet that might send Dumb to doggy heaven? As I said, there were various medications in the medicine chest but could one of these fall accidentally into the bowl? Think about it, Lewie. Rich-ard never left anything out on the top of the toilet tank, if only he would a simple careless movement might be held accountable . . . but, alas, he didn't.

Toilet cleansers? Blue stuff that came out when you dropped a tablet inside the tank, non-poisonous. Bleach, there was a big jug in the kitchen cabinet that held cleaning supplies but it had no legs, couldn't accidentally find its way into the bath, into the toilet . . . and it wasn't logical that anyone should carry it there, put it there. Was it? And even if I did find a way, would it kill? Hmmm—research needed to know that but why bother when I couldn't come up with a logical method of introduction? Wait a minute—perhaps I could finagle it with Maria, the once-a-week maid. Convince Maria that a strong dose of bleach would do wonders for the plumbing? But do it so obliquely that she couldn't possibly go to Richard afterwards and say, "The devil—Lewie made me do it."

While I pondered spring came and when spring arrived the balcony was opened. Every apartment in our building boasts a balcony with safety railings; as soon as it gets warm enough (and if the air pollution isn't too bad) New Yorkers with balconies take to the great outdoors. Chaise lounges are unfolded, chairs come out from under tarps, plants appear courtesy of the local florist . . . plants. Aha. Certain plants can be injurious to one's health but Dumb wouldn't know that. Could I convince him to nibble on the oleander, chomp on the dieffenbachia (also known as dumb cane, how fitting, Dumb, a sly cane!)?

And while I pondered that, sitting there on a chaise in the brilliant spring sunshine, my gaze fell upon an unexpected occupant of the adjacent balcony, that would be the balcony of 11 B inasmuch as we were 11 A. The newcomer, a mass of white curls accented by a jet-black nose, yapped in my direction. A friendly sort of yap accompanied by a bounce against the railing. A poodle. A young poodle from the voice, a bitch poodle from the anatomy. She'd been to the canine beauty salon, her pom-pommed ankles and tasseled tail were fresh-snow white and silky, her dark eyes sparkled, she yapped again and the tail wagged wildly. As I said, friendly. And lonesome.

Lonesome. Ah. A lonesome lady dog. And in my house was a lonesome male dog. How convenient. How terribly convenient. The plan in its foolproof entirety came to me like a flash. I went to the apartment door and looked in. Dumb was snoring on the sofa, he well knew sleeping on the sofa was forbidden but he ignored such taboos. He needed awakening. I made a sound, repeated it until his eyes became slits, his big head moved inches off the pillow it rested on. If he could speak, but he couldn't communicate of course, he would have said, "What's with you? What's the matter?"

From outside the lady poodle yapped.

Dumb's eyes opened wider, his head erect.

"Yap. Yap-yap-yap. Yap."

He yawned, stretched. Got down off the couch. Waddled to the balcony door, looked out.

"Yap-yap-yap-yap. Yip yap. Yap yip. Yap-yap-yap-yappppppp . . ."

Dumb went out on the balcony. I followed discreetly so as not to break the spell.

He stared, barked back at the poodle, one single harsh "Woof!"

"Yaaaaap!"

He moved closer to the railing, stood up against it, his dog tags dangling, his tongue dripping saliva and that's not all. An ugly sight.

The poodle flew at the railing, couldn't manage to climb

over, she was far too small. He tried the same from his side, he was too short in the legs and too heavy. They stopped for a moment, both of them panting. She started the yapping again, it sounded sad.

He backed off, took a big run toward the barrier, got his front legs over the top while his back legs scrambled. "Go for it, Dumb," I urged. "You can do it." I'd moved closer, was near enough now to give him a nudge.

He was straining now, the railing had attractive uprights to hold it firm, he was having trouble with the top of one, its shape like an inverted arrow was digging into his chest. The poodle gave a frantic leap, managed to almost touch noses before she fell back.

That was all Dumb needed. He gave one final thrust and he was over the top. I was right behind him, catching at his dangling dog tag and there, I did it. I caught it in the railing so that it stopped his momentum, it and the choke collar which began to do its thing on the points of the arrow upright. Dumb was stuck in mid-air for a moment, then he fell and dangled like a heavy pendant. His feet were scrambling, the poodle was barking loud enough to be heard down on the street but no one came from her apartment and there was no one home in my apartment but me so nobody came. Nobody at all.

"I understand that the new gal next door has a poodle," Richard explained to Marsha. "A poodle she expects to breed just once and the poodle is in heat. It must have been too much for poor old Dumb—he hung himself trying to get to her."

"Hoist on his own petard," said Marsha lightly.

Richard gave her a look, decided to let it pass. Almost. "Except that a petard is . . . wait a minute, I've got a *Roget*'s right here. Petard, petard . . . here it is. Missile. Projectile. Cannon shot. Dumdum bullet . . . Dumb Dumb bullet . . ." They looked at each other and began to titter. I was laughing too but they couldn't tell.

That's because cats can't show amusement. But believe me, we find many sources of humor in our day-to-day lives. Seemingly humdrum lives.

Incidentally, the poodle, her name is Fwances (because her owner lisps), and I have become friends now that she's been spayed. "Believe me," I assured her, "it's much better this way. You don't have to put up with those boisterous males and their shenanigans and you don't have to nurse a batch of demanding offspring. I was ever so glad when Richard had me done right away."

Fwancis (France's Princess Frances Feline) answered, "I guess you're right. But, Lewie (she likes to be formal, sometimes calls me by my full name Lewie Lewie Blooie, people name animals in such a silly manner but what can you do?) . . ." she sighed, "that big white beast was kind of cute." She can communicate because she's smart, they're the brightest of the canines, you know. She gave me a side-ways look. "I saw what you did, you know. You caused his hang-up. You grabbed his chain with one quick paw."

I shook my head. "Dumb was a sly dog," I told her. "Hoist on his own petard." And then, just to show off, "A petard is a dumdum bullet. Get it? It's a joke."

But she didn't laugh. Poodles may be the smartest of the canines but they have absolutely no sense of humor.

Life of Riley

·

Wendi Lee

As Freddy Wilson drove back to the mansion, the litany kept running through his head like a slow, steady drumbeat: "The stupid cat, the stupid, rich cat." It was not until Freddy turned into the driveway that he added, "The stupid, rich, lost cat." Parking the Mercedes haphazardly in the driveway, Freddy's only thought was to find Riley. How could he tell the lawyer that he tossed Riley out on his furry rear end without so much as a bag of kibble to his name?

The will reading had not gone as Freddy had expected. Two days after Calvin Harding's funeral, Freddy showed up at the lawyer's office at the appointed time and surveyed the room. The maid, the cook, and the gardener, along with representatives from several of old man Harding's favorite charities, were already gathered there.

Freddy Wilson had been old man Harding's companion for close to seventeen years. Since the rich old man had no immediate relatives, Freddy had been led to believe that Harding had come to think of him as the son he'd never had. Often, when they would sit before the fireplace with their brandies, Riley firmly planted in the old man's lap, Harding would turn to Freddy and, with a grand sweep of his arm around the room, would say, "Someday, Freddy, this will all be yours."

Oh, he had been given everything he wanted, Freddy thought, ruefully remembering the will-reading. After Fichter's little speech about the sad circumstances under which they must all meet and what a fine man Calvin

Harding had been, Freddy barely paid attention to the first part of the reading—the servants and charities had been given very generous sums. Harding had bequeathed the cottage on the edge of the grounds to his faithful gardener, Bert Hill. Freddy only came out of his self-induced trance when Mr. Fichter came to the bulk of the estate.

"And now we come to the last part," Mr. Fichter said, beaming in Freddy's direction. He cleared his throat and read, "The bulk of my estate, which includes the house and the remainder of my fortune will heretofore be left to my faithful companion—" Here was where Freddy stuck out his chest with pride. He was Harding's faithful companion, after all. Seventeen years of his life and he was getting his reward "—my cat, Riley."

Freddy felt his chest deflate like one of those kiddie swimming pools. He listened to the rest in stunned silence. "In the event of my beloved Riley's death by natural causes, and if there are no living relatives to inherit, the money shall revert to my companion and valet of nearly two decades, Frederick Wilson."

The lawyer put the will down, the smile still on his face, and faced Freddy. Although Freddy was tempted to punch him out, he refrained. He was curious as to why Harding had left everything to his cat.

"Well, what do you think of that, Mr. Wilson?" Fichter asked smugly. "Mr. Harding has left specific instructions that you should remain in the house. I think that was very generous of him. Of course, your duties will be to see that Riley's needs are taken care of. Your salary shall remain the same, with the usual raise every year, your expenses in regards to Riley shall be taken care of out the estate, and, since Riley cannot drive," Fichter paused to chuckle at his sorry sense of humor, "use of the Mercedes is part of the deal."

"But why Riley?" Freddy heard himself whine.

"Just before he made this will, Mr. Harding began to worry about how his death would affect Riley," Fichter explained. "He felt this was the best way to ensure a long and happy life for Riley."

"Uh, yes," Freddy managed to say, too dumbfounded to think of a better response.

Fichter interrupted Freddy's thoughts. "Well, we'll work all the details out in the next few days. I will stop by the mansion tomorrow afternoon to further discuss the arrangements with you."

"F-fine," Freddy managed to say as he shook hands with the lawyer before he left.

As Freddy got out of the Mercedes, his thoughts remained on the cat, the stupid rich cat. All his life, Freddy had been someone's servant. First he was a shoe salesman, and when he tired of catering to bunions and smelly feet, he became a chauffeur for a wealthy businessman. Then he met Calvin Harding, who took a liking to Freddy and asked him to become his valet and companion. And so Freddy had spent the past seventeen years catering to an old man's every whim, including putting up with Riley.

Riley had been just a year old, but firmly established in the household, when Freddy came into service. Freddy, who was a dog lover, had never cared for cats in general, and had never taken to Riley in particular. Of course Riley had never taken to Freddy either; over the years they had reached a tacit agreement to stay out of each other's way as much as possible.

Freddy had never understood why Calvin Harding, a wealthy industrialist, had taken in an orange alley cat with one white paw. Here was a man who could have the best of everything, cigars, brandy, cars. Yet when it came to a pet, he chose a marmalade tomcat and gave it the same treatment that would be expected if Riley were an exotic breed or had a pedigree, even to the point of letting the cat out of the house only if he were on a harness and leash.

"He's a constant reminder of where I came from," Harding had once explained while absentmindedly puffing on his cigar. "Even his name, Riley, reminds me of a fighter, someone who won't take anything for granted. If all this was gone tomorrow, Riley would be able to take care of himself."

Now Freddy regretted last night's rash decision to throw the beast out of the house. He had been so sure that he was getting Harding's millions that he had grabbed the unsuspecting Riley by the scruff of the neck and tossed him out the kitchen door. All night long, Freddy had been kept awake as Riley incessantly yeowled his anger below his bedroom window. By morning, the cat was no longer there.

Now Freddy circled the grounds, searching for a tough and wily marmalade tomcat with one white paw. He wondered if the gardener might have taken Riley in. Bert Hill had, in Freddy's opinion, one cat too many. It was a little orange-and-white tabby. Bert had once told Freddy that he kept her around not only because she was a good mouser, but she was a good companion as well.

As Freddy moved in ever-widening arcs, he called, "Riley, oh, Riley, here kitty, kitty, kitty." But Riley did not answer. Freddy spent the entire day searching the property. He passed Bert's cottage several times, but the gardener was nowhere to be seen.

In the late afternoon, just beyond the hedge that bordered the cottage, Freddy caught sight of a flash of orange. His heart leapt to his throat. "Riley," he whispered in a voice hoarse from shouting. A small orange-and-white cat emerged from the hedge and looked up at Freddy with luminous green eyes, a quizzical expression in her face. Freddy's heart sank. It was the gardener's cat, Sarabelle. Sighing, turning away, Freddy had an uncanny feeling that Riley had been there with Sarabelle, hovering just on the edge of his guardian's peripheral vision.

The day wore on and there was still no sign of Riley. Freddy began to panic. He would be entertaining the lawyer tomorrow, and if Riley hadn't returned by then, he would have some explaining to do. Freddy tried to think of ways to get around it. Telling the lawyer the partial truth, that Riley had got outside, was a possibility. But Fichter might suspect Freddy of foul play. He then thought about searching for a look-alike cat at the pet stores and the humane society, but it occurred to him that there was a chance that someone might put two and two together. After all, when he had inherited Harding's estate, Riley had been featured on the front page of the local paper. Besides, Riley's veterinarian might discover the imposter during a check-up.

By dusk, Freddy had covered every inch of the grounds, and he was now covered with mud and leaves. Just as he was about to give up, Freddy spotted lights on at the gardener's cottage. He hesitated about going to Bert with his story. If he told the gardener that Riley had got out, would Bert believe him? Freddy sighed, remembering the times Bert had been in the house to collect his pay. Riley would invariably pad into the library and coil himself around Bert's legs, purring loudly.

And every time the gardener, chuckling, would stoop down to scratch behind the marmalade cat's ears. "You must smell Sarabelle on me, old boy," Bert would say softly. "She's a good mouser, she is." How could the gardener miss the lack of affection Riley had for Freddy, and vice versa? Freddy took one last look at the gardener's cozy cottage, then trudged back to the cold and dark mansion at the other end of the property.

He had a hard time getting to sleep. Whenever he started to drift off, he would hear the loud, mournful meows of cats outside under his window. Then he would sit bolt upright, leap out of bed, and run to the window, hoping to catch a glimpse of Riley. But each time, the cats were gone by the time Freddy got into view. Then he would try to get back to sleep, but the problem of the missing cat would gnaw at him until he had paced the length of the floor a few times. He would finally crawl into bed, start to drift off, and the meows would start in again.

The dawn finally came, gray and damp, just the way Freddy was feeling. As he made breakfast, he had a sudden inspiration. Pouring a little cream in a bowl, he set it just outside, leaving the kitchen door open. Half an hour before the lawyer was to arrive, Freddy was sitting before a crackling fire, puffing on one of Harding's cigars, the kind Freddy used to cut and light for the old man. This might be the last cigar I have, the last time I can enjoy this fire, Freddy thought. I'll be out on my ear in a short while.

Riley entered the study, interrupting Freddy's black contemplation. Freddy narrowed his eyes and watched the large orange tomcat jump up on Harding's favorite chair, sniff the cushion, turn counterclockwise three times, then curl up and go to sleep.

"So you decided to join me after all," Freddy said with a false heartiness. The cat solemnly lifted his head and gazed at his guardian as if he were the lowest form of life on the planet. Freddy found himself shrinking into his chair.

After all, he had tossed Riley out on his ear, but now there he was with cream on his whiskers. The cat began to studiously clean his left paw.

"No hard feelings, eh, chum?" Freddy said in as cheery a voice as he could muster. Riley ignored him.

Fichter arrived to witness this peaceful scene, completely unaware of what had gone on the day before. Freddy silently thanked his stars that cats were unable to communicate.

"Well, everything seems to be in order here," Fichter said, looking around. "Of course, you know there is an inventory of the contents of the house. You cannot sell or give away anything in this house, or redecorate in any way, without my express permission—with the exception of your own quarters." The lawyer stroked Riley's fur. "And this fellow must go in for a check-up and grooming once a month. He's getting on in years and needs to be looked after." Riley was on his side now, yawning and stretching his four legs out, tensing them for a moment before relaxing them completely. "In any case, I don't think we need to meet more than three times a year."

After Fichter had left, satisfied that all was well with Riley, Freddy continued to chew thoughtfully on the end of his cigar, which had by now gone out. He gazed at the sleeping cat. Fichter had unwittingly pointed out something that Freddy had almost forgotten. Riley was over seventeen years old. Cats didn't live forever.

It had been a month since Harding's funeral and it was time for Riley's physical. Freddy was waiting in the outer office when Dr. Anason, a large man with curly graying hair, came out with Riley in his pet carrier. Freddy silently hoped that Riley wasn't as healthy as he looked. He had been fantasizing about the vet telling him that Riley only had a few weeks to live.

Freddy stood up to take the carrier. "How's he doing, Doc?" he asked, mentally crossing two fingers.

"He's a fine, healthy cat, Mr. Wilson. You should have him around for a long time," the veterinarian said with a smile.

"But he's over seventeen years old," Freddy stammered.

Dr. Anason dismissed Freddy's worry with a wave of his hand. "Oh, I wouldn't worry about losing him, Mr. Wilson. Cats are known to live for twenty-five or thirty years. I personally know a cat who lived to be thirty-five. Don't worry. You'll have Riley around for company for at least another ten years."

It was on the drive home that Freddy decided to kill Riley. It wasn't that he hated the cat, but he hated the fact that Riley was the heir to a fortune. No animal should inherit money. Besides, he was a dog man himself. He had wanted to get a couple of big dogs, German shepherds or Weimaraners, for company. A dog was an affectionate creature, giving unconditional love for no more than a pat on the head.

Over the last seventeen years, Riley had shown no more affection to Freddy than he would to a statue. The cat acted like he deserved to be waited upon like a king. But what galled Freddy the most was having to clean the litter box. There was nothing more humiliating than cleaning a rich cat's litter box while the cat regally looked on. No, the cat definitely had to go and if he wasn't willing to do it gracefully by dying of some cat disease or of old age, Freddy would help him along with an undetectable poison.

When they got back to the mansion, Freddy went straight to the kitchen to fix dinner for Riley. He settled on a can of sardines. The moment he opened it, the orange tom arrived and sat by his bowl, impatiently waiting for his dinner. As Freddy bent down to empty the sardines into the dish, he had to restrain himself from kicking the animal.

"After all," he cooed as he straightened up, grateful that he didn't have to cook pheasant under glass for the cat, "you are the master of this house, right?"

As if in response, the tom grunted just before diving into his dinner, dismissing Freddy's presence as if he were only the hired help.

Freddy sighed. "That's all I am, aren't I? Just the help these days. And what thanks do I get?" he asked aloud, addressing the orange cat who so disdainfully ignored him. "Mr. Harding doesn't leave me a small gift of money like the others, no. Instead he names me as your guardian, you ungrateful, miserable creature."

Riley finished his meal and sat back smugly to wash his paws. Freddy studied the orange cat for a moment, musing that Riley's left front paw looked as if he had stepped in white paint.

After completing his duties, Freddy went straight to the public library. He found the book he was looking for: *The Complete Guide to Poisonous Plants and Fungi*. He knew he couldn't take the book out; he would be the first suspect in a suspicious death when an autopsy was done on a dead Riley. Freddy didn't want to lose the inheritance through a careless oversight. He made photocopies of several entries on poisonous plants and mushrooms, one on fool's parsley and another on a mushroom called Caesar's fiber head; both of these could be ingested by Riley without arousing suspicion. Both were common to the area and Freddy was confident that finding them wouldn't be a problem.

The next day, it was still drizzling outside. Impatient to get his rightful inheritance, Freddy dressed in jeans and a windbreaker, then took the cat harness and lead from the hall closet shelf. Shaking it gently in front of Riley, Freddy softly asked, "Wouldn't you like to go out?"

The big orange tomcat stared at him, then pointedly looked out the window at the rain. Freddy got the distinct impression that Riley was reading his mind. The cat got up and turned around, his tail as high in the air as a social climber's nose, and started to stalk away. Freddy lunged for the cat and after a short but tiring struggle, managed to get the harness on. "There," he told Riley through labored breathing, "now we're going for walkies."

As he dragged the reluctant cat out the door, it occurred to him that *walkies* was a term used for dogs, not cats.

"Doesn't look like he wants to go with you," remarked a man who emerged from behind a hedge in the backyard. Even on such a crummy, gray day, Bert Hill's face was as tanned as a hide.

"It's the first time I've taken him outside the house since Mr. Harding died," Freddy explained as he yanked at the lead. Riley was trying to get to the gardener while Freddy just wanted to get on with his plan. "It looks like the rain has let up."

"You should be fine for about half an hour, but it'll start

up again soon. I wouldn't stay out longer than that," Bert warned.

What does he know? Freddy thought. Just because he's the gardener, suddenly he's an expert on the weather. Bert had crouched down and held his hand out for the cat to sniff. This was one struggle of wills that Riley won. The gardener was on his knees now, accommodating Riley by scratching behind his left ear. "That's a nice fella," he cooed. "Yeah, you like a little attention, don't you? Sarabelle sure would like to see you."

Freddy said with forced heartiness. "Since one of the provisions of the will was that Riley should never be allowed to roam on his own, I thought he might appreciate a brisk walk in the woods."

"It can't be easy for you," Bert replied mildly, "knowing that all that money and a perfectly good house has gone to a tomcat."

Although a lump of rage had formed in his throat, Freddy managed to sound casual. "It was Mr. Harding's money, not mine. I was only his companion. At least I get paid for my trouble. Besides, Riley isn't such a bad old guy." Freddy bent down to prove that they got along famously, but Riley pointedly turned away from him and stalked off toward the woods.

Bert straightened up and gave Freddy a quizzical look. "Guess he's anxious for that walk after all."

Freddy's laugh sounded hollow even to his own ears. "Yeah, see you later." He followed the insistent tug of the leash until they got into the woods.

While Riley rooted out scents under dead leaves, pounced on insects, and was taunted by squirrels, Freddy kept an eye out for his poisonous plants. Eventually, he found the mushrooms under a group of white pines. Freddy picked several of the small, brown, fibrous fungi and, after glancing around, stuffed them in the deep pocket of his windbreaker.

But now Riley wasn't ready to go back to the house. Freddy picked him up and started back. Riley protested by squirming so much that Freddy ended up half carrying the cat back to the house. When they were in sight of Bert's cottage, the rain had started again. Although the gardener's wheelbarrow was still resting on the front lawn, Bert was nowhere in sight. There were no witnesses to the cat's plaintive yeowling and efforts to break free of his guardian's hold.

By the time Freddy got Riley back in the house, the rain had drenched them both and Freddy had deep scratches and claw marks on his shoulders and halfway down his arms. The right sleeve of his windbreaker was ripped down to the elbow.

As he dabbed antiseptic on the wounds, he glowered at the cat, who sat calmly by, cleaning the blood from his paws after the battle. "First you didn't want to go out, then I couldn't get you back in here without suffering through this," Freddy said with exasperation, wincing as the peroxide bubbled in the scratches.

When he was finished tending to his injuries, Freddy headed for the kitchen, muttering, "Well, at least I won't have to put up with this much longer."

Freddy wasn't sure if cats ate mushrooms. Other than the tuna and sardines that he had always fed Riley, Freddy had never taken the trouble to find out what else Riley liked. He wanted something soft that could easily hide the taste and texture of poisonous mushrooms. After a short search, he discovered a can of crab-flavored cat food, the expensive kind, up in a cupboard. Freddy whistled as he mixed the minced mushrooms into the cat food; even Riley's pointed meowl didn't irritate him.

"Here you go, fella," he said, setting down the bowl. "Happy eating."

Freddy left Riley to eat in peace. A short time later, he came back in to check Riley's bowl and was satisfied that it had been licked clean. In the library, a sated Riley was curled up on Harding's chair by the fireplace, lazily washing his face with his white paw.

Guilt overcame Freddy's sense of greed. He hesitated when faced with leaving Riley to die alone. He had never thought of himself as a hardened criminal, killing in cold blood. Rather, Freddy saw himself as just dispatching a minor problem that stood between him and ten million dollars. It wasn't the cat's fault that old man Harding had left his fortune to the damn thing. Besides, Freddy thought as he settled into the other chair, he wanted to make sure his handiwork had left nothing to chance.

Fifteen minutes later, Riley began to look a little drowsy. Freddy leaned forward eagerly—could this be it? Someone cleared his throat, making Freddy jump out of his chair and turn around. Bert stood in the doorway.

"Just wanted to let you know that next week I'll be uncovering the tulip bulbs and planting rose bushes."

"Fine, fine," Freddy replied anxiously.

The gardener looked at him strangely. "Are you okay?" He said quickly, "I was just watching the cat."

Bert walked over to Riley. "He looks so peaceful."

Freddy's heart leapt. That was what so many people had said about Harding at the funeral. "He looks so peaceful."

The gardener bent down to scratch Riley's head, then stopped and frowned. "Say, I don't think he's breathing." He checked more closely, then announced, "He's still breathing, but barely."

"Isn't that normal for cats when they go to sleep? He is an old cat, seventeen years old." Freddy realized he was babbling.

The gardener shook his head. "My son-in-law's a vet and he says cats can live to be thirty. In fact, I had an eighteen-year-old cat and he was as healthy as a week-old kitten till the end. Maybe you should call a vet."

There was nothing Freddy could do but call Dr. Anason. He was already regretting his rash decision to kill Riley with poison. With a guardian who stood to inherit the estate, an autopsy would definitely be done on Riley and poisoned mushrooms would definitely look suspicious. Surely Bert would mention Freddy's strange behavior, and then the money would be lost.

Ten minutes later, the vet was inducing Riley to vomit. Then he pushed a pill down the woozy cat's throat and listened to his heart.

"He should be all right now," Dr. Anason said as he stood up. "Tomcats are troopers."

Freddy crossed his arms. "Do you know what made him sick?"

142

The vet scratched his head. "You took the cat for a walk in the woods today, right?"

That's right," Freddy said, not being able to resist elaborating. "He'd been cooped up in the house for three days. I thought a walk would do him good."

"Cats love the exercise," Anason enthused. "But sometimes they find plants in the woods and eat them. You'll have to be more aware of what he eats outside. I could get this analyzed," he gestured to the mess Riley had made, "and tell you—"

"No, no, that's okay," Freddy said quickly. "I'll just keep a closer eye on him when I take him out for exercise."

The vet bent over to gently rub the cat's head. "He's a beautiful animal and very healthy for his age. I'd just be careful what you feed him," the vet said, looking up at Freddy.

Two months went by since the poisoning incident and Freddy had come to terms with his subservient position. He was just getting used to the idea that Riley was going to live for five to ten more years when it happened one bright, sunny morning in June. Freddy found Riley curled up in old man Harding's chair, looking very much as if he were asleep. But he wasn't breathing.

Freddy realized he was holding his breath as well, and he let it out in one great big sigh of relief. Riley appeared to have passed away peacefully in the night. At least, he hoped the cat had done so. The first order of business was to phone Fichter, then the vet to verify Riley's death.

Within half an hour, Dr. Anason declared Riley dead.

"Well, he certainly lived a good life, such as it was," Freddy replied, upon hearing the news. He hoped he didn't sound as exultant as he felt. In his mind, he was already collecting the money, the house, and the Mercedes. All he'd had to do was wait. Riley hadn't been half bad, Freddy reasoned, for a cat.

The lawyer entered the study. "I understand our heir has died," Fichter said solemnly.

"Yes," Freddy replied, "I knew something was wrong when he didn't come to breakfast."

Fichter clucked his tongue and shook his head. "He was in such good health, too."

Dr. Anason looked up. "That he was. But all cats are different and I think the old fellow's heart just stopped pumping last night sometime."

"Of course, there will be an autopsy," Fichter said. Freddy realized that the lawyer was watching him carefully for a reaction. But Freddy had a clear conscience.

Bert appeared in the doorway with a box. Freddy looked at him with annoyance. "What do you want, Bert?" he asked impatiently.

"Well, I thought I ought to show you something," the gardener said, glancing over at Riley's still form. He suddenly looked sad. "Aw, did the little guy die?"

"Yes, and it looks like his inheritance will go to Mr. Wilson here," Fichter said. He was looking curiously at the box now. Freddy heard mewling noises coming from it.

"Aye, I guess so." Bert nodded to Freddy and said, "I'm sorry Riley's gone. He never got to see his kittens." The lawyer and Freddy moved closer. Inside, Sarabelle was curled up in the center while four roly-poly orange kittens climbed over her and each other. Each kitten sported a white left front paw.

Freddy chuckled. "Those have to be Riley's, all right. The same white paw. That must have happened the night he got out." He felt free to admit it now. "I spent the whole day looking for him. I was frantic with worry."

Fichter was frowning. "I'm sorry, Mr. Wilson, but this means that you won't be receiving the inheritance after all. Of course, you may stay on as guardian."

Freddy felt his heart drop down to his ankles. "Wha-what do you mean?" he asked in a stricken tone. "Riley is gone, and Mr. Harding doesn't have any living relatives. I'm next in line."

"You've got it backwards, Mr. Wilson. The way Calvin Harding wrote his will, it states that the bulk of his estate went to Riley first, then any living relative. Any living relative of Riley's, that is." Fichter's face softened and he stuck a finger into the writhing orange mass. "My, aren't they cute? You'll have years of employment ahead of you, Mr. Wilson. Years of enjoyment as Riley's kittens grow older. They do live for quite a long time, I understand."

Catnapper

·

Joe L. Hensley

My prospective client looked with unconcealed distaste at the fading wallpaper in my office and said: "Robak, I must have my cat back before my auntie, Miss Crystal Kingman, returns to Bington from Florida next week."

I examined him. His name was Evans Kingman and he was a true area blueblood. The Kingmans had owned most of Bington and Mojeff County a hundred years before I'd arrived in the university town to begin practicing law. Early Kingmans had been in the state legislature and in Congress. They'd built railroads and ridden as circuit judges. There was a picture of a bearded Judge Kingman hanging on the wall of the circuit courtroom. By mid-twentieth century the family had mostly died away, but the few survivors owned many stocks, bonds, banks, and apartment buildings.

I knew that Evans Kingman's "auntie" operated a white-fenced, green-grassed, thoroughbred horse farm on a thousand-plus acres north of the interstate. I'd never met her, but I'd seen her through car windows as her chauffeur drove her about town in her shiny Cadillac limousine.

I remembered from old office files that Senator Adams had settled her father's estate and that now there were only two left in the family, Miss Crystal and this thin, upset wisp of a man who sat nervously across from me.

Outside it was cold, late winter. Kingman was properly attired for the season in a thousand-dollar wool suit, a soft button-down shirt, and a dark silk tie. His cashmere topcoat was casually draped across the chair next to him.

"You want to hire me to replevin a cat?"

"I don't care how you legally do it, but I must have King Toy back before my aunt returns one week from today. I'm told you're a tough lawyer and not afraid of anyone and that's why I came to you."

I was fee-hungry and so I didn't order him out for buttering me up. Since Senator Adams had died, business had become slack in the office.

I sighed. "Tell me what happened."

He looked down at his thin, aristocratic hands. They were his best feature. "It's simple enough, Robak. I took the damned cat along in his cage because there was no one but horse help to watch him. The maid and butler are both on vacation and the chauffeur drove Miss Crystal to Clearwater for the bridge tournaments there. I drank too much at some area lounges. King Toy accompanied me and was properly simpered over by my drinking companions. I then gambled at Anthony's farm out in the county later the same night. I lost a lot of money gambling." He looked down at the floor. "I sold King Toy and his gold chain collar to Bob Anthony, the gambling-house owner, to pay my debts in cash and be out his door. I believed at the time I had to sell the cat and collar to leave safely. I was sort of threatened, if you know what I mean. No one pulled a gun or uttered a word, but I was in danger." He shook his head. "Maybe it's just that Bob likes cats. When I sobered up next morning, I called Bob to buy the cat back. I offered him twice the money I'd lost, but he declined. If you deal with him I'd pay far more than my offer. I told him it was my aunt's cat and that I couldn't legally sell it. He said that was a shame, but it wasn't what I'd told him the night before. He said he'd always wanted a cat like King Toy and intended to keep him, but that maybe he could make a deal with my aunt. I'm supposed to have her call upon return." He looked up at me hopefully. "So I came to you."

"Is the cat legally yours or your aunt's?"

"Legally it's mine. I live with my aunt and she bought King Toy for me three years ago because she said I needed something to interest me other than making bets on horses. We got King at a farm two counties north of here where a man Auntie knows raises big Maine Coon cats. He has lots of them." He smiled. "He told us there were so many of them that a few now run wild on his place. Then Auntie cared for King, fed him, loved him, and entered him in cat shows that accept his breed. I like the King, she loves him."

"This is a show cat?"

"Of sorts. A champion. Auntie Crystal loves that cat more than she loves me. She refused to have him neutered. It would break her heart if she came back and found him gone." He tried to look forlorn. "She almost might boot me out of the house and rewrite her will. I have my own money, but she has much more."

"What deal would Anthony want to make with your aunt for the cat?"

"I don't know. He's interested in her horses. Something to do with them."

"Does your aunt race her horses?"

He nodded. "Oh, yes. She had a horse in the Kentucky Derby five years back."

I nodded also. "In my opinion Bob Anthony's untrustworthy."

"Yes," he said.

I knew Bob Anthony. He was a large, tough, and clever man in his early forties who had his crooked fingers in many an area political pie. I thought he'd be in politics himself except for the fact that he'd gone to prison for scams twice when he was younger. Now he was careful, but I was sure he was also not into anything honest. It wasn't his nature.

Once, very early in my legal career, I'd appeared against him in a zoning matter. I'd done my homework, talked to my witnesses, packed the hearing with people against the proposed change, and put on a convincing case against allowing him to rezone county acreage from agricultural to industrial for some shadowy, still unknown purpose.

I'd then lost when I should have won. My clients had given up in disgust even though I'd offered to take a court appeal for costs. One of my clients later told me confidentially that he'd received some threatening phone calls about the matter.

I decided that Anthony had either paid or traded something for favorable votes. Then, to make sure, he'd had someone make phone calls to disgruntled losers.

Now, when he saw me on the streets of Bington, he smiled superiorly, having whupped me pretty good.

"Does Anthony bet horses?"

"I know he books bets, but only big ones. He lives by cutting a long-running private poker game in his house, I guess. Ten-dollar ante and half-the-pot limit. A handsome lady bartender serves single malt scotch, Beefeater's, Maker's Mark, and Russian vodka and pats around on the players. It's all very posh and pretty, but I think it's possible they cheat in the game. Anthony doesn't play, but perhaps people play for him." He looked down again. "I was foolish to go there. I'm not usually foolish. I won't be again." His eyes narrowed and I decided that not all of the Kingman blood had been leached out of him.

"Tell me about this cat," I said.

"King Toy is a Maine Coon cat. He's long-haired, tabby in color, with stripes and bars, somewhat like a raccoon. His eyes are gold. He weighs more than twenty-five pounds. Maine Coons are the largest of the domestic cats." He fumbled in his pocket and brought out a photograph. He handed it to me. In the color picture a big long-nosed, long-tailed cat stood alertly in front of a fireplace, his oval, gold eyes watching something in the distance. He looked kingly, a lot like Miss Crystal when she was in the back seat of her Caddie limo waving from its windows to the populace.

"Is King Toy a friendly cat?"

"Yes. Very friendly for a Maine Coon and not combative for an unneutered male. He likes people. I imagine he enjoys being around a gambling house because he likes noise and lights and he'll lap up beer by the bottle. Likes it better than milk."

"How much is this cat worth?"

"Not that much. Maine Coons are now officially recognized and most cat shows accept them, but they aren't the most popular of breeds. Five hundred to a thousand dollars at most. The chain around his neck would be worth about a thousand. Auntie shows him now and then, but mostly she dotes on him, talks to him, and says he makes her stock market decisions."

"Why didn't she take the cat with her to Florida?"

"The King was left to watch me," he said seriously.

"Auntie believes that cats own people and not the other way around."

"Let's say I can buy or get the cat back—would your aunt worry that I might have to tell white lies to do it?"

"Not Auntie." He shook his head firmly. "She marks the decks when she plays bridge with her lady friends at our place."

I thought about Anthony and his superior smile once more. He was a clever, crooked man who had a high opinion of his own abilities and who figured he couldn't lose. I'd heard of his poker game through local gossip. Several people had sworn to me that the game was strictly straight.

"Let me see what I can do." I named a comfortable retainer fee, which he paid without protest.

An easy way to be a winner is to see if the other side will give up before battle.

After Kingman departed I called Bob Anthony.

The pleasant-voiced female who answered the phone said he was unavailable. I left my name and said I was calling for Crystal Kingman before I prepared a lawsuit for her. I told the answerer, who now seemed flustered, that I'd wait an hour for a call back.

Anthony called back within the hour. "Robak, old chum. You called and mildly excited my secretary. Something about some lawsuit?"

"Yes. I've been hired by the Kingmans to replevin a cat you obtained from Miss Crystal's nephew. I hoped we might work things out before there's any publicity in the papers. Twice what you paid. Or I'll listen to a higher figure."

"I rather like publicity. I also like cross-suits. Good for the blood. A little birdie named Evans Kingman told me during the sale transaction that cat and collar were his property. I have witnesses and a paper he signed."

"I'll bet you do. That young man was drunk, Anthony. I think I could make a jury believe that. So how much?"

"The cat's not for sale, Robak. I believe I can present more than half a dozen witnesses who will swear Evans wasn't drunk," he answered. "He's a bad loser and a poor card player. I intend to keep my big cat."

"Mr. Kingman thinks your game is crooked."

Anthony laughed. "The game is strictly straight. Ask around."

"Gambling's illegal. I believe you know the meaning of the word illegal and I don't believe anything you do would ever be completely straight."

"Touché, Robak. The sale took place after the gambling was over. Besides, I was not in the game. I never play. I've no intention of ever seeing the inside of a jail again. Gambling, even honest gambling, is for fools and losers like you and Kingman, Robak. I merely make my place available to friends who do like games of chance. They enjoy the quiet and they like the privacy that can be obtained behind my electrified fence." He sounded almost pious.

"Perhaps the sheriff might be interested."

He laughed. "Dutchie's *my* sheriff, Robak, not yours. He knows of my game. You're most welcome to see what you can do there. I've become quite fond of this Kingman cat. I might make a deal with Miss Crystal for him if she would grant me visitation rights." He laughed, enjoying himself. "Tell her to personally call and I'll spell out my terms. I don't want to listen to your silliness again unless I decide there's good reason to do so."

He hung up abruptly.

I went to the lawbooks. I tried the statutes and cases on replevin first. Replevin, simply, is a court action to regain possession of personal property unlawfully retained. I had immediate problems with the remedy. First, I didn't think the property was being illegally retained. Second, even if I got a court order, such order allowed the person holding the personal property to put up a bond and continue possession until a later hearing. I figured Anthony would put up the bond.

I looked at some criminal laws. They seemed more productive. Gambling was illegal and had Evans Kingman lost his cat to Anthony in a poker game then we eventually might prevail. He hadn't, but there were some cases about "nuisance" gambling houses which interested me.

I left my office and walked through sunny cold to the county recorder's office. I found where the Anthony farm was in Jefferson Township by digging in huge, smelly deed books. I had a copy of the description made and took it along to the sheriff's office where Warren "Dutchie" Oldenberg, a jovial, party-line fellow, was now in charge. He was a middle-aged fence-sitter and do-nothinger. If my memory was correct I believed he'd signed Anthony's petition to change the zoning on his land. I belonged to one party and Dutchie belonged to the other. Nevertheless I planned a bold attack.

The sheriff's eyes flickered when he saw me and I wondered if I was expected.

"My good friend, Robak," he said. "What could you want from poor me?"

"I wish to officially inform you of illegal activities in our fair county," I said. I lowered my voice. "Gambling. High-stakes poker."

He smiled placidly. "I'm not a crusader against such things. Poker, like Reds baseball, is good for us old men. I prefer knowing where games are rather than having to suspect they exist. The only big-stakes game I know of would be in the home of Robert Anthony. It's a quiet, honest game, bothers no one, and I've had no complaints and many compliments. Could that be the game you speak of?"

"It is. Would you like a copy of the laws Mr. Anthony, a twice-convicted felon, is breaking?"

He smiled some more. He waved at a grinning, listening deputy. "Naah, Robak. I get my advice on criminal matters from the prosecutor, your pal Herman Leaks. And Bob— hmmm, Mr. Anthony—has paid his felony dues to our prison system long ago. Go see Herman."

Herman and I detested each other and so I shook my head. "I have a someone who played and lost in Bob's poker game and would give a deposition."

He shrugged. "If this sore loser desires to do so he might try to get Herman to accept the complaint. Herman might or might not, but either way is okay with me. If there is a complaint filed this office might then serve such papers. We do that sort of thing by mail."

"Mail?" I asked scornfully. "My client had a show cat stolen from him in the poker game on these premises." I handed him my copy of the land description. "I am informed this cat is now claimed by Bob Anthony. The cat can likely be found in and upon the land described in his deed copy."

"Heavens," Dutchie said, grinning widely now. "I've already heard something about that from Mr. Anthony. He gave me the names of some area citizens of high repute who would dispute your client's allegations."

"I see. Dutchie, I don't believe you intend to be on my side in this."

He nodded. "True," he said. "That's true, Robak. Nor would the prosecutor. He don't much like you. He likes Bob Anthony. Anthony donates big to him at election time." Remembering that other election days would surely come, he then added: "I do like you, of course. Come back when I can be of more help."

"I can't believe the game's honest, Dutchie."

"It is. I've checked. And Bob only cuts a pittance."

I nodded and left, puzzled. To make certain I was a loser I thereafter visited the office of Herman Leaks and then the office of the county judge. No one had any use for me or any hope to offer in either place. I thought about the newspapers but remembered just in time that they strongly backed the other party.

Late in the afternoon I encountered Bob Anthony on the street as I returned to my office. I thought he had waited nearby, having been told of the furor I'd attempted to cause.

He smiled with his customary superiority. "How you doin', Robak?"

I kept walking on past him. For a moment I thought he was going to take a punch at me, but he was, as always, a cautious man and let me pass peaceably. I was as large as he was and I was also ready.

To my back he asked roguishly: "Cat got your tongue?"

In the early evening, dressed for the cold weather, I drove out to Bob Anthony's place. I hid my old Plymouth on dry ground off a side trail that looked as if its last traffic had been Daniel Boone and a bear. I walked to the top of a hill and surveyed Anthony's farm. It was a handsome place. The description I'd seen described it as 140 acres. About four or five acres were fenced in high, strong wire. I could see warning signs on the wire. The rest of the farm was circled by a wooden white fence, fresh-painted and prosperous-appearing. Business seemed good. I wondered how Anthony could make enough cutting a poker game sparsely to keep all of this going.

On the large acreage I saw that there was a windsock on a pole and a leveled landing strip with many wheel tracks. Maybe some poker players flew in.

The inner electric fence was perhaps eight foot high. It surrounded a fine, patrician Georgian house and its flock of outbuildings. There was a four-car garage with a lot of as-phalt for parking beside it. There was a large brick barn. From my vantage point I could look inside the barn and see part of an inside barn wall. There was a cage against the wall. It was a big cage, new, well-made, large enough to hold a twenty-five-pound cat. It was empty.

I was cold and uncomfortable, but I remained in conceal-ment. The wind came up and the sun went down. It got colder. I shivered and kept solitary watch.

After dark, cars began to arrive one by one. I observed the routine. At the gate of the electric fence there was a phone. A call would be made, the gate would open, and the arrivee would drive his car through the gate. The gate would then swing closed.

About seven, when I'd decided to leave, a large man came out a rear door of the house. He led an animal on a leash. A cat. The cat was large, long-haired, and wore a gold chain.

He escorted the animal to the barn cage. He gave it some friendly pats, and then coaxed it on into the cage.

By better light near the parking lot I saw the man was Bob Anthony. He walked to his front door and looked around. I ducked down low. Ex-cons sometimes have the gift of knowing when they're being watched.

I waited a while longer. Cars continued to arrive. At pre-cisely seven-thirty big lights on poles turned on outside the house, outlining all brightly in their glare.

I drove home. The Plymouth heater never warmed up and I was cold. I made coffee and turned on my television set. I watched the Hoosiers beat Ohio State. In between fre-quent field goals I thought about possibilities.

I had long before made some decisions. When I could

win against cheaters with the law, then I used the law. When I could not I would use other methods.

It was almost ten when I called Evans Kingman and found him home.

"I have a couple of questions for you, Mr. Kingman. First, on your farm do you have other cages like the one you carried with King Toy inside it?"

"No. But I suppose I could get one where we bought King."

"All right. Second question then: Did you tell me that this breeder has many Maine Coon cats and that some of them have escaped and are living wild on the farm?"

"Yes. It's called *feral* and we were told that some of the cats have escaped and gone wild."

"When could we go see this cat farm?"

"You name it," he said. "I remind you that my aunt returns in six days. I have consulted some legal friends of mine in Louisville and they doubt you will be able to do me any good in that period of time. In fact they think you'll never be able to do me any good. Will you?" He sounded as if he'd had a drink or three.

"Would you still pay some money to get your cat back?"

"Whatever it takes."

"I have spent the day trying reason with Mr. Anthony and others." I thought of something. "Do *you* have any connections with the local newspaper?"

"No. We don't subscribe or read any area papers. We do get the New York *Times* and the Wall Street *Journal* in the mail. Auntie and the publisher of the Bington paper are sworn deadly enemies."

"I see. We will visit King Toy's birth farm tomorrow. You will pick me up at eight A.M. where State Road Seven meets the Interstate."

"Why do I pick you up there?"

"I don't want to be seen leaving town with you."

"Whatever," he said. I could sense he'd given up and was now resigned to his auntie's return to a horse farm *sans* King Toy.

"I will want you to arrive at the pick-up place promptly and without hangover," I ordered.

"*Really*, Robak. I'm not a problem drunk."

"I hope not. We may jointly have other work soon. You will have to be alert and ready to help from now on."

"Will that work result in getting King Toy?"

"It could."

His voice became stronger. "So be it. I will have a dry night."

"One more thing. You played in the poker game. Anger aside, did you see any sign of cheating?"

"The people I played with seemed above reproach."

"Strange," I said.

Later.

A method I'd thought of to get inside the Anthony enclave was dangerously simple. I waited until it was full dark and then I lay in a ditch across the road from the entrance. The weather was still cold and there was a fine mist of rain mixed with tiny pellets of ice that fell on me. I carried both a cage and a cat from the cat breeder. A cat slept restlessly inside the cage, tranquilized. The cage looked like the one I'd observed from afar, but I intended to check up close if I made it to the barn.

Evans Kingman nervously waited for my signal from his place of concealment. My old car was parked in a wooded copse not far from where I lay. Around me the world smelled of winter.

A bright, shiny Lincoln was the first visitor. A middle-aged area MD I knew got out of the car, used the phone, and waited for the gate to open. I knew the doctor to be a smart man and a first-class poker player. Smart enough not to play in a rigged game.

Crouched very low, I followed behind his car through the open gate. If he looked in his rearview mirror he might see me. I saw nothing to indicate that he had. I found concealment behind a tree near the gate and then in the brick barn. I crouched in a horse stall filled with burlap bags of what looked to be feed. The barn was quiet around me. Other stalls also had the feed bags stacked inside them, but there were no animals in the barn. I remembered I'd also seen no animals in the fields. I smelled peculiar smells that nagged at my memory without triggering it.

I waited. In a while I heard footsteps approaching.

I watched from between stall rails.

Bob Anthony came with the cat. I saw gold collar and gold eyes shine in reflected light.

Anthony gave the cat a fond pat. "You and I are pals, big cat. Sometime soon I'm going to make some easy racing money through you."

I smiled in the darkness.

I knew that if I was caught here there could be bad problems, but I could swear I'd come to check on the welfare of my client's cat. Thin, but possible.

Anthony put the cat inside the cage. It was a job because the cat didn't want to enter the cage. I sympathized with King Toy. The night was cold and the house had been warm and friendly. Now that had ended.

Beside me, in his cage, the cat I carried moved restlessly. I held my breath. Movement inside the cage ceased.

Anthony busied himself with removing the leash from King Toy's gold collar.

Outside another visitor car entered the gate. I shrank back into my stall as the car lights shone through the open barn door. It was 7:25. Moving-on time.

Anthony left. I waited long enough for him to make the door. I opened one of the feed bags beside me and put a handful of its contents in my pocket. I then scurried to the cat cage. The cat inside heard me and watched from his mesh door. I unlocked the door and reached in. The big cat inside batted playfully at my hand with a massive paw. I fumbled with the collar and removed it. I closed King Toy's door and secured it. The King made a mournful sound, perhaps wanting out.

The cat I'd carried was now moving more than a little as the tranquilizer wore off. I opened the door to his cage and fastened the collar around a neck that already subtly resisted it. I put the cage where King Toy's was and took the Kingman cat and cage with me to the barn door.

I saw a car approaching on the road. I made for the dark spot provided by the tree near the gate. I saw the man in the car use the gate phone and recognized him. He was the president of Bington's largest bank. I had played poker with him before and he was only slightly smarter at the game than a double bag of rocks. I resolved to make a withdrawal of my funds at his bank.

The gate opened and Mr. President drove his Buick inside and toward the asphalt parking area.

As the gate began to close and the car lights faded I ran for the opening. I barely made it. Once outside I signaled and in moments an excited Evans Kingman stopped my old Plymouth. I climbed in after putting King Toy and cage in the back seat.

"Hey King," Evans called. "We're going home for a beer."

The cat made a happy, chirping noise.

We drove. A hundred yards behind us Anthony's yard blossomed with bright lights at exactly 7:30.

"What about the collar?" Evans asked.

I smiled. "I'm not going back for it, but we may yet get it back. Wait and see."

Bob Anthony deigned to speak to me on the phone the following day.

The lady who answered recognized my voice and was cold to me but did finally agree to tell Anthony I was calling. I thought she was the handsome lady bartender I'd heard Evans describe.

Anthony sounded exasperated when he picked up the phone. "Robak, I told you not to call again."

"I only called to see if there was a way we could make a deal," I answered plaintively. "I'll admit that I checked and the cat did belong to Evans Kingman and not his aunt. He wants the cat back."

"How bad does he want it?"

"Enough to pay half again what he offered before. That's a final offer and I have authority to make it, but no authority beyond."

He was silent for a long time. "Okay. You come get the damned cat. You come alone."

"No. I'll bring one old man with me. He'll be along only to make sure I come and go without problems. I'll bring cash."

"Deal," he said.

"Thank you for changing your mind," I said humbly.

"Only because you asked real nice this time," he said.

I noted, when I picked up the feral tabby cat, that Bob Anthony had his right hand heavily bandaged. I asked no questions about the injury. Catching a cat that looked like King Toy had taken the services of three hunters and most of a day.

I paid Anthony cash and got the poker sale papers returned.

The anonymous man I'd asked to accompany me had gray hair and wore dirty clothes. He had a beard that was going from gray to white. I watched him sniff the cold air and spit tobacco juice. He examined Anthony without real interest and Anthony, after a single appraising look, ignored him.

Inside his cage the cat raged. He'd managed to rip the gold collar away and it lay in a corner.

"Crazy cat," Anthony mused. "Real crazy. All of a sudden."

"Sure," I said. "He'll maybe do better at home. Did you try beer on him?"

"Too early for beer," he said.

"Never too early for beer," my companion said, smiling.

Anthony frowned. "You representing rummies these days, Robak?"

I gave Anthony my best non-superior smile, not wanting problems. We gingerly shook hands, each of us checking to see if we got all our fingers back.

The following day the state police, without consulting Dutchie Oldenberg, using the description I'd gotten from the Mojeff county recorder, raided Bob Anthony's. They'd used a state attorney, bypassing Herman Leaks, and got their warrant from the circuit rather than the county court. They came in force during the daytime. The state troopers cut off the electric power and crashed Anthony's gate. Waiting in the back seat of a state police car was my anonymous-looking friend who'd visited Anthony's barn with me. He was undercover state police and it was said

158

fondly of him that he could both smell marijuana and fool a full-time professional drug dealer.

He'd made use of his smelling gift when he'd gone with me to pick up the feral cat.

"Damned barn is loaded with Mary Jane," he'd said on our way back. "How'd you know it?"

"Hunch," I said. "And remember you listened on the phone when I was invited to come with a companion."

"Sure."

It's good to have friends even when those friends don't include local prosecutors and sheriffs.

State police raiders estimated the street value of the bags recovered out of the Anthony barn at more than half a million dollars. A plane had flown over low during the raid, but hadn't landed.

The state boys confiscated everything in sight—house, outbuildings, furniture, cash, cards, and cars. The only thing they didn't pick up was the lady bartender, found asleep in Anthony's upstairs bedroom, but they did get her fine booze bottles. They put a protesting Bob Anthony in jail and a stern circuit judge set a high bond on him. By next day no one had met it and I heard he was screaming about a probable cause hearing and wanting a motion to suppress. His rights under the Constitution, Anthony complained, had been cruelly violated.

Bob sent someone to see me, asking me to visit him in jail, but I declined and told his messenger he should approach another lawyer since it was possible I could be a witness for or against him; I'd been on the property the day before the raid. I told the messenger to remind Bob that I'd never believed him to be an honest man even if he maybe did run an honest poker game.

Outside, on the street, the King Toy story still seemed secret and I had warned Evans Kingman against telling all or any part of it. Maybe the cat story would always stay secret, maybe not.

I didn't want to be close if and when Anthony knew all.

I thought he'd throw a cat fit.

Killed in Midstream

·

William L. DeAndrea

"**W**here the hell are we?" she asked. The air conditioner was on full blast in the rented Chrysler, but the person on the sunny side of the car still caught a laser blast of heat in the lap or shoulder or the side of the head. It had been my turn all morning; now it was Mona Tarren's.

"I'm not sure," I said. "Where's the river?"

She showed me a look of total disgust. "You mean you're *lost*?"

"No, I am not lost. I am on Highway Six-oh-nine, heading south." As if to oblige me, a rusty white-shield-on-black sign popped up on the side of the road. "I thought you wanted to know what state we were in."

"I do."

"Okay. I was daydreaming and lost track of the river. We've been back and forth across it how many times today?"

"I forget. But it's off on your side of the car. Behind those trees somewhere."

"Then we're in Louisiana," I told her.

"Thanks," she said. She almost seemed to mean it, which would be the first civil word anybody'd gotten out of her since she'd broken a nail opening the car door this morning.

Not that she'd been sweetness and light before this, mind you. There'd been the nervous pulling of the blonde-streaked hair, the tightening of the square jaw, the narrowing in the blue eyes, and the snap in the voice since we'd left New York.

I knew what her problem was; she was desperate to protect her job. Mona had left a secure but low-profile job in network news to become chief field producer for "Justice Quest," our version of the TV wanted-poster genre that's popped up over the last few years. The networks love them. They're popular with the public, incredibly cheap to produce (compared to a drama or comedy show), and they sometimes actually do some good. Furthermore, although they deal with true events in a (more or less) nonfiction way, they're produced by the entertainment divisions of the networks, rather than by news, thereby freeing them from even the pretense of considerations of accuracy and ethics and exploitation and other things that get in the way of good viewing.

Unfortunately, "Justice Quest" had come late to a crowded field, and the glut was beginning to set in. It was too much like the others. Re-enact a crime, interview surviving victims, if any, discuss possible suspects, offer a reward and an 800 number to call in tips.

The trouble was, the more glamorous the case, the richer and better connected the people involved are, the less likely they are to want to trot out their misfortunes for our amusement. There may be, in these violent times, a lot of murders out there, but the pool of *interesting* middle-class on up murders (in television, poverty is uninteresting *ipso facto*) is too small to go around.

So "Justice Quest," whose ratings were way below what they had to be to make even a cheap show viable, faced an ultimatum. Get some high-profile society murders to feature, complete with interviews, or say goodbye.

And now this was it. Somewhere on an island in the middle of a minor tributary of the Mississippi River lived a man who'd been at the center of one of the most gruesome murder cases in history. Him and his cat, who'd also figured in the case. Mona Tarren needed him, bad, or she was out of a job altogether. I was supposed to get him for her.

My name is Matt Cobb. The sign on the door says Vice-President, Special Projects, but that sounds a lot more impressive than it is. *Special Projects* was the euphemism some forgotten genius came up with to describe what we do, which is namely everything too ticklish for Security, and everything too nasty for Public Relations.

This, however, was semi-personal. I'd been begged to do it by Jack Hansen, an old friend who had made the jump from local crime reporter to anchor of a network prime time show and didn't want to go back. "You can do it, Matt," Jack had told me. "You charmed this guy once, after all."

"Yeah," I said. "But I was a lot cuter then."

The name of the man on the island was Earl Rushton. Yes, *the* Earl Rushton. No, you can't just walk through a particularly heavy door just off Fifth Avenue in New York and see him whenever you feel like it. You never could do that, anyway. At Earl Rushton, as at Harry Winston and the other very tip-top jewelry establishments, one and one's bank account need to be accepted for an appointment before one gets to see the rocks. However, while Earl Rushton Limited is still in business at the same address, one will find it was sold shortly after the holocaust to a Belgian conglomerate.

"The holocaust" is what the tabloids, with typical class, called it. "THE GOLDEN HOLOCAUST," read the headline in question, probably because of the poison gas involved. If you asked me, it was still going a little far.

Not to say that the carnage wasn't plenty bad enough. Twenty-seven dead, four paralyzed, tens of millions of dollars worth of diamonds taken. The press finally settled on thirty-five million as the figure, although that was probably high.

And I knew Earl Rushton. At least, I'd met him and had a meal with him.

Not as a customer. I wear a Timex watch, and that's as far as any discussion of jewelry you ever have with me is likely to go. But Earl Rushton is a prominent alumnus of Whitten College, in upstate Sewanka, New York, which is also my alma mater.

It got to be my alma mater because I got the scholarship—the one athletic scholarship that little bastion of academic rectitude hands out each year. Part of the process was a meeting with a member of the scholarship committee. In my case, that was Earl Rushton. He took me to the Four Seasons for lunch. He probably wanted to see if the po' boy would be flustered by the place. The only thing that threw me was the fact that there were no prices on my menu. I later learned that there are special menus for the host which do have prices. The way it was, I figured first you ordered, then somebody gave you an estimate.

Anyway, I remembered to use my silverware from the outside in, and I didn't belch at the end of the meal, and Rushton seemed to be satisfied. Conversation was easy, since all he wanted to talk about was basketball, and I could talk basketball in my sleep in those days. If I'd been a little bigger (I'd topped out at six-two) I would have been looking for a more prominent school to play for, education or no education.

Rushton seemed like a nice-enough guy. I never formed any vivid memory of him. I never spoke to him again after that afternoon. He apparently approved of me, but he hadn't kept in touch.

I had tried to tell this to Mona, and to Jack Hansen, but desperate people don't listen well. There's the old proverb about a drowning man grasping at a straw. You're supposed to nod sadly and sympathize with the poor guy. Now I was having a look at things from the point of view of the straw, and that was no fun either.

It was about ten minutes later when we found the turnoff toward the landing. A kid of about seventeen wearing cut-offs, a work shirt, and battered deck shoes over bare feet was waiting for us.

He waved us to a stop. I rolled down the window. Hot, wet air poured into the car like dog breath.

"Are you Mr. Cobb?" he asked.

"That's me," I said.

He grinned. "And you must be Ms. Tarren. Pleased to meet you. I watch your show all the time. I'm Lew Rushton. You're a little early, but Granddad won't mind. He told me to bring you as soon as you came."

"That's nice of him."

"Don't be too sure of that. He said he just wants to get it over with as soon as possible."

Lew directed me to the only building near the landing, a six car garage made of no-nonsense concrete blocks, with tough metal doors and serious locks. I drove in; we got out of the car. It was no cooler in the darkness. When my eyes adjusted, I saw several expensive cars and wires for burglar alarms.

Lew saw me looking. "Rings at the sheriff's office about five miles down the road," he explained. "Grandmom sometimes throws a party for the local gentry, you know, and since the only way out to the island is by boat, the cars have to be well protected."

I found the kid interesting. With his sun-browned skin and tousled blond hair, he could have been Huckleberry Finn, until he opened his mouth. That was pure eastern prep school, en route to Hahvud. Or Whitten College. We had our share of accents at Whitten.

On the other hand, he was much too chatty to go with the accent. My experience with the crowd in question has been that they hand out personal details like hundred-dollar bills, but Lew Rushton seemed to like to talk just to hear himself.

It was the same in the launch heading toward the island, but now he was concentrating on Mona.

"Your show is the most popular thing going at school, Ms. Tarren," Lew said. "I recognized your name from the credits. Granddad just said you and Mr. Cobb were from the network." He looked at me. "I haven't seen your name in the credits."

"I take extra money instead," I told him.

Mona slapped my arm. "Don't listen to him. What do you like best about the show, Lew?"

"The phone number at the end," he said. "We use it to play Baffle. We do it with all the shows, but we like yours the best, because you've had some incredibly heinous crimes lately."

"Baffle?" Mona asked. "How do you play that?"

"Oh, we wait for you to do a story on something really good, like a child dismemberment or something. Then we think of somebody whose guts we hate who sort of fits the description, and we turn him in. We had one guy actually picked up for questioning by the FBI. It was fabulous!"

Mona looked sick. "That's Baffle? How—how often do you do this?"

"Oh, at least once a week. Remember, there's four shows on the air like this now, so there's usually at least one heinous crime we can hang around somebody's neck. Baffle stands for 'Bust a Fucker for Light Entertainment.' "

He sighed as if he couldn't wait to get back to school, and drove the launch with a smile on his face. Looking at Mona's face, I wanted to laugh; looking at Lew's, I wanted to knock his head off.

The boy spoke again before I could do either. "Hey, that was a pretty heinous crime at my Granddad's place ten years ago, wasn't it? Are you going to do that one? I hope so. I was only a kid when it happened, and nobody'll tell me the details. I looked up all the microfilm I could find in the library here, at school, and in town over there, but all I got out of that was that somebody put a gas bomb in the place, my Granddad would have bitten the big one if he hadn't slipped out the back door to chase the cat, they got away with a lot of goods, and that one of the people who got killed was my father's girlfriend."

I noticed that Mona had surreptitiously turned on her pocket tape recorder. I wasn't so sure Lew Rushton hadn't noticed it, too.

"That was no big deal," he said. "I mean, I met her, but I don't really remember her. My father had divorced my mother long before. She married somebody else. Lives in Hong Kong now, I think. I might see her again when the Red Chinese take over in 'ninety-seven and kick her butt out of there. That'll be weird."

He turned to Mona. "You probably know all this already, though, right?"

"I've done some research," she conceded.

"Then you know my dad ate a bullet about three months after Wanda—that was the girl friend—bought it. *That* was a bummer." He grinned. "As your generation used to say."

We were close enough now to the island to make out details. The main house was a rectangular white wedding cake, loaded with curves and columns, sitting in the middle of a spectacularly lush, green lawn. White gravel paths curved gracefully through the green. It occurred to me that an island would be a frustrating place for anybody who likes to walk in straight lines.

Lew said, "Uh-oh."

"What's the matter?" I asked.

"The boat's not there?"

"Of course not," I said. "It's here."

Lew looked at me quizzically, then gave me the benefit of the doubt, deciding I couldn't possibly be that stupid and must be kidding.

"Not this boat," he said. "The oyster boat."

"Oyster boat?" Mona echoed.

"Hey, I think I've given you a scoop, after all. It's not a crime, exactly, but it's something nobody back East knows. Granddad couldn't get the jewelry business out of his blood, no matter how disgusted he got with the whole New York scene after the holocaust thing and my father's suicide. So he's trying to grow pearls."

"Here in the river?" I asked.

"Round the back of the island. Says one of the reasons he bought this place years ago was that he always had it in the back of his mind to give it a try. He's been studying everything about how the Japanese do things for years. Finally got hold of the right kind of oysters just before the trouble back in New York. So he was ready for the big move, you know?"

"Sure," I said, although I hadn't even known there were oysters that could live in fresh water. "Any success?"

"Nah. But the old boy keeps trying. What the hell, he's old and rich, this keeps him in shape."

"Where shall we wait for Mr. Rushton?" Mona asked.

"No need to wait. I'll swing around the island and bring you out to the oyster boat. You'll probably get more time with him that way."

"Oh," Mona said. "But I wanted to get a picture of the cat, too."

"The cat'll be there. Wherever Granddad goes, Phluphy goes. That's P-H-L-U-P-H-Y. Grandmom got the cat and wanted me to name it, so I did. I had no imagination as a kid. Grandmom was horrified I wanted to call such a fancy cat Fluffy, so my dad came up with the spelling to make everybody happy. Funny, the way he turned out to be

Granddad's pet. He never gave a damn for animals until about three weeks before the attack, when he started taking Phluphy to the office."

"And the cat wound up saving his life!" Mona said. She was showing signs of excitement—if she could land this story, she'd get the crime freaks, *and* the cat lovers, who were legion. And the Baffle players, too.

The oyster boat was a low, flat job with a railing around the deck, a control center with a canopy over it, and a tiny outboard motor. Earl Rushton was aboard. He wore a maroon Izod-Lacoste alligator shirt, crisp yellow bermuda shorts, immaculately white deck shoes, and white cotton socks with maroon and yellow stripes at the top. How he managed to keep all that dry and do what he was doing was beyond me.

What he was doing was dredging the river bottom, the way the clam diggers in Long Island Sound do it, with a dustpan-like thing on the end of a long pole. He would pull the thing onto the deck, avoiding the drips of water, dump the oysters into a pink plastic bucket, then lower the dredge back over the side, its handle resting neatly in a little chain-and-clip contraption attached to the railing where he stood.

There was a blob of silver-gray on the deck about four feet behind him and to the right—just out of range of the drips.

He welcomed us on board with embarrassed courtesy.

"Mr. Cobb; Miss Tarren. Is it time for our appointment already?" He raised his wrist, and I saw he'd caught one oyster already—a very expensive Rolex.

"Past it, Granddad, actually," Lew said.

"I'm so sorry. I see so few people these days, I lose track of the time."

I looked him over. My previous meeting with the guy had taken place about the time his grandson was born, but he didn't look any different. The hair was still polished silver, and seemed to stay in place by magic. The face was tan and smooth, and the lines in it, though perhaps deeper, only added character. The wardrobe was different, of course, but he still hung those clothes like a Man of Distinction in those old liquor ads.

167

The only difference was his hands. That day at the Four Seasons, I had been aware of a callous-free handshake and perfect nails. Now they were the hands of a diamond miner rather than a diamond merchant. Marinated in river water and rubbed against oyster shells for ten years or so, they were rough and broken-nailed.

He held up an oyster in one hand and a metal tool in the other. "I apologize for not shaking hands." He showed even white teeth in a grin, then bowed to Mona.

"Do you mind if I go on with this? I can explain it if you like."

Rushton looked affectionately at his grandson. "Did you laugh?"

"Not this time, Granddad," Lew said.

"I'm surprised," the old man said. "A lot of people have tried to culture pearls in this country. Nobody's succeeded, and maybe I won't either. But it passes the time."

He put the metal device near the rim of the oyster and squeezed the handle. Slowly the shell opened. "Had it made to my own specifications," he announced. "One thing I couldn't learn how to do was to open the shell without killing the animal." He took a look inside, gently pushed the shell closed, then pitched it back into the water. "No luck," he said. "I'll keep trying, though. It's my patriotic duty."

I would have bet good money Mona had her tape recorder going now, too.

"How's that, Mr. Rushton?" she asked.

"I spent forty years in the diamond business. That means I spent years dealing with a South African–Dutch monopoly. There's nothing you can do about that. The diamonds are in the ground where God happened to put them.

"But there are oysters that can thrive in all sorts of environments. The best ones to eat live in cold, salt water. Some of the best cultured pearls come from oysters that grow in warmish fresh water, like we have right here. The Japanese—and other Asians—have been at this for hundreds of years, and if you think they're zealous about protecting their car industry, you don't know the half of it. So I've got a lot of catching up to do. Besides, as I said, it passes the time, keeps me out of my wife's way, gives me some exercise, and still leaves me plenty of time for reading."

He lifted up the oyster rake, and dumped the as-yet unchecked oysters back in the river.

The cat went nuts. It sprang to its feet and ran to the rails, making loud angry meows. It looked at Rushton and gave him more of the same. Very indignant, Phluphy was, silver–gray fur bristling for emphasis.

I didn't know if I was glad or sorry I hadn't brought Spot along on this trip. Spot would have given the cat an excuse to bristle. He doesn't like cats.

I don't mind them myself, though I prefer dogs. The important thing to remember about a cat is that this is an animal that will eat four hundred dollars' worth of caviar, if you let it, then knock over your garbage can to get at a pork chop bone. Cats are interested in themselves, period. I respect that, and cats seem to respect me for knowing that about them, and we get along fine.

What I have troubles with are cat lovers, the kind of people who think cats sit on their laps to give them affection rather than to suck up some body heat. The kind who say things like "little oozy poozy," as they rub their face against the cat's fur.

Actually I can't stand people who treat dogs that way either.

I was thankful that Rushton didn't go so far as to say "little oozy poozy," but he got pretty bad. He scooped the Persian up and held it to his cheek, and said, "What's the matter, Pluphkin? Something scary in the water?"

The cat showed impressive fangs as it meowed in his face.

"Okay, kitty, we'll get you right home. I have to talk to these nice people, anyway."

Phluphy didn't want to know. He meowed louder.

"Lew, take us home, won't you? I'll see to Phluphy."

He tucked the cat under his arm like a football, and he subsided long enough to use his rough little tongue to lick the oyster juice off his master's (a term you have to use loosely with cats) hands.

During the quiet interval, he asked me what I heard from old Whitten College. I told him not much lately.

He'd mentioned a murder that had taken place last time I was there. I told him I remembered it, too. He said he heard on the news that I had solved it, and I said that was sort of true, and that was all we had time for before the cat started a ruckus again.

The oyster boat pulled up to the dock. Lew jumped out and tied us up, then offered a hand to Mona, who took it and gave him a charming smile. I didn't blame her for smiling. We'd already been here longer without being thrown out than I'd thought we might be.

The old man, still carrying the unhappy and very noisy cat under his arm, hopped ashore. "Lew will show you to my sitting room," he said. "I have to get some dinner for Phluphy."

I looked at the building. The place still looked like Tara. "Does your grandfather have any help on the place?"

"Only the Jacksons live in—she's the housekeeper and cook, he's the butler and chauffeur, sort of. This is their day off. Heavy cleaning, stuff like that, comes in by the day. Why?"

"Just seems like an awfully big place for a millionaire to clean himself."

"Don't worry about that," Lew grinned.

I mentioned that the caterwauling had died down.

Lew nodded. "Phluphy always gets like that when he expects to be fed. Shall we go in?"

Inside we had to wait for a while. Mona amused herself by lining up camera angles.

"Of course, we'll have to get the cat. Everybody loves cats. And that chandelier. And we'll have the kid for pathos—lost his father as a result of the tragedy. This is going to be great." She swung around, making a frame in front of her with her thumbs and forefingers like an old-time director. "We'll start the piece with Rushton walking through that archway—"

At that moment, Earl Rushton walked through the archway in question. He looked as if he had let the network wardrobe department dress him for Mona's benefit—blazer, spotted shirt, white slacks. He even wore an ascot. The personification of the typical viewer's idea of what a rich person wears around the house.

He had a little dish with him, with something in it that clattered, like jordan almonds.

He asked us to sit down, placed the dish on the coffee table. It didn't contain jordan almonds. Instead it contained some lumpy gray–brown things that shone dully in the sunlight.

"I thought you might be interested in these," he said. "Some of the pearls I've gotten from the river." He smiled and shrugged. "As you can see, we still have a long way to go."

"That is a sort of . . . unusual color," Mona said.

"The color's not important. We can adjust that with the food we put in, and the chemical mix of the water. It's that shape that's the problem. Unfortunately, the oysters don't care. We put an irritant inside, and they cover it with something smooth—nacre, we call it—and as soon as they're comfortable, they stop. There'd be no pearls at all if oysters could just spit."

We laughed politely.

"My wife'll be joining us in a minute, if you don't mind. She's getting us us some tea."

Son of a gun, I thought, he really did feed the cat himself. Of course, why you'd indulge a creature who got so nuts during a boat ride that you had to head back to shore was beyond me, but what the hell.

Soon, Mrs. Rushton joined us, carrying tea things. She also belonged to the formal-around-the-house set. She was wearing a dress of perfect Barbara Billingsley-as-June Cleaver design, complete with pearl necklace. Not lumpy brown ones, either. She was a tall woman, and robust, with a handsome face. If nature hadn't blessed her with two perfect gray streaks in her dark chestnut hair, some friend had blessed her with the name of a genius hairdresser. I could see Mona nodding slightly, lining up camera angles for Sheila Rushton, too.

I was hoping for a chance to remind her we hadn't even broached the subject of the show yet, but it wasn't really necessary. Things went swimmingly. Rushton and I talked for a few seconds about dear old Whitten, then Mona launched her spiel about how "Justice Quest" had helped catch dozens of criminals, but that the worst crime of recent decades still unpunished was the holocaust at Earl Rushton, Ltd. She could make no promises, but there was a *chance* the network could help, and wouldn't he please let us try?

And incidentally hype our ratings and save our jobs, I refrained from adding.

Rushton frowned, bit his lip, and at last said, "Why not? Of course. When do you want to do it?"

Mona's control was good. Her eyes widened with surprise and delight only for a few seconds before New York Career Girl was back in control. Without missing a beat she said, "At your earliest convenience," she said. "I could have a crew out here tomorrow, if you like."

Rushton's grin was tinged with sadness. "I think that's just a *little* too early, Ms. Tarren. How about—oh—one week from today?" He spoke to his wife. "Is that okay with you, dear?" he asked. "Is the whole idea okay with you?"

"I think it's marvelous," Sheila Rushton said. She turned to us. "It eats at you, you know, to have something like this happen. It's been worse for poor Earl than for me."

"What do you mean?" Mona asked, all concern and soft sympathy. She was already in film–interview mode.

It was Rushton who answered her question. "The idea that I was spared, Ms. Tarren. That's what eats at me. The diamonds were insured, and even if they hadn't been, I could have stood the loss and still lived quite comfortably.

"But the human life! Over two dozen human lives, all my employees, longtime customers and friends—"

"Your son's fiancée," I said.

Rushton nodded, seemingly as sad about her as he was all the others. I could see it. Time and death have a way of glossing over people's bad points.

"All of them," he said. "And the killer had every right to expect I would die, as well. He put the canister of gas right where it would be sucked into the air conditioning and spread through the whole establishment."

"But the cat saved your life," Mona said.

Rushton smiled in spite of himself. "That's right. Of course, at the time, I thought I was saving his. There was an outside door from my office to a courtyard between our building and one on Sixth Avenue. On nice days I used to open it from time to time. Air conditioning can get so stale—I like to leaven it with fresh air."

It took a strong effort to keep me from loosening my tie. There was no air conditioning on in here, either. Rushton was easy to please, I thought, if he considered the air of either midtown Manhattan or that of an island in the middle of a swampy river "fresh."

"Anyway, I opened the door, and Phluphy—he was just a kitten then—jumped out. I'd never been responsible for a pet before, and I had that exaggerated fear of all new pet owners. I was so afraid he'd be crushed by a car or attacked by a dog—and then my grandson would never forgive me. So I chased him outside. The cat kept me hopping around that courtyard and back alleys—in a full business suit—for over half an hour.

"Of course, just minutes after I'd left, the gas bomb went off."

Rushton swallowed. "The office door had locked automatically behind me when I left, and the door was impregnable. When I finally caught the cat, I had to find my way through an alley to a side street, then walk around the block to Fifth Avenue to get back into the building.

"That's when I ran into the police and fire department. The thief or thieves had already been in the store, of course. They put on gas masks just before their timer let out the gas, then helped themselves to the jewels. No one ever saw them. The police and emergency vehicles were there simply because a passerby had been sickened by a slight whiff of gas coming from under the front door and had told a traffic cop."

He shook his head. "And that was that. The thieves have been very clever. No identifiable stones have turned up on the world market, no unusual number dumped on the market at one time. I still have connections in the diamond world, and I check with them from time to time. Whoever did this must be living frugally, selling the goods one or two at a time."

"That could be the strangest thing of all." I hadn't meant to say it, it just popped out. Now that I had, manners compelled me to explain myself.

"It just seems a little odd that someone would commit a mass murder like that just to live frugally."

Rushton took a deep breath of unfresh river air and said, "Cobb, we've both come a long way from Whitten, but I'm older and I've seen a lot, and I tell you there is no fathoming what goes on inside the human mind."

He rubbed one eye. "Besides, what seems frugal to me might be extravagant to someone else, no?" He slapped his knees with his hands. "By God, I think this is going to do me good. I've hidden these feelings for so long, get them out in the open and maybe we can deal with them once and for all. Care to stay for dinner?"

"It's very kind of you," Mona said, "but I'd really like to start back right away and begin getting things ready for filming the interviews. In fact, If you'll let me use your phone, I'll call New York and tell them the project is a go."

Sheila Rushton stood up. "I'd better help you in the early stages, my dear. We're quite primitive here. If you want to make a credit-card call from the house, you have to go through the local operator."

Rushton and I made small talk until they came back. It reminded me of that lunch at the Four Seasons. Everything superficial and friendly on the surface, but the man was looking at me in a way that said he was searching for something in me. All he would have found at that point was a vague sense of unease. Something I'd heard or seen this afternoon wasn't hanging together with the rest, and it bothered me.

Soon Mona was back, and we took our leave. Lew reappeared to ferry us back to the rented car.

"I take it he agreed," Lew said.

It wasn't a hard guess. Mona's smile glowed visibly in the twilight.

"I'm surprised," Lew went on. "He never even talks about it."

"Said he wants to get his feelings out in the open," I told him.

Lew was deadpan. "Feelings? Granddad? Seems weird, but maybe that's it. Anyway, I'll have to lay down the law on this case to the guys back at school—no Baffle on this one. On this one it would be nice to get some real results."

All the way back to the motel, Mona didn't once ask me what state we were in. What she mostly said was, "Isn't this *terrific*?"

What I mostly said was, "Uh-huh."

"God, I wish we'd had a film crew with us today. I hope he's that good next week when the film is rolling."

"You never asked him about his son's suicide."

"I don't want him to use it all up! I want that reaction fresh. I also didn't ask him about the possibility of an inside job."

"I thought the whole staff was killed."

"Two people had the day off, one was out sick. The sick one was in the hospital, one of the guys with the day off had an alibi—he went to the track with friends, but the other one got some heavy questioning by the cops before they decided he just didn't fit it. If we use him, we'll probably change his name."

"Not to tell you your job or anything, but check into the proverbial disgruntled ex-employees, while you're at it."

"We will," she assured me. "The cops did at the time, but we'll dig deeper."

We got back to the motel, which was pretty elaborate for where it was, with a separate garage for vehicles and all, plus a restaurant where the food was actually edible.

Mona celebrated with a couple of Gibsons before dinner, and talked about how great it would be, how this was going to turn the show around.

I said I hoped she was right and ate my pork chop.

It was still early when we were done. Mona said she wanted to get some work done, and that was fine with me. I went back to my room, turned the air conditioner on full (by me, no air warmer than sixty degrees can possibly be fresh), jumped into the shower, got out and dried off, watched some college hoops on ESPN, and went to bed. Driving always makes me tired, and we had a long haul to the airport tomorrow.

About midnight, there was a knock on the door.

"Go away," I said cordially, but the knocking went on. I got out of bed, put on a robe, staggered to the door, and opened it to the extent the chain bolt allowed.

Nobody there, but the knocking sound continued. Curious. Then I heard Mona's voice say, "Matt, it's me. Open up, I need you."

I had not exactly expected this would happen, but I flattered myself enough to include it in the possibilities that Mona, with the drinks in her, might decide to declare a little cozy celebration involving the two of us.

She was a very attractive woman, and in earlier days, I would have jumped at the chance and whatever else there was to be jumped at. Now, however, I was officially Going Steady with a young woman who happened to be the network's largest single stockholder. Roxanne was the best thing that had ever happened to me, and I wasn't about to mess that up. The idea was to get it across to Mona without winding up with her hating my guts.

I unbolted the connecting door and opened it a little, about to explain the good news that there were still faithful men in the world, and that I was one of them, when my eyes focused enough to see that she already had company.

A big, sandy-haired guy with a mustache, a butch cut (I could smell the wax), and an incipient beer belly was in the room with her. His right hand was behind his back, under the flap of his seersucker jacket, undoubtedly ready to unholster a gun. His left hand held a black leather case with a silver star pinned to it.

"You Cobb?" he asked.

"Sure am," I said. "What's up?"

"I'm Investigator Paul Albrick. Sheriff's department. I'd like you and Ms. Tarren here to get dressed and come along with me, if you would."

"Are we under arrest?"

"No, nothing like that. I know you Easterners hear 'southern' and 'sheriff' and start thinking about fire hoses and back rooms and lynching parties. But there ain't nothing like that going on. My daddy's the sheriff, and this parish wins awards, he runs things so clean. Look, if you want a lawyer, you can have one; even though y'all aren't suspected of anything, okay?"

He was as earnest as a kid talking to the father of his first date. I tried not to let it fool me. We weren't suspected of anything, but Albrick had done a fine, professional job of approaching us, all the same.

"Nah," I said. "We can save that for later, if necessary. Okay with you, Mona?"

"Sure," she said, though I sincerely think it was a simple desire to stay on the good side of the cops that kept her from *screaming* for a lawyer.

It was curiosity that was driving me. "Before we go anywhere, though, we do want to know what this is all about."

"Some trouble at Rushton's Island," Albrick said. "Somebody rowed or poled out there, socked the grandson, and stole the cat."

"Oh, no," Mona said.

"How's the kid?" I asked.

"Doc's with him. No telling, right now. Anyway, we're doing all the routine, question everybody who's been there, you know, and the sheriff sent me to fetch you. I'll be waiting outside till you get dressed."

I decided that if I was crossing the damned river again tonight, I wasn't going to climb back into a suit to do it. I put on a pair of jeans and a pullover shirt, and suggested Mona go casual, too. Only trouble was, I'd already left my Nikes in the rental car. I asked Albrick if we could stop by the garage and pick them up. He said sure.

Mona had a dress on ("I didn't *bring* any casual clothes"), but she did have on a pair of canvas espadrilles, which was a lot more practical in a boat than high heels. Albrick walked us to the garage so I could get my sneakers. I walked up the ramp toward the rental car, and saw that there was something wrong. I called for Albrick as I ran up to the car. I stopped about ten feet away from the nose of the thing and looked.

Liquid, black-looking in the fluorescent light, had trickled down in snaky tendrils from the windshield. Written on the hood in big ragged letters was the word DON'T. Clinging to the windshield itself like an obscene parody of those suction-cup Garfield toys was the gray Persian, Phluphy. His head had been smashed, and he'd been cut open down the belly. One yellow eye leered at us.

I heard somebody gulp. Might have been me. I turned away. "Well," I said. "That solves half the mystery."

* * *

Albrick didn't laugh, but he didn't smack me in the mouth either, so I figured I came out ahead. Driving down the highway, after the investigator had arranged to have the kitty corpse guarded and to get the lab boys out there, Albrick had a remark of his own.

"It looks," he said, "like someone don't want y'all doing this TV show, don't it?"

Mona came back at him with a very commendable load of the First Amendment, the Communications Act of 1934, and the Accepted Canons of Journalistic Responsibility, but that wasn't the point.

We got the point later, right after we were taken to the island in a sheriff's launch.

Mrs. Rushton met us as soon as we walked in the door. "Thank God you're here!" she said. "Use the phone in the hall. Call New York right away. Call off the filming!"

Mona's media persona finally got the better of her diplomacy. She looked at Mrs. Rushton and said, "Are you insane?"

It made sense from Mona's point of view—the network arrives—more violence—great television—ratings! TV people sometimes forget that real people have feelings. TV people tend to forget that reality exists.

Of course, a response like that was a good bet to *drive* someone like Mrs. Rushton insane, and I was wondering what to do about it when Earl Rushton came down the main stairs and saved the day.

"Lew's conscious, dear. He's asking for you." His wife dropped everything and ran upstairs.

"How is he?" I asked.

"Thank God, the doctor said he's going to be all right. It wasn't so much that he was hit so hard, it was that he hit a rock when he fell." Rushton shuddered in visible relief.

When he stopped, he said, "But Ms. Tarren, while my wife is perhaps a bit hysterical, she's absolutely right. Helping you with that TV show now would be out of the question. I won't take a chance with my grandson's life." He shuddered again.

"Maybe we'd better sit down," I said.

"Please do. I'm going back upstairs to Lew."

"Can we talk just a minute? I can appreciate your concern, but *we* were the ones who were warned."

"I take it as a warning to all of us. It was my grandson who was attacked. Our cat who was butchered. Poor Phluphy. He never hurt anyone."

"How did you know about that?"

"The sheriff told us. His son radioed it in."

"That's right, he did."

Rushton left us and went upstairs. He was soon replaced by the sheriff in uniform, a carbon copy of his son except that he had some gray under the butch wax and more beer under the belt. He led us, politely but thoroughly, through our day, asked if we had witnesses for what happened after we got back to the motel. I told him sure, the waitresses at the restaurant would remember us having been seen at dinner too late to have made another round trip to the island and done the mischief that was supposed to have been done.

The sheriff nodded. "As a matter of fact, she does. Lab boys say there's no cat hairs in your car, neither. So I suppose y'all are off the hook."

Then he took off his hat, said "May I?" and wedged himself a seat on the sofa between Mona and me.

"Look, Cobb," he said. "I been on the phone to New York about you. Why don't you just sit here and think awhile while I do my job, and we'll see if you come up with anything."

"That's not the way it works," I began.

"Look," he said, rising. "The only lever I got on you is that the police launch ain't leaving the island again till I'm ready to go myself, and that ain't for hours yet. I know this ain't no big murder case like on your show, ma'am—watch it every chance I get, by the way—but Rushton pays about half the taxes in this parish, and I'd appreciate any help I could get. Just think it over, all right?"

"Sure," I said.

"Good," the sheriff beamed. "Deputy Packson is at the door if you need something."

"Also to keep us from making a break for it, right?"

The sheriff chuckled and walked off. I sat down to think.

"Tell you what *I* think," Mona said.

"What?"

"I think I should have listened to my mother and become a secretary."

"Baloney," I said. "When this is over you'll realize you loved it. Nobody goes into this business without a huge ego and a love of adventure, no matter how sick."

"Not even you?"

"Especially not me. You think it's not a kick to have a lawman in a place you never heard of ask you for help?"

"All you have to do now is deliver."

"Right. So let me think."

I thought. I thought about the cat. Why smear the cat on *our* windshield? I mean, I have no love for cat killers, but we really didn't give a damn about the creature, except for Mona's probable delight if it turned out to be telegenic. But there was something off, something wrong about the cat that bothered me all day. Something that had happened on the oyster boat . . .

Sure. And then the rest of it started to fall into place. Everything. All the way back to New York.

"Cobb," Mona said. "Are you alive?"

"Huh? Yeah."

"It's been hours, you know, nearly sun-up."

"Complicated thing."

"You spent all this time thinking about the cat?"

"About the cat, and an insect."

"Insect."

"The wicked flea."

"What the hell are you talking about?"

"Sorry, it's a joke. Bible quote—'The wicked flee where no man pursueth.' That's what happened tonight. That's why the cat was killed."

"You've got something?"

"I've got a headache. I've also got a bunch of ideas so crazy they almost have to be true."

"Almost?"

"One of them, at least, can be checked. Deputy Packson! I need to talk to the sheriff."

I talked to the sheriff for a long time. For a while I thought he was going to give me a medal. For a while

I thought he was going to throw me in jail. Finally he said, "I can't go into court with a bunch of noise like that. I can't even mention it to Rushton."

"I can."

Sheriff Albrick was silent for a long time. Finally, he said, "Yeah. You do that, Cobb. I don't want no comebacks on this."

"Unless I'm right."

"Right. Then I adopt you as my second son. But you mess this up, you are an orphan, you got me?"

"Yeah. Well, before I go off to find out if I can call you Daddy, let me run down what's supposed to have happened here on the island tonight. The help had the night off, and weren't around. Mrs. Rushton took a sleeping pill and went to sleep early, about nine o'clock. Lew went for a nighttime cruise on the river about the same time. When he landed, somebody jumped him, hit him, left him there."

"I told you all this."

"Just making sure. About an hour later, Rushton hasn't seen the cat or his grandson for a while, so he calls out the back door. He gets no answer, gets nervous, starts looking around. He finds Lew, who mumbles something about hearing the cat snarling before he passes out again. He runs to the house, calls you and the doctor, and here we are."

"Here we are."

"Okay, hold on tight."

I caught Rushton in his study upstairs. He was sitting in a reclining chair, looking at a gem catalog.

"Never really gave it up, did you?"

He looked up at me. "What? Oh, this? Just keeping up. Same with the pearl business, just keeping up."

"How's Lew?"

"He's going to be fine, according to the doctor. We'll just keep him in bed for a few days."

"That's got to be a relief."

"You can't imagine."

"Bet I can," I said. "Mr. Rushton, what would you say if I told you I snitched one of the pearls you showed us this afternoon?"

"You didn't," he said. I was silent and he went on. "And

even if you did, what difference does it make. They're worthless, anyway."

"You mean if I asked for one now, you'd give it to me?"

"No. Not now. I find your manner offensive. What's gotten into you, Cobb?"

"Something I saw the cat do."

That hit home. Rushton blanched, but said nothing.

"I didn't think about it at the time, you know. It bothered me, but not enough to keep me working at it. It was just that it struck me odd that the cat would act all betrayed, would start demanding a meal in the middle of the river. Cats get used to routine, don't they? That cat was accustomed to being fed when you dredged up a bunch of oysters. You never gave a damn about the oysters. The metal gadget was shiny and brand new, but there was a well-used knife right near you. You usually cut the oysters open, right? Then took out the pearl and fed the oyster to the cat. You didn't do that this afternoon, because you didn't want us looking at the pearls. You didn't even want us looking inside the oysters, did you? Because the seeds, the centers the pearls are built on, weren't covered yet."

He eyed me steadily. "I have no idea what you're talking about."

"You knew I didn't snitch a worthless pearl because you counted them. Why keep track of the number of worthless pearls? And why do you keep worthless pearls in a wall safe?"

"I still have no idea what you're talking about."

"No? Well, try this one for size. The sheriff is going to get a warrant for your pearls, and he's going to X-ray them. And he's going to get an expert to tell him what the shadow pattern of the seed is."

"I see."

"Yeah. Me too."

"How do you know?"

"The cat on the windshield. A warning, sure, but why that? Slashed tires would have been just as effective, and a whole lot less messy. An excuse to call off Mona's film crew? All you had to do was to change your mind. But then I latched on to the one thing I wasn't supposed to notice—that warning also served to *eliminate the cat*.

"See, old fellow alumnus, I think you know more about me than you let on; you could certainly find out. You saw me wondering about the cat, you worried that I might put something together. Or if I didn't, somebody else would. So the cat had to go. But you decided to make use of him. You've gotten more use out of that cat than most people do, I'll give you that.

"But you didn't mean to hit your grandson so hard. Probably you were just going to stun him, then tie him up. You knew your wife would be out of it with the sleeping pill she took. You got the cat, killed it—where? Now that the lab boys know to look, they'll find traces of blood in a tub drain, or on some isolated part of the island. When Lew hit his head on the rock in falling, you could have called off the plan, hidden the cat, and called off the most horrible part of your plan, but you go through with your plans no matter how horrible they are, don't you?"

"You're telling it," he said. His voice was very quiet.

"You drove off to the motel—Lew had told you what our car looked like, no doubt—left your grisly message, and zoomed back here, 'found' your grandson, and spread the alarm. You made up that bit about Lew telling you he'd heard the cat snarling, knowing he'd be excused for not remembering saying it or hearing it.

"Good superficial effects, Mr. Rushton, but they don't stand up. You called my attention to the goddamn cat, and that's when I got it."

"Got what?"

"Well, everything I've told you so far, for starters."

"Well, even if you were telling the truth, what could you get me on, cruelty to animals? My grandson would never press charges."

"You forgot about the pearls, Mr. Rushton. Those X-rays are going to show diamonds in the middle of those worthless pearls. The diamonds supposedly stolen from your establishment ten years ago. You're going down for insurance fraud, at least, even if nobody can prove murder. But more than that, you're going to lose your wife, and your grandson. I'll tell Lew. This is no game of Baffle."

"What?"

"He'll understand. Of course, we wouldn't really even

have to wait for the warrant. Brilliant idea, hiding precious gems *inside* worthless ones. All we need to do is dissolve one of the pearls in vinegar or wine—*oof!*"

Without giving a hint, Rushton shot out both fists, caught me below the ribcage and knocked me over. Instead of trying to get past me, he ran for the bathroom at the end of the study. The door slammed, and I heard a bolt slide home.

I tried the door. It was no ordinary bathroom door. Rushton had been ready for this, maybe for years.

"Get away!" he said.

"Where are you going from here, Rushton?"

I heard phones ringing in the house. A few seconds after they stopped, Deputy Packson appeared with a slightly bewildered expression on his face.

"Mr. Rushton's on the phone, sir. He wants to talk to you, but only on one of the downstairs extensions."

"Okay, he's locked in there. Watch the door. But from a distance. He's tricky."

I went downstairs and took the hall phone, the one Mona had called New York from. I could see Sheriff Albrick backing out of the kitchen with that extension's receiver in his hand. "Yes, Mr. Rushton, he's on the line now. Here he is, go ahead, Cobb."

Albrick was giving me dirty looks, which I ignored.

"Go ahead," I said.

"I got you that scholarship," Rushton said. "That diploma got you your job. I sowed the seeds of my own destruction."

"I was the smallest part of that. You did it all yourself."

"I suppose so. It doesn't matter."

"Why don't you come on out of the john and talk about it?"

"Let's just talk on the telephone for a few minutes."

"Why did you do it? Business was good. You could have just retired. Why did you kill twenty-seven people, your employees and customers?"

"To protect my son. I had to kill that worthless bitch he was planning to marry. She would have destroyed him. Made him a weak fool. I couldn't let that happen. I thought if I just arranged something horrible enough, she'd be lost in the shuffle."

I looked down the hall. Albrick looked like he was having trouble standing up. I felt a little woozy myself.

Rushton was still talking. ". . . too late, of course. She'd already made a weak fool out of him. He *killed* himself over her, can you imagine that? *My son* killing himself over a tramp. If he was that far gone he's better off dead."

"You killed twenty-seven people to break up your son's engagement?"

"Cobb, I'd kill a *million* people to protect what's mine."

I was speechless. Rushton laughed into the silence. "I told you, Cobb, you can never know what's in another person's mind. Now listen. The combination on the wall safe is 22-35-51-33-19. In about twenty minutes, have the sheriff tell one of his men to put a few bullets through the window here, then wait another half hour before anybody tries to go in."

I heard a hissing noise. "Bye bye, Cobb. Tell Lew I did it for him . . ."

There was a thump and a sharp click as both Rushton and the receiver hit the floor.

"Simple," I told Mona on the plane back to New York. "He deliberately cultivated the cat to have an excuse to be out of the building when the gas went off. He'd already stolen the diamonds a few at a time. Didn't even steal them—they were his. Sneaked them out of the store. Then he called the fiancée, told her he wanted to talk to her, maybe he could come to accept her yet, and so forth. Then he beat it out the back with the cat, but not before he was sure his target was on the premises."

"He—he was *evil*, Matt. Pure evil."

"Ought to make for a great show."

"Jesus, how crass can you get?"

I just smiled.

"How did Lew take it?"

"How do you think? Pretty damn bad, but better, I think, than Albrick took to the notion that he was the custodian of thirty-five or so million dollars in diamonds until the insurance company gets there."

"Did you tell Lew what his grandfather said?"

"That he did it all for him? I did not."

"Why not?"

"How'd you like to think twenty-seven innocent people, one guilty bastard, and one cat were slaughtered because somebody loved you?"

"I see what you mean." She chewed her lip for a few moments. "Matt?"

"Yeah?"

"I think we'll leave it out of the show, too."

"Okay by me," I said, and settled back in the seat to try to go to sleep.

Leaving Cornucopia

·

D.C. Brod

The day Tom Lloyd stomped his way into Harley's Tap was one of this town's dreariest. And that's saying something. Cornucopia's in the northwest corner of Minnesota and in mid-January the days are real short. To make matters worse, the sun had spent the last three weeks behind thick, gray clouds. It made me want to take an airplane somewhere—anywhere—just to fly above the clouds and see the blue.

The only good thing you could say about the weather was that it was great for business. Between the short days and half the town being out of work, lots of folks wind up at Harley's trying to drink the dark away.

Lots of times I'm the only woman in the place and I guess it can get pretty rough, but I know how to take care of myself. Harley's always telling me, "Anyone hassles you, Annie, just come see me." I prefer to settle things myself, which I'm pretty good at, seeing as I've been doing it since my mom took off with some salesman when I was fifteen. Of the two taverns in Cornucopia, Harley's has the better clientele. Still, it's a tavern. Whenever one of the customers has too much to drink and gets a little frisky, I just dump a beer in his lap. With a job like this, you've gotta draw the line real fast, and I want to make sure I'm the one drawing it. Especially where Harley's concerned. He's got a knack for remembering what's owed him and forgetting the rest.

Harley's a real piece of work. His name's actually Harvey, but he figured Harvey's Tap just didn't sound like the place a guy would go to knock back a few shots. Then, when folks started calling him Harley, he didn't bother to set them straight. Finally, he'd get mad when somebody called him Harvey. I still do it sometimes, just to get his goat and show him that I know where he came from. He really doesn't look like a Harley. What he looks like is a pumpkin. His skin's real pale and he's got this red-blond hair, teacup-handle ears and a grin that covers half his face. Thing is, about the only time he smiles is when he's leering at some woman. He wears black all the time, which really makes him look like a jack-o'-lantern, lots of leather, and boots—always boots—the kind with silver studs and buckles. Usually he's got a cigarette hanging out of the corner of his mouth. Sometimes it's lit.

You have to know how far you can push Harley. I'm careful about that. Not only does he outweigh me by at least a hundred and fifty pounds, but I've heard stories. Some think his wife, Mary Beth, went too far when she told him she'd been sleeping with Jimmy Holt for the last year and a half and didn't care who knew it. A couple weeks later when Mary Beth and Jimmy disappeared, most figured they'd run off together. That may be, but it's real easy for me to imagine Harley killing the two of them and dumping the bodies way out in the woods. But then I think there's no way, even if he'd wanted to. Harley's got a pretty good track record for thinking big and producing small.

He's always saying that someday he's gonna add on to the place, or he's gonna sell and move to St. Paul where he'll open a bigger place that'll charge cover. Or how he's gonna get me in bed. In a pig's eye, Harley. Maybe I should be scared of him, but I'm not. I've seen the way he bootlicks the mayor and the sheriff or anyone who's in a position to give him either trouble or a break. He's real tight with the deputies who all happen to be regular customers. I've never seen any of them pay for a drink. That's Harley's business, but they don't tip either. In a town hard hit by the recession, Harley knows what a gold mine the bar is and he wants to keep it that way. That's why he put a pool table in the back room, even though the room is so dinky it's hard to make a shot from some angles. And then he has me dress in these short skirts and tight sweaters, figuring I'll attract more customers that way. Harley's like an overprotective pit bull when it comes to this place. Maybe it's a defensive thing with me, being a decent-looking woman pushing twenty-five and all, but the first thing I look for in a person is what's weak about him. Take the incident with the entryway, for example.

For the last five winters I've been telling Harley how he needs to build an entry, but since the cold wasn't keeping anyone away, he wouldn't see it. I'd tell him how bad it got waiting tables without the benefit of whiskey shooters to keep me warm, but he'd just grin and tell me to quit complaining. Finally I told him if he didn't install one, I'd start wearing jeans and sweatshirts. Then, just to show him I meant business, I followed through with a pair of baggy jeans and a sweater down to my knees. The next day he called Fred Carson about building the addition.

Now, some of the cold gets trapped in the entryway, which helps, but what I really like about it is the sound it makes. When someone opens the outside door, there's this *whoosh* as the air collects, and I've got maybe five seconds to guess who's coming in. Some days I like to imagine it's Kevin Costner. Maybe he's way up here looking for some place to film a movie that's supposed to be set in Siberia. He'll take one look at me and tell his assistant to fire Julia Roberts. Those are usually the snowy days when it feels like I'm serving prison time. But mostly I'm more practical, hoping it'll be some nice guy who'll just want to take me someplace warm.

The second he walked in, that's who I thought Tom Lloyd was. It had been a quiet night—maybe ten people— like Mondays usually were and I was behind the bar, drying a beer stein. Harley was in the storeroom and Haywood Henderson, a scrawny old farmer with one glass eye, was the only customer sitting at the bar. A few of the tables were full, but even the folks into heavy drinking were quiet about it. The jukebox was playing "All My Exes Live in Texas" and Haywood was telling me about his wife Edna's gout, when I heard the *whoosh*. One ... two ... Boots stomped off snow ... three ... Please be someone new ... four ... Everyone in the bar turned toward the door ... five. It opened and in walked a man who looked like he'd stepped out of a Marlboro commercial. I swear he was a sight for sore eyes. Right away I knew he wasn't from around here. Not only do I know everyone in Cornucopia plus most of their cousins, but this guy had way too much color to have spent the winter under these clouds. He took off this great-looking black Stetson and, knocking the snow off it, checked out the bar. Then he shrugged out of his jacket and dropped it on an empty stool, set his hat on top of it and sat on the next stool over. He pushed a shock of sandy-colored hair off his forehead. His beard parted and his teeth flashed white in a smile as he asked for a Moosehead. Not only did he have a great smile, but he had really nice eyes—kind eyes.

Haywood swiveled around in his chair so he could check out the newcomer. I popped open his beer and poured it down the side of a glass, figuring this wasn't the sort of man who sucked it up out of a bottle.

After a brief but thorough scrutinizing, Haywood nodded at the man. "Snowin' out?"

He'd been watching me, but now he turned to Haywood. "Sure is. They're saying we're in for about four inches tonight." If his drawl was as fresh as it sounded, he was from the South.

Haywood shook his head like the weather let him down again. "It'll be more." He swallowed the rest of his beer and pushed the empty glass toward me. "You from around here?"

"No. San Antonio. Just came down from Winnipeg. Had some business up there."

Haywood raised his bushy eyebrows. "Helluva drive."

The other man shrugged as he swallowed some beer. "Don't like to fly and the trains don't run on my schedule." He glanced out the window at the snow. "When it started coming down pretty good, I decided Cornucopia was as good a place as any to spend the night." He was watching me when he said that, and as I put Haywood's refill in front of him, I prayed for a blizzard worse than the one we had twelve years ago. We'd been snowbound for nearly a week then.

I gave Haywood a shot of Jack Daniels, hoping to shut him up. "One on the house, Hay. To keep you warm."

He winked his good eye at me. "Why, thank you, Annie, you're a compassionate woman."

"Annie," the newcomer said. "That's a nice, old-fashioned name you don't hear by itself very often."

Smiling, I sort of shrugged it off. Didn't seem right to say thank you when I had nothing to do with naming me.

"I'm Tom. Tom Lloyd."

"Nice to meet you."

I was searching my brain for something unstupid to say when, out of the corner of my eye, I saw Haywood pull some bills out of his pocket. "Hey, Eighty," he said. "How 'bout a game?"

Tom twisted on the bar stool and looked behind him into thin air. "Check out the guy on the floor," I suggested and he dropped his gaze. There was Eight Ball, in all his glory, in the middle of his after-nap cleaning ritual. Just then he was trying to get at his underarms. Even if he weren't so gifted, Eighty would be a special cat. For one thing, there was his appearance. He was big—I'd once weighed him and he was close to twenty pounds—and had unusual markings. Big tortoiseshell spots covered most of his back and tail, one leg, his chest, and exactly one half of his face. That was what really caught the eye. His face always reminded me of a half-full moon—the cat in the moon. But I guess what I liked most about Eighty was the way he'd come in the office where Harley let me take my breaks and curl up on my lap while I read. Sometimes it was the best half hour of my day.

He'd wandered into the bar a year ago. At first Harley wanted him out, which Eighty wasn't at all agreeable to. (He hates the cold as much as I do and doesn't set his paw out the door until spring.) I'd have taken him home in a second, but I rent a room from Mrs. Agnosti, who'd never hear of it. She's got a snotty little poodle that's so hyper it pees every time the floor creaks. I think she figures an in-your-face cat like Eighty would have it living in a puddle.

Most of the bar emptied into the back room behind Haywood and Eighty. Tom gestured in that direction. "What's going on?"

"That's Eight Ball." I smiled. "He plays pool."

Tom arched an eyebrow. I nodded and he turned at the sound of balls cracking. "He any good?"

"For a cat, he's really good."

"This I gotta see." Tom lifted his beer as he got up.

It really was something. It was also the main reason Harley tolerated Eight Ball. Like I said, Harley was ready to throw him out the second he stepped in the bar, but everyone was cooing over him (he knows how to work a crowd) and I managed to convince Harley to let him stay for a while by telling him the cat might be his answer to the mice that had invaded the storeroom. And for a week or so Harley kept close tabs on the rodent population, then figured the cat must be eating the mice, otherwise he'd be starving to death. I never told him I left food for the cat every night in the ladies' room. Then one day when Harley and I were getting ready to open the bar, we heard the crack of balls from the back room. We both looked at each other, wondering the same thing: if we were the only ones here, then who was playing pool? We went back and there was the cat, sitting in the middle of the pool table knocking a ball into a pocket. He'd play with it first, batting it between his paws and jerking his head back like the ball kept surprising him. Then he swatted it in, went over and peered down the hole. Finally, he stuck his front paw down after it, trying to figure where the damn thing went. He spent some time fussing at the hole, making these little frustrated grunts. After coming up with no answers, he went back to the balls. Sometimes he'd sink the ball with one swipe, but mostly it took two or three tries. Once he'd cleared the table of the six balls that had been left from the night before, Harley racked the twelve up again and broke. The cat jumped out of the way as the balls scattered over the table, then went back to batting them into the pockets. Since then we'd learned he was only good for about two games before he got bored. But the crack of the cue ball against the others always brought him into the little room. It didn't take Harley any time at all to figure out how to make money off Eight Ball's talent.

Careful to keep my voice low so as not to disturb Eighty's concentration, I explained to Tom as we watched ball after ball drop in the pockets. "Harley charges everyone a buck just to watch. If you want to bet, there's a couple ways you can do it. Either bet on which pocket he'll put a ball in. Now, that's never as easy as it sounds. Eighty doesn't pay much attention to which pocket is closest. You can also bet on how long it takes him to clear the table. Usually it's under five minutes, but I've seen it take him a lot longer. Depends on his mood. Afterwards, everyone counts their winnings and Harley gets ten percent off the top. On busy nights he can make upwards of a hundred dollars." Tom looked at me sharply. I lowered my voice to a whisper and added, "He claims he uses the money to feed and take care of Eighty."

"Does he?"

"I guess. But how much can a cat eat?"

Harley was always getting offers for Eighty. A couple months ago, some guy offered him a thousand bucks. I saw Harley's little eyes flash for a second. Actually, it was longer than a second. It took him maybe thirty to figure out he could easily make that off Eighty in a good month. I was glad Harley turned down the offer. First, I didn't like the man. He was dressed in real fine clothes and kept flattening his tie against his chest. But also, Eighty's about the only thing around here worth showing up for.

Tom watched for a couple more minutes, then shook his head and went back into the bar. I followed, figuring he was looking for another drink, but when he took the stool again I saw that there was still some left in his bottle. Frowning, he slowly added it to his glass.

"Something wrong?" I approached from behind the bar. "Don't you like cats?"

"I love cats. It just seems ..." He hesitated. "I don't know."

"What?"

"Well, Eighty's like a circus bear, you know? Doing all the work and getting damned little to show for it. Doesn't seem in a cat's nature, you know."

"I guess in a way. But he's not doing anything he doesn't want to do." I paused. "Besides, what would he do with the money anyway? Blow it all on catnip?"

Tom nodded, thoughtful. "I suppose you're right." Then

he smiled at me. "How long have you lived in Cornucopia, Annie?"

I rolled my eyes. "Forever. Longer even."

The game broke up then and folks started filling the tables again. Somewhere along the line we'd picked up a few more customers. That seemed to always happen when Eighty started whacking those balls. The big cat hopped up on the bar and arched his back as I stroked him. Then he rubbed his nose against mine and gave me a little lick.

"Get that cat off the damned bar!" Harley's voice boomed from the back room.

For the rest of the night, while I was pouring beers, Tom stayed at the bar talking to me. He offered to walk me home, and even though it was my turn to lock up, said he'd wait.

The last thing I did before leaving was put food out for Eighty. This was always the hard part. He hated to be left alone, and even though he had a fresh bowl of Tender Vittles waiting for him, he'd meow and fuss, rubbing up against my leg. Then he'd walk back and forth in front of the door as though that might keep me from leaving. One time I stood outside the door and heard these sad little meows coming from inside. It's enough to break your heart. Now when I leave I hum something just so I can't hear him.

Tom walked me back to Mrs. Agnosti's through the snow. At one-thirty, it was still coming down hard. Cornucopia's kind of a pretty town in the dark, when it's snowing and you can see the big flakes in the glow from the street lights. There were at least eight inches on the ground and I hoped by morning there'd be no way out of town. I live just a block off Main Street and it took us about ten minutes to walk the distance. He was telling me about his work as a computer salesman, but I was having trouble concentrating, thinking about something he'd said earlier.

When the conversation lapsed, I said, "What you were saying about Eighty tonight?"

"What? Oh, you mean about him being a performing cat?" He chuckled. "I guess I didn't mean anything by it. Still . . ."

"What?"

"I don't know. He's a proud cat. You can tell by the way he carries himself. Just seems demeaning."

"We've all gotta do things we don't want to do."

Tom settled to think about that for a minute. Then he laughed softly. "I guess he doesn't mind. I mean, he's doing it for you, not Harley."

"What do you mean?"

"It's pretty obvious. No matter what Harley says or thinks, he's your cat."

"Maybe." I liked the way that sounded. "But Harley'd never hear of it."

We'd reached the steps to Mrs. Agnosti's house. I expected Tom to ask if he could stay with me. I guess I was hoping he would. Mrs. Agnosti had rules against cats, but not men. There are at least three that come calling on her all the time, and I'm not sure but I think one night all three of them were in her bedroom.

But when he didn't follow me up the first couple steps I turned and looked down at him.

"Goodnight, Annie," he said.

"Are you leaving tomorrow?"

"Will you be here?"

'Where else?"

"Then I'm not leaving."

If a meteor had nailed me into the ground just then, I'd have died happy.

It stopped snowing during the night, but Tom Lloyd stayed the next day and the day after that too. He took me to dinner at the Farmer's Inn, Cornucopia's best restaurant. I had prime rib with baked potato, piled high with sour cream. Tom had some kind of broiled fish.

That night at Mrs. Agnosti's, I invited him in, and he smiled like a little kid who just got a bike for Christmas. We made love with the lights on. And the whole time, he kept telling me how beautiful I was—every part of me—until I actually felt that way. Afterwards I turned the light out and as we lay crammed together in my single bed, he told me he'd have to be leaving in a couple days. "Called my boss, told him I was snowbound. He's okay. Said to take my time. But I can't push too hard." I was glad he couldn't see my face because I swear the second the words were out of his mouth, my eyes flooded.

Neither of us spoke for a while, then he said in a quiet voice, "You'd like Texas." I tried not to make much of that, but my heart started banging away in my throat and I didn't trust my voice. He gave my shoulder a squeeze and sighed, falling back into the pillow. "I know. This is your home. You can't leave."

I swallowed the lump in my throat, realizing I had this one chance to set him straight. "Um, no. I mean it is, but I don't want it to be. Not always. You know I like the warm. I told you that."

"But to live there?"

My next three words were the hardest I've ever spoken: "You asking me?"

He laughed softly. "Yeah, I guess I am. I can't promise anything, Annie, but I'd sure like to try."

"Me too." I wanted to squeal, but figured that would break the mood.

"Harley's gonna miss you."

"He'll get over it."

Tom started chewing on my ear. I thought of the regulars at Harley's. Of Hay, Ned, Winkie and . . . and Eighty. I let out a little gasp. "What about Eighty?"

"What about him?" He breathed in my ear.

"Well, it doesn't seem right leaving him."

He stopped chewing and I could feel him looking at me. "Who says you have to leave him?"

"Are you kidding? Harley would never let him go."

"Why tell him? Besides, like I said the other night, Eighty's more your cat than Harley's." I could hear the smile in his voice. "What would Eighty want?"

That night, after we made love again, we planned the liberation of Eight Ball and Annie. Since I was locking up the next night, it would be easy. Tom offered to buy a cat carrier, even said he'd go to the next town for it so no one in Cornucopia would think anything was up. Afterwards I made Tom tell me all he could about San Antonio. I could feel the heat rising in me as he talked and I couldn't believe it would be a matter of days before I was there.

* * *

My last night at Harley's Tap was easier than I thought it would be. No one there was a friend in the real sense—I wouldn't tell my deepest secrets to any of them. I got some teasing about Tom, but that didn't bother me. Hell, it was all true. Whenever someone would ask me what was up between the two of us, I'd just smile and keep on humming "Streets of Laredo."

The plan was for me to take Eighty when I left, stop at my place and load my stuff in my old Cutlass, then meet him at a motel midway between Cornucopia and Oberon, the next town south. We'd stay there the night, sell my car as soon as we could and then the three of us would be on our way.

I'd asked Tom why we were stopping so close to town and he said he'd rather drive in the day. This way we could get an early start. "Besides," he'd said, "no one's gonna be looking for you until you don't show up at Harley's." I was a little worried about Harley coming after us, but Tom figured once we crossed over into North Dakota, Harley wouldn't have any connections with the cops and we'd be home free.

Walking out of Harley's Tap for the last time was like shutting the door on my whole life up to that point. No matter what I did, I couldn't go back to Cornucopia. Eighty yowled at the cold. He didn't much care for the cat carrier either, but it was a nice one. Real roomy. It looked like the kind they use for animals on airplanes. "Yeah," Tom had said, "I think it is. But that's all they had. Cost enough. But look, it's like he's got his own cat house."

The motel Tom picked was the Sunset Inn. It reminded me of that *Psycho* motel—a bunch of little cubes attached to each other. But Tom explained we were better off at a place like this than the Holiday Inn because we could park right outside the room and no one would notice if we sneaked a cat in.

When I got there, I let Eighty out of his carrier and put out his litter box and some Tender Vittles. Then I hugged Tom for a long time.

When we finally pulled away from each other, he said, "I'll bet you're hungry."

"Starved."

"Well . . ." He stepped into the bathroom and pulled out a cooler. "Ta-da!"

"Oh, thank you, thank you, thank you." I reached out for the sandwich.

"You can thank me later. Now eat."

It was turkey with cheese and he poured me a glass of Coke from a half-full liter. I stretched out on the bed, munching the sandwich. Eighty was there next to me, patting my leg with his paw. I pulled off a piece of turkey. "I feel like Bonnie. Do you feel like Clyde?"

He laughed. "Not quite. But almost." Then he jumped up and got his jacket. "I almost forgot. The guy at the office said he'd dig up a map for me. You finish eating. I'll be right back."

I balled up the sandwich wrapper and tossed it for Eighty a couple times. He wasn't in the mood, and I guess I wasn't as hungry as I thought I was. I got up and checked out the room. The bathroom was one of those tiny ones where you can barely turn around. The bed was a double. A couple feet separated the foot of the bed from a small dresser with a TV on the end near the door. The whole place smelled musty. I figured I might as well get used to it. For a while, anyway. Texas was a long way off. I pushed the curtain back and peered out into the parking lot. You could only see part of the sign from here and the office door. Next to the office was a phone booth and I did a double take when I noticed someone was in it. Two-thirty A.M. seemed a funny time to be running out to a pay phone. The booth wasn't more than twenty feet way, and I could make out a navy jacket and a cowboy hat. Even though the person's back was to me, who else would be outside our motel room at this hour wearing a blue jacket and a Stetson? I continued to watch and in another minute he was off the phone. When he turned to open the door, I saw it was Tom. What in the hell? I let the curtain drop and leaned against the wall. Eighty was on the bed, paws curled up under his chest, and he watched me with half-closed eyes.

"Why the hell would he use a pay phone when there's a perfectly good one in the room?" Eighty blinked. "I know. Dumb question. He doesn't want me to hear." I began to pace the room, jerked the door open, saw no sign of Tom and closed it again. Maybe he did have business at the office. Eighty narrowed his eyes. I pushed the deadbolt in place and dragged Tom's suitcase out of the closet. When I came right down to it, what did I know about him? Nothing except he had nice eyes and a good line. Since when was I so trusting? Packed in his suitcase were several pairs of jeans, heavy shirts and sweaters, but no suit. That seemed kind of odd seeing as he was supposedly in Winnipeg on business. In the side pocket I found an envelope with the name "Thomas Leonard" typed on it. Inside was a round-trip ticket between Fargo and Los Angeles. It looked like the L.A.-to-Fargo half had been used. Also in the envelope was a rental car agreement for a green Skylark. I reached into the other pocket and felt something like a bracelet and I pulled out handcuffs. Further back in the pocket was a small revolver. What in the hell? I had to think. I closed up the suitcase and jammed it back in the closet. Okay. So big deal, he'd planned to fly back. To Los Angeles? Then I remembered what he'd told Haywood in the bar that first night. "I hate to fly," he'd said. My blood ran cold and my face got hot at the same time. I began to pace the room again, hands against my cheeks. Why lead me on? What was the point? Just then, Eighty brushed up against my legs, arching his back. Oh my God. He'd left Cornucopia with two things he hadn't come with: me and Eight Ball. If he didn't want me, what was left was the answer: Eighty. He was sniffing around his cat carrier. Of course. He didn't buy an airline cat carrier because it was all they had left. He bought one because he needed one! My knees turned to rubber and I sank onto the bed. I had to think, but realized I also had to throw up. I retched into the toilet, but nothing came up. Oh, Jesus. Don't think about Tom or whatever his name was and what he did, just think about what you have to do. How did I get so dumb all of a sudden? Take Eighty and get the hell out of here. Before I could force anything but flashes of light into my brain, I heard a key in the door. I ran over and slipped the deadbolt off.

Tom gave me a funny look when he stepped in. "What's with Fort Knox?"

"It's just motels. They remind me of *Psycho*." I tried to giggle, but it came out a whimper.

Just to have something to do, I sat crosslegged on the bed and ate some more of the sandwich. It was like chewing sawdust. Tom chatted about San Antonio and how far we were going to drive the next day. Then, so he wouldn't notice how I'd forgotten how to talk, I told him I was tired, which I was. When Tom started to get amorous, I told him the sandwich didn't set right and convinced him when I puked it up in the toilet. He got me some Coke, but I waved it off. I didn't want anything from him. Not anymore. I pulled the spread over my shoulders.

"You gonna sleep in your clothes?"

"For a while." Finally, he left me alone. I lay there with Eighty curled up against my stomach and tried to figure out how and when Tom was going to dump me. My thoughts started getting mushy. I tried to stay awake, but every part of my body felt weak and my eyelids were so heavy.

The next thing I knew, I thought the room had exploded. I bolted upright and saw Tom laying across the end of the bed. He was wearing his hat and coat. Eighty was yowling, but I couldn't tell where he was. The room was freezing and I saw the door was open. Standing in the doorway, filling the space, was Harley waving a gun at Tom. He saw he had my attention and pointed it at me. I just sat there, my mouth open, and couldn't move. Once I saw the look in Harley's eyes and that jack-o'-lantern grin of his, I had no doubts about what had happened to Mary Beth and Jimmy.

Tom moaned a little and tried to sit up. Harley put a boot against his chest and pushed him back down. He grinned at me. "Looks like someone was leaving without you, Annie."

Tom was up on his elbows now, wiping the blood off his nose with his jacket sleeve. "Listen, Harley."

"Shut up, Lloyd," Harley said, but he was still staring at me. His eyes were so wild they could've started fires. I wished the bed would swallow me up. "A friend of mine saw you leaving with that carrier. He figured it was kind of strange and followed you here." He chuckled. "And you thought it didn't pay to water the deputies." Then I heard Eighty, yowling from somewhere near Tom. Harley turned to the noise and Tom moved fast. He bounded off the bed and then he was standing there holding Eighty's carrier out in front of him.

"Here, Harley. Take him. A damned cat isn't worth dying over."

Harley looked at Tom, puzzled, then smiled again real slow. "You're a smart man, Lloyd." He reached for the carrier.

I swear I never thought before I moved. If I had, I never would have believed that 115 pounds had much going for it against a 275-pound wall. But I threw myself at Harley and must've caught him off balance because he fell against the dresser and the TV. Then Tom was on him too, and the three of us wound up in a pile in the corner. I untangled myself first, pushing Harley's arm off me. As I crawled backward, I put my knee right down on the gun, and picked it up. I kept my eyes on Tom as he pushed himself off Harley.

"Jesus, Annie." Tom was bent over Harley now with his hand cupping the big man's chin. I crawled across the bed and found Eighty's cage. He looked a little dazed but, on the whole, better off than the rest of us. Tom took Harley's wrist in his hand. "I think he's alive. He just must have hit his head on the TV or something." He got up and closed the door, turned and saw me pointing the gun at him. He managed a look of disbelief. "Annie, what are you doing?"

"Where were you going?"

"I . . . I was just loading up the car."

"At four A.M.?"

"You wanted to get an early start, didn't you?"

I made him move back toward the bathroom. "You've got five seconds to tell me what this is all about, Mr. Tom Leonard. One . . . two . . ." He opened his mouth and closed it again. "three . . . four . . ."

He held up his hands. "All right. Here it is. I was hired by a guy who saw Eighty about a month ago. He wants him for a film he's producing."

I remembered the man in the suit and how Harley turned down his offer. "Why Eighty? I mean he's smart and handsome, but it seems like a lot of trouble."

Tom sighed and I couldn't tell whether he was disgusted

with me or someone else. "Do you have any idea how hard it is to get a cat to play pool?"

"What do you do for this guy? Besides steal cats?"

He hesitated, glanced at the ceiling, then sighed. "I train animals for, uh, movies, TV, things like that."

"Oh, I see. So you know first-hand about circus bears, don't you?"

He didn't answer.

"The man you work for. That's who you were on the phone with outside. Isn't it?"

"Annie . . ." he faltered, then shrugged and said, "I was paid to come get him."

"Steal him, you mean."

"Aw, that's not it. Really. This guy made a nice offer to Harley. He turned him down. Once Harley think's he got something someone else wants, you know he wouldn't settle. Not for anything reasonable."

"Oh, I get it. If it's not for sale, it's okay to steal it."

"That's not what I mean and you know it." He hooked his thumbs in his pockets. "Besides, who are you to talk? You're the one who took him."

"Yeah, but not for your reasons."

I realized the gun was shaking and brought my other hand up to steady it. "The gun and the cuffs. You wanted to make damned sure you were rid of me. Didn't you?"

He held his hands out toward me, palms up, like he was offering me something. "I wasn't going to use the gun."

"What were you gonna do if I woke up?"

"That's what the cuffs were for." He said that like it excused him for everything, but then when I didn't back down he added, "I wouldn't hurt you. Why do you think we were staying here, for God's sake? I didn't want to leave you stranded in the middle of nowhere."

I swallowed hard. "This is all really touching."

Tom took a deep breath and released it. "Look, Annie, I'm sorry. You think this is easy for me?" He shook his head in regret. "You and me? I just didn't realize how much I'd started to care."

That did it. Sometimes it takes me a while to hit my limit, but I know when I'm there.

I left Harley leaning against the wall, out cold, and Tom

handcuffed to the toilet, hollering threats, which rolled off me like rain. As I threw my stuff together, I was feeling pretty indestructible—like if anyone tried to stop me he'd get zapped faster than he could say, "Oh, shit." But then, just in case I was wrong about that, I yanked a couple important-looking wires out of their cars' engines.

It's been daylight for an hour now. We stopped outside Fargo, North Dakota, for gas and a map, and I bought some sandwiches, pop and Tender Vittles. The old Cutlass is humming along real nice as Route 89 takes us south. I'm back to feeling mortal again, but that's okay. Eighty is sacked out on the passenger seat, paw curved across his eyes to keep the sun out. As long as I keep him warm, he won't complain. I know just how he feels.

Cat House

·

Melissa Mia Hall

Each morning a different victim sprawled across her porch, sometimes in pieces, sometimes exquisitely intact, hardly dead, hardly dead at all.

"Oh, Kittykins, I'm not impressed," she'd say and then off she'd go to find a sack to put the poor creature in. Then she'd take it to the garbage can out back. It was a most disagreeable habit. Katy didn't know what to do to dissuade the cat from delivering such awful compliments. She'd tried spanking her, yelling, throwing her off the porch—nothing worked. Dead squirrels, dead birds, dead mice, dead rats. She half expected a dead dog or even a dead cat next. And what if she killed a skunk—oh, the delicious odor anointing the polished red brick. How delightful and horrid. Kittykins was only one year old, a delicate feline with essentially a sweet and intelligent disposition. The thought of those tiny paws tearing into anything amazed her. Her luminous green eyes, her calico-tiger coloring, her romantic purrs all conspired to give the cat such a gentle look. It was almost impossible to consider Kittykins as a cold-blooded killer. Instincts, of course, it was just her natural instincts. Nothing to get out of whack over.

And she never ate her victims. For instance, she enjoyed playing with squirrel tails. She was absolutely cherubic as she tossed the tail in the air and rolled over like a trained circus dog. Such a darling.

But this morning, as she scooped up a mangled sparrow, the latest prize, Katy shivered. She loved birds. It was getting out of hand, entirely out of hand. "I'm afraid, Miss

Kittykins, I will have to give you away or take you to the Humane Society—" The cat licked her paws, feigning disinterest. "You see, I don't want this for dinner. I have some perfectly good frozen chicken breasts that I honestly prefer to sparrow meat." Katy held the bag with the bird away from her body. "I'm so tired of this." She had never intended to keep a cat—she'd just showed up the day she moved in, thin, starving—a small, helpless kitten. It would've been cruel *not* to feed her.

Besides, she had been lonely. After the break-up with Jack, the idea of starting over in a new city with a new job and a new house had been wonderfully appealing. But the reality of starting over cold was different from an idea. You can't touch an idea. And ideas were silent abstract things you couldn't see. No colors in an idea. Or smell, Katy reminded herself, looking at the bag of dead sparrow.

"Okay. I won't quit feeding you but you know that dry cat food you don't like particularly—well, don't think I'm going to rush out and get you some stinking gourmet canned food anytime soon. Got it?"

The cat strolled off the porch and into the bushes.

"And I'm sick of those dirty little mounds in the flower beds, too!" She chased after the cat, swinging the body bag. But Kittykins had disappeared into a clump of gardenia bushes she had just planted, hoping they wouldn't have a late freeze.

"Damn you!" She went around to the back of the house to deposit the bag into the big blue garbage can. She weighted the lid down with an extra brick. "This is my life—" she said, smiling in spite of herself.

She checked the hanging baskets on the patio and decided to take them into the shed in case it froze tonight. Maybe it wouldn't but she couldn't afford to replace them. She worried about the gardenia bushes. Maybe she'd toss a sheet over them. Just to be safe.

Eventually she went back into her house, her new house that she'd been living in for a year. It still didn't feel like a home just yet. The kitchen, especially—a monument to the latest in European equipment—felt alien and uncomfortable.

Katy stood in the kitchen and remembered her old

kitchen with Jack, the wooden cabinets a warm rusty-brown, the old round table and the blue curtains. The African violets on the windowsill. The braided rug. The giant turkey platter on the wall. The sink always full of dishes. The coffee pot always with at least two cups of stale coffee in it. This kitchen gleamed. It was very clean, primarily because everything was white. A very modern kitchen with up-to-date, built-in wizardry. That was one of the selling points of the house. The kitchen had just been totally redone by the former owner, a woman Katy met once, briefly, at the realtor's office. A recent divorcee, the woman had been very cool about the kitchen, detached. The realtor had laughingly referred to the kitchen as the reason for the woman's divorce of her fifth husband. But Katy didn't think it was the kitchen's fault. The kitchen was supposed to be the heart of the home and this kitchen had never come close. Katy hoped she could change that.

She touched the cold sink with a speculative finger. She couldn't change the basic style of the place but she could liven it up with some color. But more than anything, the kitchen cried out for voices. She'd bring in a table of golden wood to replace the white table and benches. A family table. But no family. Katy's throat tightened. No crying. No crying now. Her eyes filled. It made her angry, her fist fell on the drainboard. "Get out of here—" She grabbed a Coke and headed for the microwave popcorn. She popped a bag in the microwave and then headed for the TV. The Academy Awards were on. Hallelujah.

Old Oscar time. She could handle that. The familiar scenes recalled other houses, people sitting around the TV screen, each one composing their own secret acceptance speeches. "I want to thank my mother—" Katy swallowed painfully—gone, her mom was gone, "And my dad—" also gone, but good riddance, "Also God and my ninth-grade English teacher—" who was possibly gone. She put away the popcorn frantically and ran to the kitchen for another bag. "Come on, hurry, I might miss something!"

The bag bulged upwards. Katy grabbed the hot bag and sprinted back to the bedroom where her best TV sat in state, angled into a corner between two huge lawyer's bookcases.

"Is this a great life or what?" Katy munched on her popcorn and wondered why she hadn't seen half the movies up for nominations. She stretched out on her bed and pretended to enjoy the spectacle. When she was a kid she had even watched Miss America and liked it. When she became a socially and culturally enlightened teenager, she had been suitably horrified by the Oscars and crowns for beauties. And now she was cheering for the Best Actor. Her eyes blinked sleepily at the screen. Of course there was a difference between Oscars and crowns. But it was all acting, wasn't it? The phone rang. Katy bolted up, excitedly. She loved getting phone calls. Especially now, so far away.

"Hello?"

Nobody on the line. A dead connection? "Hello? Erin?" Her sister Erin called after ten P.M., to save on the charges. Silence. She replaced the phone in its cradle and turned back to the TV. "Well, that's funny," she said aloud—she'd gotten into the habit of thinking out loud when no one was around. Lonely-people-do-lonely-things Department. She should write a Glamour article about it. Or Redbook or Elle or what is Cher wearing tonight? Oh God. Katy clapped her hands.

She drained the rest of her Coke and tried to concentrate but the screen blurred and shifted. She was watching her past. The new house and the professional movers unloading the truck. The emptiness of the house being filled with half of her life, the half without Jack. She kept wondering where the old wingback chair was or the vintage thirties reading lamp. The ungodly sculpture Jack won in a poker game. Jack hadn't called. Not once, just to see how she was making out. She heard a horrible noise. Her fingernails hooked into the Star of Bethlehem quilt she bought at a crafts fair before she left Long Beach. The cat. Cat fight. Kittykins was protecting her turf. Kill 'em, Kittykins. Kill 'em good.

Movie music swelled and applause filled the room. Katy jumped up, her chin posed in an Audrey Hepburn lift. Frozen, she listened intently as something heavy hit the side of the house. Her hands held on to a section of the quilt. The snarling sounds ceased and an ominous silence descended outside. The cat fight was over. If Kittykins had died, she would die.

Katy turned off the TV and went into the hall. She stood in front of a tacky photo collage full of fading color prints and stark, more eloquent black-and-white prints her mother had assembled a long time ago. The dim light made it impossible to see the faces in those prints, but Katy could feel them. There was reassurance in those unseen faces. She could feel her mother's smile, her grandmother's eyes. Old Granddad leered in one corner, caught telling one of his silly cornbelt jokes. And her sister Erin held her hands wide in a twelve-year-old burlesque routine masquerading as amateur gymnastics. Katy felt so lost standing there. Her eighteen-year-old senior picture held her tightly; the features on that scared face had been transferred to her thirty-three-year-old face.

Go check on the cat. Katy moved down the unfamiliar hall and turned into the living room. An unpacked crate stood in the center. It had been standing there all year, a box of paintings, prints and photographs that had not been hung. The white walls made a statement. Simplicity. Unadornment. Purity. Emptiness.

This house. They used to be called "airplane bungalows" —built in the thirties, Katy thought that's what the realtor had said. And the neighborhood was so homey. There was a neighborhood watch association. It was safe to jog around here and there was a playground just a few blocks away if you had children. Katy suddenly ran to the door and wrenched it open with one quick, desperate pull. She'd forgotten to lock it. She had been sitting there, in her bedroom, all alone, with the door unlocked. "Damn it, Katy, you stupid ass—" But the glass door was latched. She undid it and switched on the porch light. She looked down on the large heap on the porch and immediately switched it back off. Then she closed both doors and locked them.

"I need rest." Whatever she had seen could wait till tomorrow. Her stomach couldn't bear the prospect of hauling away that big a victim. "It's just a dead cat," she said softly. She didn't want to know if it was pretty Kittykins. She didn't want to know.

* * *

The night did not pass quickly. Katy was up at all hours, using the bathroom and popping antacids and sure-fire headache remedies that forgot to catch fire. She tossed and turned incessantly, twisting her Eileen West gown up around her waist. By five A.M. she gave up and threw her quilt back. Her bedroom fan fanned her loose hair and chilled her bare shoulders. The house was still dark. She went through the rooms, turning on lights.

She heard a cat yowling a familiar yowl she identified with Kittykins. Relief flooded her features. She started for the back door. The cat dishes were on the back porch. She got the cat food and went outside. Kittykins was not there. She was probably at the front door waiting for her to acknowledge her most recent gift. Katy's stomach flip-flopped. A garbage sack, then. And her garden gloves. Or better still, the plastic gloves beneath the sink. Katy really didn't want to do this. But it had to be done and she went back to the front door.

It wasn't a cat. Or a dog. Katy stood looking down into the dim light. The dark heap stirred, amazingly still alive. Kittykins stared up at her proudly, defiantly, standing on her latest trophy, tail straight up, eyes vibrantly green. She miaowed sweetly.

It was much, much larger than a cat or a dog. But she hadn't thought it could be this—this—

"Oh my God."

The head turned to the side. One eye opened. The profile had a certain similarity to—

"Jack?"

He needed help. She had to call 911. Kittykins kept walking up and down him, purring. "Get off of there!" Katy knelt beside him, took his pulse and tried to get control of herself.

"Are you dead?" she said, thinking he might very well be dying and had been, for several hours, while she pampered herself in a warm bed. "Oh God, Jack, what happened?" She remembered the cat fight and the thump. Had he been hit by a car—? She looked out to the street and now saw his old blue BMW standing neatly by the curb. Why she hadn't noticed it before struck her as completely absurd. Obviously he'd been mugged and beaten so severely—

Kittykins hissed as the man's left hand twitched and raised to touch Katy. "Help—me—"

"Oh, Jack, you're alive." She checked him carefully. "I think your leg is broken. Listen, you stay here and I'll go call someone to help, okay?" She wadded the black plastic garbage sack into a pillow and stuffed it under his head. "I'll be right back—" She ran and got a real pillow and her quilt, came back and tried to make him more comfortable. She wondered what the neighbors would think, especially the old bag who lived across the street. "It's the effect I have on men," she said as she went to use the phone. The cat slipped inside after her. If Katy had seen her, she wouldn't have allowed it—Katy didn't want to mess with litter boxes, but she had to tend to Jack until the medics came, and the cat's entry went unnoticed.

"I can't believe you drove all the way from California."

"I can't believe I did either." Jack appeared wonderfully vulnerable in casts and voluminous bandages." She adjusted his pillows and put a straw in his beer.

"So what happened?"

"I got the shit beat out of me."

"Well, I can see that—but out there, last night—"

"Some bastard beat me up and took my wallet and then those cats came." Jack's one unswollen brown eye grew round as a marble. "You wouldn't believe it."

"I heard them yowling and all."

"No kidding. I was terrified. Didn't you hear me scream?"

Katy shook her head.

"I thought they were going to eat me. And that cat—that cat of yours stepped in—I've never seen so many cats in my life. I passed out—I've always loved cats—" Now Jack shook his head.

"What do you mean—were they really going to—you know—eat you? I can't believe that—"

"Naw—of course not."

Katy felt suddenly awkward. For a moment, Jack's voice had the old argumentative nasal twang, the just-about-to-get-nasty tone she had hated so much, that had led to such bitterness between them. Those hot words worn out from too many problems—her job, his job, the question about children—neither of them ever willing to back down from any fight. They had always persisted in such a way that no one ever won. No one ever won. But they had always enjoyed making up. Hadn't they?

"I miss you." Jack huddled against the pillows and scrambled for a cigarette.

"I thought you were going to quit."

He shrugged painfully. "Stress."

Katy thought this was where she was supposed to scream, "Yeah, sure," but couldn't summon the strength. She waited for Jack to get defensive but he just looked at her with a small smile playing across his lips.

"Katy, where's that cat of yours?"

She hadn't see the cat since early morning. She hadn't fed it. The cat had totally slipped her mind in all the commotion. "Well, I don't know."

"Maybe you'd better check on it."

"Her."

"In a way, I think I owe her my life."

"Jack—" Katy did not believe the story about a cat gang descending upon him like a plague of locusts, ready to devour him, although his stomach was temptingly soft in the middle. "You stay there and I'll go check on her."

"Yeah, I'm really going somewhere," Jack snarled.

Katy went in search of the cat. Hauling food outside, she called out for Kittykins. Usually just the sound of the back door opening was enough to send the cat jumping off the roof or tripping off the nearest tree limb. She waited a long time, but the little cat did not appear.

A sense of acute loss assailed her. The bowl of food stayed untouched. Katy sat on a patio chair and waited. From time to time, she called out "Kittykins!" and she got up several times and looked behind bushes and strained her eyes staring up into crisscrossing tree limbs. Kittykins was gone. There was a feeling about the backyard. An emptiness. Katy finally gave up and went back inside. The white kitchen greeted her with a rosiness Katy had never noticed before. And it was warm. She'd fix tuna fish or salmon for dinner.

She walked leisurely back to Jack, who was snoring. He'd come back for a reconciliation. He wanted to live with her. He could work here as well as he could work on the Coast. It didn't matter where he lived as long as he was with her. She wanted to believe that. She knew he was trying to believe it.

Katy suddenly felt a presence, someone watching her. She was standing in the living room. A sound. "Kittykins?" Somehow the cat was inside. She longed to see those luminous green eyes. The box with the pictures. Kittykins loved boxes. When it was cold she had lived in a nest of cardboard boxes in the garage. She was so cute playing in them, jumping in and out, toying with the flaps. "Kittykins?"

Katy looked inside the crate and saw her own eyes reflected in a round glass that used to hang in the house in California. She realized her eyes were exactly the same uncanny shade as the cat's.

"Katy! *Katy!*"

She turned away from the box, frightened by the frantic tone in Jack's voice.

"What? What is it—what's wrong?"

"It's on me . . . get it off. It's sucking my breath—"

"You're dreaming. Jack—" She held him gently in her arms. He was like a child. He cried in her arms. She stroked his hair and kissed him. She had never seen him cry.

"Tell her I'm sorry."

"Tell who, Jack—?"

"You—you—" He opened his eyes. "Did you find the cat?"

"No, I'm afraid not—"

"You won't—I mean, you can stop looking—" Jack said softly, clinging to her like she was a life preserver.

"You had a bad dream—" she said, licking the salt from his lips.

"She's here," he mumbled.

"Jack, no—"

Then the house purred.

Neutral About Cats

•

Jan Grape

People aren't neutral about cats, they either love them or they hate them. But honestly, I *have* always been neutral about cats. It's just I've always felt cats would rather be left alone. I respect that. Sometimes, I'd rather be left alone.

The flight steward on my flight from DFW to Austin reminded me of a cat. His movements were smooth and fluid as he made his way down the narrow aisle of the 727. His hair was that orange-gold color of Morris in the cat food commercial. But what added to the perception was the way he made a funny humming noise each time before he spoke, almost like a purr, and he blinked when he looked at you as if he were wearing new eyes.

I watched as he paused to hand out a pillow or a magazine or check the seat backs and upper storage racks, and thought he acted exactly like a cat pausing to rub against the doorjamb while leading you down the hallway to the food bowl.

A cat lives at my house now, been there about a year. A young black tomcat, with long spindly legs and golden tiger eyes. I named him Sam Spade and call him Spade.

I was on my way home from attending a meeting for private investigators in Pasadena, California. My name is Jenny Gordon and I'm a P.I. My partner C. J. Gunn and I own G&G Investigations in Austin, Texas.

C. J. had gone to this P.I. convention last year, and she had insisted I go this year. "You have to go. You need to catch up on all the technological advances, Girlfriend."

C. J. is a sharp ex-policewoman who thrives on new technology.

"You know I have the mechanical brain of a horned toad," I said. "Even when I see that stuff, I don't understand what it is or how to use it and besides . . ."

"Besides nothing. How you gonna learn if you ain't exposed?"

"I don't need . . ."

"Get with the program, Girl. We gotta compete with the big boys." A big smile had spread across her cola-nut-brown face as she closed her deep brown eyes briefly and obviously remembered some aspect of her trip last year. "And besides, my dear . . . these meetings always harbor at least one or two of the best-looking hunks. A little R&R wouldn't hurt your disposition none."

She was right, as usual. I had needed a little vacation and once I got there enjoyed meeting people and talking shop. The technology things were mind-boggling, but there were a couple of intriguing gadgets. Like sunglasses with mirrors on the inside to let you see what's behind you and a gizmo you hook onto your telephone that changes your voice when you speak. It can make you sound like a man or a little old lady or even a child. Could be useful when you have to keep calling the same telephone number for different information.

The hunks? Well, there *was* one guy from the L.A. area who really turned me on . . . but that's another story.

The flight from L.A. to Dallas had been routine, the usual drinks, a semi-hot meal—roasted chicken breast with mushrooms and rice. And as usual, the veggies were limp and bland and the cookie dessert was dry, but this airline's use of stainless steel silverware instead of plastic and ceramic coffee mugs made the meal seem better than it actually was. It had been a long time since I'd seen such niceties, except in first class where I never ride unless someone else pays. I was impressed.

I'd bought a new Tony Hillerman paperback to read and the three-hour flight passed rather quickly, that is, until we got over the Dallas Metro area. We got caught in a holding pattern and circled DFW for fifty-five minutes because of bad weather.

The airport at Dallas is huge, several terminals, miles and miles of gates, but if you're continuing on with the same airline, you can catch a cart over to the gate you need if it's too far to walk. You don't even have to go through Checkpoint Charlie again if you're on a connecting flight. I rode a cart over to the gate I needed and discovered all the flights were backed up because of the thunderstorm. Luckily I had the book.

Finally, at eight P.M., three hours late, the flight to Austin boarded. It's only a short hop once you get airborne. The plane was about one-half full, and my seat was four rows from the back. I always feel safer in the tail section and this time I didn't have a seatmate. I was tired and glad not to have to talk to anyone. All I wanted to do, for this one-hour flight, was finish my book.

I wasn't exactly alone. The galley ended across the aisle from me—the male steward and the young female Hispanic attendant, also working this section, were up and down the aisles, in and out of the galley. A young couple sat in front of me and a couple of guys sat somewhere behind.

When the steward brought the glass of white wine I'd ordered, I noticed his name tag read "Ringo." If that's not a cat name, I thought, it should be.

Cat's names should fit the cat. For instance, my cat, Sam Spade, is nosy, he's always poking his nose into things and P.I.'s have a tendency to do that, too. So naturally I think Spade's name suits him perfectly.

For years I'd satisfied my natural curiosity by working as a radiological technologist (a high-toned name for an X-ray technician), looking inside human bodies, helping to diagnose what was wrong. That curiosity transferred easily into looking inside people's lives when my P.I. husband was killed and I took over his business.

The curious Mr. Spade came to live with me one night about ten months ago. Before Tommy died, we had lived in a middle-class neighborhood house instead of the apartment I have now.

A friend from that neighborhood, Glenda Knipstein, was a big cat lover—strays came to her door on a routine basis. It wasn't unusual for her to have a dozen cats around. She swears, "There are cat paws out on the highway, that only cats can see, which point the way to my house."

Anyway, the tiny black kitten showed up at her house one cold rainy night, and since Glenda tries to find good homes for strays, she managed to talk me into taking him.

I never knew exactly what made me consent. She had asked me to come over for lunch one day and I'd barely gotten inside and sat down when this little black ball of fur jumped up into my lap and began kneading his tiny claws on my sweater. About a minute later, he curled up and purred himself to sleep. He slept the whole while we ate. When I was ready to leave, the kitten woke up and looked at me with big blue eyes and Glenda said, "Why don't you take him with you? Just until we find out where he belongs."

Of course the kitten's owner never showed up and Spade decided to stay. The grown-up Spade now has golden eyes, but I've never forgotten those startling blue eyes in that tiny black kitten face. Glenda takes care of him when I'm away. I will admit he's good company for someone living alone, but I'm still neutral about cats.

Despite the earlier bad weather, the plane ride was smooth. Thunderstorms sweeping down from the Panhandle can move out quickly. I sipped my wine and read, getting to the final chapters.

I'm not sure exactly how long I'd been reading when a commotion and a woman's scream jerked me away from the Southwest scenery and the Navajo policeman in the book.

A flight attendant, from the forward section, I supposed, made a terse announcement over the speaker.

"Ladies and gentlemen: Everyone please remain calm. Cooperate fully. Do as you're told and no one will be hurt." The speaker clicked off abruptly.

The steward, Ringo, was walking slowly, coming towards the rear. Someone was walking behind him. Two or three passengers were standing in the aisles at about the mid-section of the aircraft, and I heard snatches of conversation buzzing around the cabin.

"What's happening . . . ?"

"What's going on?"

As Ringo and the person with him passed each row, however, all conversation stopped and the standing passengers sat back down immediately. Everyone settled down, faced forward and no one protested.

Ringo was walking in a strange manner—sort of what I'd call straddle-legged. As he got closer to me, his odd gait became apparent. A short stocky man wearing a red ski mask was shoving Ringo along. The man's arm snaked around Ringo's neck and rested on a shoulder near the steward's throat. Something metallic glinted in the man's hand.

When they got nearer, I could see a small rivulet of blood on Ringo's throat, blood running down his neck was spreading to the collar of his white shirt. He'd been cut, but not badly.

"Do like the man says and don't anyone move," Ringo said through stiff lips, as they passed the Hispanic girl standing in the galley doorway and moved on past me to the plane's rear. The fear on Ringo's face was as easy to read as a large-print book.

The girl made a whimpering sound when they passed.

"Everyone empty your wallets and purses. Take off all your jewelry, too," Ringo said in a low quavery voice. He grunted and repeated the words louder, more firmly.

There were some muttered words I couldn't understand and Ringo, obviously prompted by the assailant, spoke to the girl. "Esperanza, get some pillowcases. You and the other attendants fill them. If you don't do exactly as you are told, my throat will be cut."

A few more muffled words were uttered, and Ringo said, "Get everyone's money and jewelry. When those cases are full bring them back here."

The girl, Esperanza, didn't move or speak, her eyes were wide and unblinking. She was rooted to the spot as if someone had poured a quart of glue over her feet.

Personally I felt some relief. I'd been afraid we were being hijacked to some Middle East country. An ordinary garden-variety robbery didn't seem half bad somehow.

Esperanza still hadn't moved or spoken. The girl's scared to death, I thought, and in a low conversational tone said to her, "Esperanza, get yourself together. You've been trained to handle emergencies. You can handle this situation."

There was a long silence when I thought she'd slipped off into never-never land, but she finally faced the two men and said, "Yes. I'll do it. Please don't hurt Ringo."

Esperanza opened an overhead compartment, took down a pillow and pulled off the pillowcase, then another and another. She stripped a dozen or so.

"Start up in the first cabin. When the cases are full, bring them back here." Ringo's voice sounded stronger.

The girl did as she was told and the flight attendants up front helped. In a few minutes, Esperanza brought bulging pillowcases to the rear and grabbed up more empties. Ringo told her to hurry.

When the girl finally stopped in front of me, holding out a pillowcase, I put what was left of a twenty-dollar bill inside, it was the only cash I had in my billfold. Fortunately I was wearing only costume jewelry, a couple of silver rings. No need trying to explain they weren't worth anything, I thought, and slipped the rings off and also unfastened the clasp on my thirty-nine-dollar Timex watch and dropped all three in the pillowcase. Let Mr. Bad Guy sort out the fake stuff from the good stuff.

The masked man muttered again and Ringo said, "Don't forget your earrings, lady." He must have been standing directly behind me, but I didn't look up.

Damn Sam. I had forgotten my earrings. Tommy had given me diamond studs for our first anniversary. They had a lot of sentimental value, but the two small diamonds weren't worth much money-wise. I hated to give them up, but it was pointless and dangerous to argue. I stifled my anger the best I could, pulled the earrings out of my ears and bit my lip to keep from saying anything.

As I dropped the earrings in the pillowcase, I noticed a change in the speed and sound of the jet engines. The wing flaps made that awful grinding noise and I became aware we were descending quickly. The pilot made no announcement over the speaker, but Ringo and the bandit must have realized what was happening, yet nothing was said.

Esperanza moved to the rows behind me and after a few moments she said, "That's all."

"Put your diamond ring in there, too, Esperanza," said Ringo.

"No. Not my engagement ring," she said. "I won't give up my ring."

"Give . . . it . . . to . . . him," said Ringo.

"No. I won't." Her voice cracked as if she were crying.

The jet engines grew louder and I couldn't hear any more.

A male voice said, "Oh my God." It sounded like Ringo, but I couldn't be sure.

I craned my head around a little and saw Ringo and the masked man locked in an embrace, but I couldn't see the girl.

A chime sounded and the FASTEN SEAT BELT sign came on and other chimes sounded all those messages for the flight attendants.

Feet shuffled, A male voice said, "Don't . . ."

It could have been Ringo's voice or it could have been the bandit's, I had no idea.

There were some grunts and then, something that sounded like two pro-linebackers in football pads banging together on Super Bowl Sunday.

I hoped Ringo had jumped the bandit and wanted to lean out in the aisle and look but was afraid my actions might be misconstrued.

Long seconds passed, but the only noise was from the screaming engines.

When Ringo didn't shout out that everything was okay, I had a horrible feeling he was on the receiving end of that blow and was unconscious or worse.

Suddenly the plane landed, bouncing once before settling to a smooth drive down the runway. I could feel the sensation as the pilot applied the brakes and the plane slowed. The engine noise revved down.

What had happened to the masked man? And to Ringo and Esperanza?

When I could stand it no longer, I glanced back over my right shoulder to the rear of the plane, but could see nothing.

While this happened, the plane began to transverse the air field rapidly. The flight attendants up front were conspicuously absent. Only the airplane itself made a noise. It was as if the plane, pilots and passengers were all robots.

Briefly, I felt I was in the Twilight Zone, the only human alive in the whole airplane, then a baby started to cry, but the sound was quickly silenced. Next, I heard a muffled cough and a sniff from somewhere in front of me. Normal human sounds made me feel a bit better, but not much.

Somehow we must have been given immediate clearance, both for landing and taxiing. I assumed we were at Robert Mueller Airport in Austin, for what that was worth.

The plane slowed and stopped. It was too dark to see outside, but I didn't think we were at the gate yet.

A shuffling noise came from the back. Metal scraped and that sudden breached-vacuum sound of an opened Exit door was unmistakable. Thumping, bumping noises sounded and I had a notion the bandit jumped out. The airplane began moving again and you could tell the Exit door was still open.

The plane was still taxiing when I heard a faint call for help. The voice was low, only the people in the rear of the plane could have heard it.

That sounds like Ringo, I thought, and throwing caution out, I turned slightly and looked. I saw a pair of feet and legs. The remainder of the person couldn't be seen.

A voice gasped, "Help ... us ... please." It was definitely Ringo's. He groaned and coughed.

I unfastened my seat belt and got up, holding on to the seat backs, and moved slowly toward the rear—ready to sit down if the masked man was still there.

The two men, in separate rows sitting behind me, just sat and neither would look me in the eye. Bastards, I thought, don't want to get involved.

The girl was on the floor—between the seats—of the last row. Her upper body was flat on her back, her legs and feet flopped to the side. She wasn't moving and her face was pasty-white.

If her chest moved, I couldn't see it. She had a huge gaping hole just under her left breast that slanted upwards towards her neck. The blood wasn't gushing out, but that area was covered with it and puddled beside her.

I knelt and felt for the carotid artery, grateful that I had enough training to know where to look. The pulse was there, but barely.

She needed immediate care. More care than I knew how to give, but I opened the luggage bin overhead and found a pillow and some blankets. I spread one blanket over her legs, another across her chest and shoulders, and took a pillow and placed it directly over the bleeding area, pressing down slightly.

Ringo asked for help again as the plane jerked to a halt. I almost lost my balance, squatting on my feet in the aisle. I grabbed the armrest, leaned back a little bit and peeked around the panel. I sure did hope the knife-wielding bandit had jumped out of that open Exit.

Ringo was alone, on the floor near the Exit door, lying on his side. He rubbed the back of his head and struggled to sit.

I placed my left hand back on the pillow over the girl's chest area and pressed gently. "Don't try to sit yet, Ringo." I couldn't see any blood except what had been on his collar earlier. "Did you get stabbed or cut?"

"No. Just conked on the head." He sat up and I saw sweat pop out on his face. "I think I'm okay."

He retched and had to lie back down. Probably has a concussion, I thought.

Movement and excited voices pierced the silence and I looked to the front of the plane. People were crowding the aisles. Most were craning to look this way.

A male voice said loudly, "Everyone stay calm. Please sit down and be quiet a minute." The voice was firm, but not angry. "Let me through, please, I'm the captain.

"Let me get back here and see what the situation is. Sit, please, everything's okay. Your bandit jumped out back there, but the police are after him."

When the captain reached the rear of his aircraft, he looked like Superman to me. It didn't take him long to get the injured on the way to the hospital; Esperanza was loaded into a Life-Flite helicopter and Ringo taken off by ambulance.

In a few minutes the passengers were calmed, and we learned the rest of the story. The senior flight attendant, who had been working the first-class cabin, had managed to get a message to the captain during the first few moments of the incident.

The captain had called the Austin tower, got emergency clearance to land, and ordered police and medical help. They were waiting when we landed. It had been easy from his standpoint.

An airport policeman had seen the masked man jump out onto the runway and had chased him into the baggage area. While he was out on the tarmac, the bandit lost two of his pillowcases full of booty and police had recovered those.

About the time the ambulance left with Ringo, the captain announced the bandit was now in police custody. Everyone cheered, except me. Oh, I was glad he was caught, but I was too worried about Esperanza to feel like cheering. She had lost so much blood, I knew her life was in jeopardy.

Everything else was predictable. Those people who for emergency reasons had to be someplace else were questioned and sent on their way—the remaining passengers were taken to a V.I.P. lounge and given drinks and food.

Since the crime had been committed on an airline, the FBI would have charge of the case eventually, but their headquarters are in San Antonio. An agent was on the way, but the Austin police questioned people and handled things for now. APD said we would be released when that was completed.

Some people were furious about being held, but there was nothing to be done about it. The harrowing ordeal was over, we were safe, the crook in custody, the injured being cared for, and that was the main thing.

The next morning, I slept as late as Spade would allow. He had chewed me out royally when I'd finally made it home a little after one A.M. Whenever I had to be gone, I had to endure his complaints for two days after returning.

I had tuned him out, piled into bed and zonked without moving until a black paw started batting at my hair. When I poured his food into his bowl, he barely thanked me.

"That's the way you're gonna be, huh?" He ignored me, tail standing up as straight as an arrow. I picked him up and tried to scratch him under his chin, but he twisted and jumped out of my arms and beelined it outside—out through his kitty door.

"Okay for you," I said. I started the coffee and toasted an English muffin, ate and went in to take a shower. As I stepped out onto the bath mat—showered, shampooed, legs and underarms shaved—the telephone rang. It rang four times before I could get head and body wrapped into bath towels and answer.

"Jenny?"

"Yes?" For a moment, I didn't recognize the voice. It was my friend from the old neighborhood. "Glenda? Is that you?"

"Yes, it's me. Uh . . . C.J. told me you were back home."

Her voice sounded odd, like she was crying or close to it. "Glenda, what's wrong?"

"I need to see you."

"You want to come over here?"

"Yes, and Jenny . . . I really *need* you. My brother has been arrested. They think he robbed that airplane last night. The one you were on."

"Damn Sam. Well, get on over here." I knew Glenda had an older brother, but I'd never met him. He was a bit of a loner and didn't visit her much when she and I were neighbors.

Glenda arrived fifteen minutes later, just as I finished blow-drying my short mop of hair. She is a year or two older than my thirty-five years, with strawberry blonde hair in a pixie cut and she doesn't know what it is to watch her weight as she's blessed with a great metabolism. She has a cute rather than pretty face, with a sprinkling of freckles across her nose and cheeks. Her best features are her big brown eyes. She shows a lot of caring in those eyes.

She's married to a swell guy who likes cats as much as she does and they don't have any children. If I had had a sister, I would like her to be like Glenda.

Glenda tried to pet Spade, but he ignored both of us. I poured coffee for her and she sat down at the kitchen table.

Spade suddenly got feisty, dug his claws into the carpet, then scampered back out the kitty door and attacked my pecan tree. He must have scratched and dug at the bark until his claws were sharpened to needle points because when he came running back inside and leapt into Glenda's lap; he promptly stuck one of those needles into her thumb, drawing blood.

We cleansed her wound and while she read the morning newspaper accounts of the plane robbery, I put on a little makeup and finished dressing.

She told me her brother James, a Pan Am ticket agent, had been laid off when that airline went belly up. He had gone to work in the baggage department at the airport while he tried to get a job with another airline. He was the man the police caught last night in the baggage area.

"James *was* on that flight, Jenny. He'd been out to L.A., job-hunting. When the airplane landed he was sitting up near the front, just behind first class, and got right off. He said he was already late for work. He walked back to the baggage section and went into the men's room. They caught him when he came out."

She continued and fought to hold back the tears. "No one is sure what the man looked like before he put the mask on over his head. Since the plane was half-empty, people had moved around locating places to sit so they would be the only person on that row. So no one knows where the masked man had been sitting originally.

"James is about the same size as the bandit—I'm told there were six men on the plane who fit the general description and James has one of those faces that no one ever remembers.

"He didn't have a ski mask, but I think it was found in the lavatory wastebasket. He did have a pocket knife. Our dad gave one to him when he was twelve years old, and he always carried it. And he's in debt because he took a cut in salary, but Jenny, I swear to you, they've got the wrong man."

"Glenda," I said, "there's probably not much I can do. I'm sure the FBI . . ."

"Jenny, I want to hire you to clear my brother." Tears spilled down her face and dripped on her blouse. "My brother is one of the kindest people I know. He wouldn't hurt anyone ever. His first wife did him really dirty and if he was ever going to hurt anyone it would have been her.

But he just went on with his life. He has a girlfriend now and he's a happy person."

She wiped her eyes and smiled. "James only has one big fault that I know of—he doesn't like cats. He's a dog person and I forgave him for that a long time ago."

"I want to help, Glenda, but with the FBI in charge, I don't know where to begin."

"I'll pay you. Whatever it takes."

"It's not the money," I said. "And besides, I couldn't charge Spade's godmother."

My telephone rang and it was my partner, C.J. Her news was not good.

"One of my contacts at APD just called," C.J. said. "The girl flight attendant just died."

Glenda was looking at me.

"Oh, shit," I said. "That doesn't help, does it?"

"Glenda must be there."

"You got that right. Listen, I have company, I'll call you back in a little while."

Glenda was going to have to know and I decided the news should come from me rather than from some news reporter. "Glenda. I . . . uh . . . there's no easy way, but you have to know. The flight attendant died this morning."

"Oh, poor little thing." When the full implication hit her, she furiously beat her fists on the kitchen table. "Oh no, no, no. They will charge James with murder. Jenny, my . . . my mother can't take that. It could kill her."

"I know . . ." Her mother had had a heart condition for years.

"The police or FBI or whoever is in charge seems determined to nail James' ass to the courthouse square. Please help us."

All I could do was promise to try and find out what I could.

It would be difficult to get information from APD without the help of my friend, Lt. Larry Hays of the homicide department. Larry had been my late husband's partner until Tommy resigned from APD and opened his own investigator's office. Hays could usually be counted on for help, but he was out of town on some special assignment. My only plan was to nose around headquarters and hope to find someone to pump.

Austin Police Department headquarters sits directly beside Interstate 35 and between Seventh and Eight streets. My apartment and office are both located in the northwest part of town, just off Loop 1 and a few miles from downtown. Loop 1 Freeway, known to the locals as Mo-Pac (it was built alongside of the Missouri-Pacific Railroad), gave me a straight shot south into downtown Austin. From there I'd have to get over on Eighth and head east to the Interstate.

Austin is built on and surrounded by hills, limestone crags and ledges on the west side which climb up to the Edwards Plateau, and gentle rolling hills on the east side leading into the fertile Blackland Prairie. The unusual topography is because of an ancient escarpment, Balcones Fault (running north-south) and the meandering Texas Colorado River (running northeast-southwest), and both bisect Austin. In my opinion, this city is in the prettiest part of the state and the scenic Mo-Pac drive is usually a pleasure to make.

Today, however, I was too concerned about how to help my friend to enjoy the view, but when I found a parking space right next to the police building, it seemed like a good sign and lifted my spirits.

At one time I knew most of the men in homicide, but in the three years since Tommy left, a number of new faces had appeared. One was a detective named Ken Richards. Detective Richards might have the information needed, I was told when I inquired at the front desk.

Richards stood six feet four, towering over my five feet six inches, and yet nothing in his manner was intimidating. He had dark brown gray-streaked hair cut military style, and he looked to be in good shape. His face, tanned or windburned, looked friendly and I guessed his age to be early fifties. He was dressed in dark gray corduroy Levis and a pale blue dress shirt with a paisley tie. A wariness was noticeable in his dark eyes, making me believe they didn't miss much. The cops I've known who have been on the street for years get that look.

I introduced myself, showed my I.D. and could tell he

wasn't impressed by my P.I. license, a fact I've learned to ignore. I told him I had a personal interest as I'd been a passenger on that plane, but that I also had a client. Was there any way he could help?

"Well, you've come to the wrong place, Ms. Gordon," Richards said. His voice was deep and he had a strong Texas twang. "The FBI has taken over and about all I can say is that we have two suspects in custody."

"Two suspects? James Knipstein's sister is a friend of mine and she's the one who's hired me. Who's the other suspect?"

His eyes narrowed and I could see he had all but dismissed me. "Sorry, Ms. Gordon, um . . . uh . . . there's really nothing more I can say. You need to contact Agent Brown . . ."

It was time to invoke my friendship with Larry. "Lieutenant Hays is a friend of mine and . . ."

Sudden light dawned on his face, "Hey, are you Tommy Gordon's widow?"

"Yes."

"Well, why didn't you say so?" His attitude changed totally as he placed me into the cop-family category. "Tommy was a good cop. I rode with him a few weeks when he first came out of the academy."

He led me into an office, waved me to a chair, sat behind the desk and we chewed the fat a little longer about the early days, getting on first-name basis quickly. Eventually we got back around to the case. "What's the deal here, Ken?" I asked. "Why two suspects? We only had one masked bandit."

"The second man, Roger Cantu, is a University of Texas student and he was found in the baggage area a short time after Knipstein was arrested. Cantu was about three feet away from where part of the loot was stashed. They first thought he was an accomplice, but when he was picked in a line-up as the actual bandit by some of the passengers, their thinking changed."

"Then why hold Knipstein?"

"Knipstein was also picked out by some passengers. But none of the passengers could pick between those two. And no one except that flight steward, Ringo, heard the suspect's voice clearly and he's still in the hospital with a concussion. He's been so broken up by the girl's death, the doctors won't let anyone talk to him."

"And this FBI agent . . ." Ken seemed to be debating with himself about something and probably the fact that he'd known and liked Tommy was the deciding factor. I could tell it in his face when he decided to say more. "Hell, I don't know. There was a time when I could work with the G-men—some of the old-timers—but a lot of these new ones with their college degrees, they think street cops are incapable of original thought."

He got up and began pacing the room. He soon stopped and looked down at his feet, which were a gigantic size and encased in a pair of the biggest sneakers I'd ever seen outside of a pro-basketball arena. Somehow they were not discordant with the way he was dressed.

"You know, Jenny," he continued, "I don't like it when people get killed, especially young people, and I have a strong desire to be personally involved in catching the murderer. But crimes committed on airplanes are the private jurisdiction of the FBI and I've been given orders to back off. One thing I do know how to do is follow orders."

"I wonder why I haven't been called in on those lineups." Sounded like someone wasn't doing his job right. Maybe that's partly why Richards was so put out with the FBI agent. In all fairness, however, someone from the FBI may have tried to reach me at my office and I'd been unavailable.

"I suppose you'll be contacted, but who knows. College books don't always teach what goes on in real life," he said. "Well, let's see what we have. Two suspects, both on that flight. Both fit the general description. Both were caught in the baggage area."

"But James had a reason," I said. "He worked there."

"He was not supposed to be working that day." Richards frowned and sat back down, picking up a pencil and doodling on a note pad.

I knew Glenda well and couldn't imagine her brother capable of committing a crime, but how could I prove otherwise? Having a sister who's a wonderful person doesn't cut any ice with the police. "Ken, this may sound stupid, because I don't even know the man, but I just don't think Knipstein is involved. This man has never been arrested. I mean, what's his motive?"

"It's a puzzler, all right. The lack of a motive bothers me, too. Both men have jobs. It just seems senseless to me.

"Both men refused to take the lie detector for some strange reason." He stopped doodling and looked at me. "This G-man is convinced that Knipstein is the one because they found a knife in his pocket."

"But James' knife was a pocket knife and those are allowed on airplanes, aren't they?"

"Generally no one questions a pocket knife, especially if the blade is only three or four inches long. On the other hand, Cantu didn't have a knife."

"Maybe he got rid of it."

"Maybe. You know, there is one thing that bothers me."

"What?"

"When something odd shows up in a case, I get a tingling along the back of my neck, and Cantu had a strange-looking rock in his pocket when we arrested him. Now, it might not mean anything, but I got one of those feelings when I saw that rock."

Richards seemed to be talking to himself, shaking his head; thinking. "No. I don't know what it is about that rock."

"What kind of rock?"

"Who knows rocks?"

"Maybe he pretended it was a bomb or a grenade when he first grabbed Ringo," I said.

"None of the passengers mentioned anything like that. All they talked about was that knife, although no one could describe it."

"Well, I didn't actually see a knife either, but I saw the damage it did first hand."

Richards got up and walked to the doorway. "Yeah. But even now while we're discussing it, I'm getting that tingling feeling again." He rubbed the back of his neck as he spoke. "Uh . . . let's go down the hall a minute." He took me to the evidence room and requested to see the stuff taken from Cantu's pocket.

When the stuff came, Richards picked up the rock. It was

flat on one side as if it had once been attached to a block of wood. It reminded me of something my grandad had used to sharpen his pocket knife on when he was whittling.

"It looks like one of those things to sharpen a knife with," I said.

"Yeah. That's what it is. A whetstone! Why would a guy without a knife have a whetstone?"

"Beats me." And for some silly reason I remembered this morning with Glenda and Spade. Remembered how Spade started digging on my pecan tree, sharpening his claws. And that led to thinking about those stainless steel knives on the L.A.-to-Dallas flight. "Richards, I just had the craziest idea."

His face was still puzzled as he looked at me.

"Is it possible Cantu sharpened one of those knives the airline uses for meals?"

"Don't they use plastic?"

"This airline didn't. Not on the flight from L.A. to Dallas."

"But the bandit pulled the knife on the flight to Austin, not on the one to Dallas." Richards still looked as if he thought I was nuts. "Anyway, he would never get it past Checkpoint Charlie when the Austin plane boarded."

"You don't have to go through the checkpoint when you make a connecting flight. He could have taken the knife from the first flight, gone into one of the men's rooms in Dallas and sharpened it to a fine point and strolled on board with a lethal weapon in his pocket."

His thinking got up to speed. "And, before he jumped off, hid it on that airplane. That way he wasn't caught with a weapon."

Richards and I walked back to his desk and he contacted the FBI agent in charge of the case.

It wasn't easy at first to convince the agent, but after they found the knife and came up with all the other evidence—like a motive and the lab report on James Knipstein's knife being negative for blood—James was released.

At the office the next day, I was feeling a little blue as I made out the final report for our files. It would take some time to get over seeing the girl, Esperanza, covered in all that blood. I couldn't think of anything I could have done to save her.

Then Glenda and her brother, James, came by the office. He was short and stocky with reddish-brown hair thinning on top and they both were grinning from ear to ear.

"I really appreciate your getting me out of that mess, Jenny." James had a high squeaky voice. He held out his hand. "I've never been so scared in my life."

I shook his hand and motioned for them to sit on the sofa in our reception area while I leaned my backside against my partner's desk. C.J. was out trying to get photos on an insurance scam case she was working. "You probably would have been cleared anyway. The FBI found out Cantu had once dated Esperanza. He was furious when she dropped him and got engaged to another guy. The robbery was just a cover-up for killing her."

"All I know is that FBI agent was determined to pin it on me. I'm not sure he would have checked Cantu out so thoroughly if you hadn't come up with that knife idea."

Glenda smiled. "You know what tickles me? Spade helped you solve the case." She got a knowing look on her face as if anything smart that cats did was certainly to be expected.

"Well, yes," I said. "I guess he did."

Glenda and James wouldn't leave until I promised I'd come over for dinner on Friday night. Spade was invited, too. Glenda said we'd all have Gulf shrimp.

After they left, Detective Richards called to say he had some diamond stud earrings and other stuff I might want to come down and identify.

And Ringo called to invite me out for dinner on Saturday night; I accepted.

Things were looking up—but I'm still neutral about cats.

Buster

·

Arthur Winfield Knight

Peg holds Bud's cat up to her face, her thumbs under Buster's front legs, his body dangling like a sausage. Buster's back feet bicycle as he tries to squirm free, but Peg has a firm grip on him.

"What a nice kitty," Peg says.

Buster hisses, and I know how he feels. I don't like Peg, either. She's always complaining so it's hard for Kim and me to understand why Bud's so infatuated with her. Maybe anyone looks good after Marion. When he was married to her he'd come home from work and she'd say, "Oh, it's you," and make a farting sound through her teeth. That went on for a couple of years, and we don't understand why he took it.

Buster tries to claw Peg and she half-throws him to the floor. He stands there for a moment, stunned, then runs across the room and peers out at Peg from beneath a chair. He's cinnamon-colored and has a fat face, as if someone has been giving him steroids.

Peg ignores Buster and puts an arm on Bud's shoulder. She says, "I want to devote the rest of my life to making this man happy."

Kim and I like Bud—I've known him since high school—but we think Peg's desperate. She's in her late forties and has a greater chance of being kidnapped by terrorists than she does of finding another husband.

Bud and Peg met at the office in San Francisco where they're insurance underwriters, and she came home with Bud for the first time three weeks ago, just before Kim and

232

I came west for the summer. Bud and I grew up in Petaluma.

In a few minutes we're supposed to leave Bud's condo and go to lunch with a woman from a local paper who's going to interview me. Bud said he'll tell her he and Peg constitute my fan club. It's about right for a writer. A fan club of two.

Peg spent the first two weekends on the couch but made it to Bud's bedroom this weekend. She's turning a night of sex into a lifetime commitment and talks about moving in with Bud before the summer is over.

As usual, Bud's compliant. He says, "I just go along with the program."

That's been his downfall all his life: going along with the program, no matter whose it is.

His father always told him he'd go to college in San Francisco, then come back to Petaluma and take over the insurance business and he did.

Bud's first wife told him they'd have two kids and they did, then Lil left him to raise them. One night he came home from the Elks and the babysitter was in his bed, naked. Marion said, "Get in," so he folded his clothes neatly, draping them on a chair; six months later, he married her.

Kim says he needs a benevolent dictator, but Bud hasn't found one yet. Maybe it will turn out to be Peg, but more and more, we doubt it.

We think Peg's a liar. According to her, she's seen everything, been everywhere: Mexico City, South Dakota, Florida, Georgia. Done everything: spent a weekend with Willie Nelson in Texas, been the lead singer and played guitar in several country-and-western bands.

"I wish you'd sing for us," Bud says. "We want you to play something."

I think Buster could carry a better tune if you stepped on his tail. Peg's voice is abrasive.

She says, "My shoulder hurts."

I wonder how that affects her voice, but I don't ask.

In a few minutes we have to go meet the lady who's going to interview me, and she and I will do most of the talking. I wonder how Peg will stand it, not being the center of attention.

* * *

Bud and Peg came to see us every Saturday and Sunday when we arrived in Marshall, but they only come on Sunday now since Peg says she's "jamming" with her old music teacher on Saturday afternoons.

When we met Peg, she loved to tell us how she got by on four or five hours' sleep, but increasingly she complains about being tired. She and Bud sleep in until noon on Saturday and Sunday when she stays with him; they take Old Nellie, her car, to San Francisco together on Monday mornings and she drives him back to Petaluma on Friday nights. Other days, he still takes the bus.

Bud said he'd never commute to the city, that people who did it were stupid, but "Here I am commuting," he says cheerfully. After twenty years of mismanaging the business he inherited, he sold what was left of it and got what he calls a "real" job.

The cabin Kim and I have rented is on Tomales Bay and we see egrets and blue herons each morning when we go out onto the deck to drink our coffee. Kim loves the egrets particularly and hunts for their plumes—they lose them as mating season progresses—under the eucalyptus trees where they nest a hundred yards or so from our cabin.

I don't think Bud cares about the egrets but he stands on the deck with me, lighting a cigarette and coughing tightly. "This is paradise," he says as we watch the fog come in over the azure water. He mirrors the sentiments of the woman in charge of the post office three miles down the road. The other morning she wrote, "Ho hum, just another day in Paradise" on the community chalk board.

Inside, Peg says, "I'm so tired of working for Harry that I'm ready to tell him to fuck himself." Peg's three favorite words are *shit, fuck* and *God*. "I'm ready to tell him to shove the job. You know, when I fell and broke my shoulder, I even phoned Harry from the hospital, letting him know I wouldn't be in that day, and the bastard deducted it from my pay even though the accident happened when I was on my way to work."

Kim and I have heard the story a dozen times, maybe more.

"I don't have to take that kind of shit from anyone," Peg continues.

The sliding glass doors separating Bud and me from the front room are open so it would be easy to hear Peg even if her voice weren't so shrill. I watch her sip her wine. Even though she's sitting in a large leather chair, one that you almost sink into, her body is somehow rigid.

"I took enough shit when I was married the first time. Twenty-one years I put up with a husband who liked to beat me. I would have left him sooner if it hadn't been for our daughters. Then all three of them decided to stay with him after our divorce." Peg raises her hands, gesturing, almost spilling her wine. "God give me strength. Sometimes I don't know how I've survived.

"My second husband was ten years younger than me. He came from an old family in Bodega Bay but he was addicted to drugs and he spent *my* seventy thousand dollars on cocaine before I left him."

I wonder where Peg got seventy thousand dollars, but I try not to listen. Her life is a long list of grievances against ex-husbands, lovers, bosses, an accounting of wrongs done to her by parents and children. A sad ballad played over and over again. "My seventy thousand dollars." That is another favorite word of hers, perhaps her favorite: *my, my, my.* She always seems to be saying: Look at me. And, over and over, she's told us how "hot" men are for her. A cop in the city threatened to give her a ticket if she wouldn't put out for him, a lover in Georgia locked her into their trailer because he couldn't get enough of her, because he was insanely jealous, she says, but she escaped.

I try to imagine Peg being pursued. She covers the lines in her face with makeup but it only calls attention to them. Her severe blonde hair is cut shorter than mine, and her wire-rimmed glasses look like they might have come from a military supply store. She exudes the warmth of a mannequin but, still, Kim and I try to like her. At least she's given Bud something more to do than iron his shirts on the weekends, something more to do than go to the Safeway, something more than to walk his decrepit springer spaniel. Bud with his bad feet and his fourteen-year-old drooling dog with its gray chops.

Marion was good for Bud when they first went out, good for his two girls, but things changed. It began in bed and ended with her farting through her teeth each time she saw him. It could happen again.

Bud leans against the railing, and even in the diffused light he seems old. I can see his father in him.

Bud says, "Peg and I were making love yesterday when Buster jumped onto the bed. Peg was on top so I couldn't tell what happened exactly but, all of a sudden, Buster was flying through the air like he was jet-propelled and he slammed into the closet door so hard he knocked it off its track.

"Peg said she was just ready to come when it happened, but Buster sort of put a damper on things.

"The rest of the day, Peg kept trying to make up to Buster, giving him fresh milk and some Star Kist tuna, but he just hissed at her and stayed under the kitchen table. Finally, I think Buster got on her nerves. She says she really loves cats—she has two Siamese at home—but she's beginning to think Buster's retarded."

I think Buster might be smarter than his owner but, as my father-in-law says, opinions are like assholes— everybody has one—and even though Bud told Kim and me he hoped we're good enough friends to tell him what we really think, I know he doesn't want our opinion about Peg.

When my mother grew up in Penngrove there was a small bar and gas station called the Twin Oaks about a quarter of a mile down the old highway from her house. I remember driving past it when I was in high school and college, and maybe there'd be a car or two parked there. Generally the lot was empty and I imagined the odors of gas and oil seeped into the barroom, mixing with the smell of beer.

Now the gas station is gone, but the bar still remains. On weekends there might be up to a hundred cars in the lot because there is "live" country-and-western music there. Every Friday night, Old Nellie is one of the cars in the lot and Bud and Peg are inside, sitting three or four tables back from the band.

Peg drinks Margaritas and Bud drinks old-fashioneds and, if they talk at all, they have to yell at one another to be heard over the music.

Tonight Kim and I are with them. She's drinking white wine and I'm drinking beer and we're listening to a band that "opens" for Alabama. I've never heard of Alabama but opening for them seems to be a big deal.

Peg says her arm's still sore but it doesn't seem to hinder her from lifting her Margarita and she nods, her head wreathed in smoke, as she keeps time to the music. The band plays songs like "Your Cheatin' Heart" and "Take These Chains From My Heart" and "Cold, Cold Heart," and I want to say, "This group sure has a lot of heart," but I don't think Peg would appreciate it.

When the band breaks, Peg goes up to the small raised stage and talks to one of the band members, then she goes back to the ladies' room.

Bud has always been easy to talk to—we drove across America together the summer we graduated from high school and we were roommates for a semester when we were in college—but suddenly there are gaps in our conversations. Suddenly the past seems more pleasant than the future, at least the future Bud and I will share.

Last time Kim and I went to Bud's, Buster threw up on the living room rug and Bud picked him up by the tail, throwing him outside. "I don't know what the hell's wrong with that cat," he said. "He's been puking all over the place."

"Maybe you should have him put to sleep," Peg said.

Funny, Buster was never sick before Peg arrived on the scene, and I thought about the professor in the history department at the college where I teach in Pennsylvania. He'd been arrested for poisoning cats with tuna mixed with antifreeze, but Peg wouldn't do that. Not even if she hated Buster. No, I shouldn't let myself become paranoid just because I didn't like Peg. She wasn't a cat killer. Was she?

Peg comes back to our table and says, "Someone tried to pick me up when I came through the bar."

Bud smiles. "It happens all the time."

Kim and I just nod.

"I'd better marry her before someone else gets her," Bud

says. More and more, the word *marriage* enters his conversation. A few months ago, he said he'd never get married again, that he was eventually going to get out of the insurance business and go north to open a bait shop and call himself The Master Baiter.

"The guy in the band I was talking to thinks there might be an opening for me," Peg says. "Maybe in the next six months. By that time I ought to have the strength back in my hand. My arm shouldn't be bothering me by then. I'll be able to bring in some extra money."

"Yeah, and I can sit here half-crocked spending the money she makes," Bud says. He's half-crocked now, but that's probably the least of his worries. He thinks Peg will solve his problems, helping him make the mortgage payments on his condo, providing him with another car besides his own. The engine's ready to go on his old Chevy and he holds the lining on the ceiling up with safety pins; it is the way he holds his life together.

Peg tells us she's put five thousand dollars into Old Nellie, that it's a "damned good car" even if it is old, even if the window on the driver's side keeps falling down, even if the valves clatter and it burns more oil than it should. Bud has told me Peg's even willing to help him pay off Marion.

"How can I pass up a deal like that?" he asked.

"I guess you can't," I said. I wanted to say: Stick to being The Master Baiter, but my nerve failed.

Kim says we have to warn him about Peg. It's our duty as friends. I say he doesn't want to hear it, but I don't think that will stop Kim for long. She says she wears her heart on her sleeve. I say she blurts things out.

Peg used to insist we hug her every time we left, even if we were only going to the grocery store for ten minutes—"I need my hugs," she'd say—but this time she just nods as we get up to go and the band begins its next set.

Peg's on the phone when we arrive at Bud's. The receiver is pressed to her ear and she holds one hand over the mouthpiece. She says, "Goddamn it, I hate that woman. But I love her."

We've been here before when she's talking with her

adopted mother. Apparently she has agonized talks with her, long distance, every evening. "Shit, shit," she says, banging her head against the wall.

Apparently Bud has accepted these evening conversations as part of the program since Peg moved in with him two weeks ago. Apparently they don't seem strange to him. He just says, "Marion and her mother always had conversations like that," (Marion was adopted, too) but he doesn't seem to draw any inferences from that. Maybe he'll think about it more once he gets his phone bill.

Kim and I talked about these calls earlier and she said, "I can't imagine a grown woman phoning her mother every night."

I said, "You ought to. You have a lot of insane discussions with your mother."

"I was twenty-three then." Kim's thirty-seven now.

Peg's still banging her head on the wall. "But, Mom . . ." She's crying while Bud shoves the handle of a broom into the automatic garbage disposal, trying to dislodge some broken glass. "Shit, one of the girls must have broken a glass. Shit."

His springer spaniel scratches at the door from the kitchen to the backyard, its huge nose pressed against the glass, and Buster runs around the room, meowing, in a circle.

"Shit," Bud says again. "I'm picking up Peg's bad habits. I never used to swear like this." But you can tell he almost delights in swearing. Possibly it's the most daring thing he's done in a long time.

Peg drops the receiver for a moment, watching it dangle from its cord. She lights a cigarette, taking a deep drag while she listens to her mother's voice. It's harsh, scolding.

Kim holds her hand out to Buster and says, "Here kitty, kitty," and Buster sniffs her fingers. Kim says, "His nose is dry."

Peg picks up the receiver again, sighing. She looks old in the fluorescent light. Makeup fails to hide the lines the cigarettes have cut into her face.

Peg claims her one goal is to make Bud happy, and for a while I think she succeeded, but little things get to Bud in a way they didn't prior to Peg moving in with him. Now he yells at the dog, "Quit pawing the goddamn glass," as if it can understand him, and for a moment I think he's going to run over and kick it but he's too busy jamming the broom handle down the garbage disposal, too busy picking out pieces of glass. He cuts his finger and says, "Shit," then he tries to turn the garbage disposal on but it just hums. "Goddamn those girls."

This is the first time we've ever heard him swear at his daughters.

Buster throws up on the linoleum, but I don't think Bud or Peg notices.

Peg says, "Mother, you don't understand," as she crushes her cigarette into an ashtray, then she stretches the cord until I think it's going to break. She goes into the bathroom between the kitchen and the living room and I hear something thump. Maybe she slammed down the toilet seat.

The dog begins to bark and Bud's sweating now. His glasses slide down the bridge of his nose.

Peg screams, "That's a fine thing to tell your daughter. A fine thing. Just tell me, where were you when I needed you all those years, huh?"

Buster throws up again and falls over, writhing. His sides are heaving and a kind of dry sound comes from his throat, like someone letting the air out of a balloon.

Bud drops the broom, rubbing his hand on his shirt, then he notices the blood on it. "Fuck," he says.

Kim goes over to Buster, picking him up gently, but I can tell it's too late. There are tears in her eyes.

"Buster's dead," she says, but Bud is shoving the broom handle down the garbage disposal again and Peg is banging her head on the wall.